Helen Black g................., west Yorkshire. At eighteen she went to Hull University and left three years later with a tattoo on her shoulder and a law degree. She became a lawyer in Peckham, and soon had a loyal following of teenagers needing legal advice ar d bus fares. She ended up in Luton, working predominantly for ldren going through the care system.

len is married to a long-suffering lawyer and is the mother of ns.

HARD AS NAILS

HELEN BLACK

CONSTABLE

CONSTABLE

First published in Great Britain in 2020 by Constable

13 5 7 9 10 8 6 4 2

Copyright © Helen Black, 2020

The moral right of the author has been asserted.

*All characters and events in this publication, other than
those clearly in the public domain, are fictitious
and any resemblance to real persons,
living or dead, is purely coincidental.*

A CIP catalogue record for this book
is available from the British Library.

ISBN: 978-1-47212-988-8

Typeset in Bembo by Initial Typesetting Services, Edinburgh

Printed and bound in Great Britain by Clays Ltd, Elcograf S.p.A.

Papers used by Constable are from well-managed forests and other responsible sources.

MIX
Paper from
responsible sources
FSC® C104740

Constable
An imprint of
Little, Brown Book Group
Carmelite House
50 Victoria Embankment
London EC4Y 0DZ

An Hachette UK Company
www.hachette.co.uk

www.littlebrown.co.uk

HARD AS NAILS

Chapter 1

5 October 1990

Key worker Hemma's got a new rule. Well, she calls it a 'policy' but it's the same thing. Basically, she's got sick of putting everyone right when they get her name wrong like two thousand times a day, so now she won't answer anybody unless they pronounce the H. What she gets for her trouble is a lorry load of huffing by all the kids in Orchard Grove.

'Huh-Emma, can I have a travel pass?'

'Huh-Emma, someone's nicked my hair spray.'

'Huh-Emma, Jordan's having a wank in the telly room and I want to watch EastEnders.'

It's like we've got a group case of asthma and I'm thinking Hemma regrets instigating her policy, but she can't back down now.

'Huh-Emma,' our Jay shouts. 'Have you heard from that solicitor?'

Hemma gives him a tight smile. 'No, Jay, I haven't. But trust me, as soon as I do, you'll be the first to know.' She turns to me. 'But I have got something for you, Elizabeth.'

I could tell her that I've got my own policy about names and that no one ever calls me that. But I can't be arsed. There's some guideline about not being too casual with kids in care for fear that we start to look on staff as our mates. It's a load of bollocks if you think about it. They insist on using the names our mams and dads gave us even though most of us don't have anything to do with our mams and dads. But, like I say, I can't be arsed to argue.

'She's called Lib.' Of course, our Jay's always got enough energy to argue. 'Everybody knows that.'

I flick his ear.

'Ow,' he says.

'Please don't do that, Elizabeth,' says Hemma. 'We don't accept violence in the unit, as you're well aware.'

Me and Jay look at each other and crease up. Most days it's like a cage fight in here. There's a new lass, Michaela, who battered both her roommates the first night she arrived because she said one of them farted. In the end both girls moved out so Michaela got a single by default. Hemma's not renowned for her sense of humour, so she walks off.

'Huh-Emma,' I call after her. 'You said you had something for me.'

She nods, reaches into her pocket and hands me a letter. I'm hoping for something from Fat Rob. He's already sent two since I left Manchester, and although they're only short, they're dead funny and it always cheers me up to think he's living his best life over the Pennines. My heart sinks when I see thin pale blue paper marked HMP. I only know one person in prison, and I don't want to read anything he's got to say to me.

Later, in my room I stare at the unopened envelope. Through the wall I can hear our Jay chatting with Michaela. He shouldn't be in there, but at least she's laughing and not thumping him. Yet. Neither of us wanted to come back here, but I knew that Jay was just going to get himself into real trouble in Manchester and that he wouldn't leave without me. I suppose we were lucky that two places came up together in Orchard Grove. The lad who had my room before me got sent to secure for robbing an arcade. Him and his little brother somehow managed to get away with about a grand in fifty-pence pieces. They got caught dragging their bags onto a bus because they were both too young to have passed their test. Anyway, that left this room for me.

I think I'm just going to bin the letter. Whatever Connor wants to get off his chest, he can sodding well keep it in. This is the lad who said he loved me, who said he wanted to look after me, and when he got nicked for dealing drugs he wanted me to take the blame. Rob was so angry with *him that he's not spoken to him since, and they were friends years before they even met me.*

Next door, Jay's voice has dropped low and I know what's coming. I bang on the wall. 'Do not even think about it,' I shout.

'Why do you care?' he yells back.

'I don't give a shit, Jay. I just don't want to listen to it.'

I hear a few squeaks of the bed and something that might be a cough. I thump again. 'Don't make me come in there.'

'For fuck's sake,' Jay mutters, and a door slams.

I wait a few seconds to make sure he has actually left Michaela's room and that it's not just some charade, then breathe a sigh of relief. It's not as if I got any privacy when I lived with Rob. I mean, we shared a bedsit with no bathroom. We got used to ignoring each other's comings and goings. But that's a far cry from listening to your brother shagging.

I lie on my bed and stare at the ceiling, wondering what Crystal and Frankie are up to. The solicitor says she's pushing hard for a contact session, but they always say that. Then I pull myself together and take out one of my books. Hemma's convinced she'll have the paperwork sorted for me to go back to college next week and I don't want to fall behind in the meantime.

Present Day

When Liberty pulled up outside the Black Cherry, Rebecca's Audi was already in the car park.

'Shit.' She pasted on a smile. 'Hi, Becca.' Her voice sounded ludicrously cheerful even to her ears.

Rebecca didn't answer but gave a curt nod, then went to her boot and popped it open. She was wearing a navy windcheater with pink polka dots and a pair of brown chinos, sensible and comfortable, as she retrieved a plastic box. Then she stalked back to Liberty's Porsche and dumped it on the bonnet.

Liberty yelped and jumped out. The 911 was getting on but

she loved that car like an old family dog that peed on the rug but still made everyone laugh. A tangle of chargers fell out of the box onto the paintwork. Liberty grabbed them and stuffed them back inside on top of three Welcome to Playa del Carmen mugs, one without a handle.

'That's the last of it,' said Rebecca.

'Could you two not talk this through?'

'There's nothing to say.'

Music seeped towards them as someone opened the door to the club. Liberty and Rebecca turned to the sound and saw one of the dancers with a packet of fags. She shoved one between her lips and pulled off her Cleopatra wig before lighting up. Liberty gestured for her to go back inside, but the girl held up her cigarette. 'Break.'

'Don't make me ask twice,' Liberty shouted. The girl huffed, but did as she was told, nipping her cig and putting it back with the others. When the door closed, Liberty turned to Rebecca. 'You could try counselling.'

Rebecca snorted. 'Can you imagine Jay speaking to a shrink?'

'I don't think they use shrinks.' Liberty slid the box off the Porsche, praying there were no scratches. 'Although that might not be a bad idea. He's struggling since Frankie died. We all are.'

Rebecca's shoulders softened. 'I know that.' She paused as if trying to remember why she was there. 'But I also know that he's shagged virtually every dancer in the club.' She pointed at the door. 'Probably that one just now. Can you imagine how stupid that makes me feel?'

'You're not the stupid one.'

Rebecca tucked her hair neatly behind her ears. She was all wrong here, like one of those odd-one-out puzzles where the clues were meant to be subtle but stuck out like a sore thumb. 'Tell him I've seen a solicitor.'

'Becca! Please don't do this,' Liberty said. 'You're truly the best thing that ever happened to my brother.'

Jay's wife shook her head. 'There's no point stringing this out. We both know that Jay's not going to change, but I don't want to have to find out about it any more.'

Liberty stumbled into the club, slammed the box onto the bar and slumped onto the stool next to Crystal. She snatched her sister's drink and took a gulp. 'Just Coke?'

Crystal patted her pregnant bulge. Mel poured a couple of fingers of Jack Daniel's into a glass and slid it at Liberty. Then Mel poked about in the box, holding up a cocktail shaker still in its cellophane.

'You been hitting eBay again?' Crystal asked.

'It's not funny.' Liberty knocked back her bourbon. 'Becca won't change her mind. This time she's definitely divorcing him.'

Crystal inspected a pair of clean gardening gloves with the words 'The Lawn Ranger' embroidered on the cuffs. 'Do you think our Jay's ever cut the grass?'

'Straight after he painted the shed,' said Mel.

Both women cracked up. In spite of herself, Liberty joined in and helped herself to another shot. Even the thought of Jay gardening was hilarious. Who the hell had bought him the gloves? The girl from outside tottered towards them in a pair of high-heeled gladiator sandals, the laces crossed so tightly the string dug into her shins. She had the jet-black Cleopatra wig back on.

'I can go outside now?' she asked. When Liberty nodded, the girl glanced at Mel. 'I can get my phone?'

Mel pulled a shoebox from under the bar and lifted the lid. Inside were at least fifteen mobiles. She offered it to the girl, who grabbed a Samsung with a cracked screen and scuttled away.

'I bet they don't like this new regime,' said Liberty.

'They can like it or lump it.' Mel sifted through the phones, double-checking they were all off. 'No one's recording anything that gets said in here.' She held up her palm. 'And I know you think I'm paranoid, but I'm too bloody old to get sent down, that's for sure.'

'What about the punters?' Liberty asked, pointing at a bloke by the stage: he was ignoring the dancer in cat ears, twirling her tail, as he flicked through Facebook on his phone.

'Too far away. And there's the music. But the girls are here before we open and when we're shutting. Plus, they're up at the bar, in my chuffing face night and day.'

Crystal was wearing the gardening gloves and waved one at Mel. 'What if one of the dancers sneaks in a second phone? Thought of that?'

The girl on the stage was now naked except for the cat ears, one foot on the floor, the other wrapped around her neck.

'If she can hide it and still manage to do that, good luck to her,' said Liberty.

Mel refitted the lid on the cardboard box and slid it back under the bar with a sniff. Since they'd heard about Mads, the county-lines kid being sent in to spy on Ricky Vines, they were all feeling cautious, but Mel was taking it to a new level. There was no doubt in Liberty's mind that if she looked at Mel's search history, there'd be links on how to sweep for bugs. She finished her drink and checked the time. Seven fifteen. 'Gotta go.'

Mel picked up Liberty's empty glass and slung it into the dishwasher. 'You're still trying to find her, then?'

'Frankie would have wanted me to,' Liberty replied, and left the club.

Liberty drove across the Crosshills until she arrived at an all-night chemist, windows full of handmade signs for bargain bubble bath. She pulled over and watched the youngers outside as they crowded around a phone that one was holding. By the looks on their faces they were watching something funny.

When an addict appeared, fizzing with anxiety and need, one of the kids peeled himself away from the screen and took the cash. Then he whistled and another lad on a bike circled around and pedalled towards them.

The door to the chemist opened and a young woman appeared, black baseball cap pulled low over her eyes, hood over the cap. It would have been hard to tell she was female except Liberty knew who she was. Without warning the girl slapped the younger holding the phone on the back of his head and his cap fell to the floor. He shouted out in annoyance but picked it up and put away his phone.

When Liberty hooted her horn the group looked up as one, but only the young woman moved towards the car and got in.

'Tia,' said Liberty.

'Told you before, you shouldn't come down here.' Tia pointed at the youngers. 'Let me tell you, this lot aren't keeping a proper eye out for the feds. Too busy watching some fight on YouTube.'

'Who pissed on your chips?'

Tia kissed her teeth. 'They get on my nerves. Don't matter how many times I tell them, they just keep doing the same things.' She reached into her jacket pocket and pulled out a box of Canesten. 'Plus, I've got the worst case of thrush.'

'Yoghurt's good for that,' said Liberty.

Tia bared her teeth. 'How is eating that stuff going to help?'

'You don't eat it.'

Tia looked down at her crotch. 'Oh, my days, you cannot think I'm going to put it up there. I mean what about strawberry seeds and that?'

Liberty closed her eyes. Any conversation with Tia was like entering a parallel universe. Frankie always said he was going to strangle her, but it might end up being Liberty who did the deed.

'I was just passing so I thought I'd check in on you.'

Tia patted Liberty's knee. 'Thanks, Mum.'

'Fuck off,' Liberty replied, with a smile.

'I appreciate it,' said Tia, 'but I don't want you getting nicked.'

Liberty nodded. Once upon a time, she'd been a teenager without anyone to look out for her. Bad things could happen to kids in that position. She didn't want bad things to happen to Tia.

Through the windscreen they could see the lads were back watching the video. Tia growled and opened the door. 'Where're you off to, then, Lib?'

'St Stevens,' said Liberty.

Tia rolled her eyes. 'Still trying to find her, I take it?'

'Yup.'

'Why are you even bothering?' Tia asked.

'Because Frankie would have wanted me to check on her, like I check on you.'

Tia stuck out her tongue and jumped from the car. Liberty watched her best dealer jog across the street where she batted the phone out of the younger's hands with a mouthful of expletives.

Rose Angel rolled her hips, making the nylon of her hi-vis jacket squeak. She needed to see the physio again but getting an appointment was murder. Typical that after all the injuries she'd sustained over the years making arrests, jumping fences, disarming nut jobs, she'd put her back out dragging an unconscious man behind a bus shelter.

The radio on her shoulder crackled but there was no message. Good. She scanned the length and breadth of Carter Street. Everything was quiet and she hoped it would stay that way.

Adam came out of Scottish Tony's with a polystyrene cup in each hand and something wrapped in foil held in his armpit. He handed a cup to Rose and let the mystery package drop into his now free hand. 'Burger,' he said. 'Assumed you didn't want one.'

Rose took a sip of tea. 'I'll wait until I get home.'

Adam rolled back the foil, took a bite and groaned. 'I told him I didn't want any bloody tomatoes.'

'Do you want to get a fresh one?' Rose asked.

'Nah,' Adam replied, and flicked the slices of tomato from his burger onto the pavement. A sliver landed on his boot and he wiggled his foot until it flew off. They walked up the street towards the squad car. 'We'll have to find someone soon.'

Rose sighed. The chief super's new policy was that patrollers had to make at least one stop-and-search each shift. It was part of the new war against drugs and weapons. Trouble was they had to choose who to search with care. With no Taser between them, and most back-up at least ten minutes away, they didn't want to target anyone who might cut up too rough.

On their first shift together, Rose had marched off in the direction of a couple of lads openly dealing on the corner, but Adam had pulled her back. He didn't fancy spending the night in A and E, he told her, and rolled up his sleeve to show her a jagged scar where he'd been stabbed the previous summer. She'd hardly been able to make it out through his copious ink and he'd had to run her finger along the huge black panther that covered most of his forearm so she could feel the ridge, like she was reading him in braille.

'Do you think they'll ever issue you with a Taser?' she asked him.

He shovelled the last piece of burger into his mouth and laughed. 'They're like Man U season tickets,' he said. 'You put your name down without hope or expectation.'

'Thought you lot hated Man U.'

He got into the car. 'We do, but they can't give away tickets to Leeds with a free haircut.'

Rose got into the passenger side and put on her seatbelt. Then they drove to the Crosshills to rummage around for someone to notch up their numbers. Someone among the hopeless and the homeless who just might have a bit of gear on them so they could get an arrest at the same time. Ruining already crap lives and shattering trust. The job was a good 'un.

'Tell me again why we do this,' said Rose.

'I'm too thick to take my sergeant's exams,' said Adam. 'And you got sacked from being a detective for locking up one of the Greenwoods.' He wagged his finger at a man pushing a shopping trolley. 'What about him?'

'If you think I'm putting my hand in his pockets, you've lost the plot.'

'C'mon, Rose.' Adam winked. 'Give the poor bloke a thrill.'

She was about to tell him to get lost when her mobile beeped: email incoming. She checked it and froze as she read the unexploded bomb the words contained.

'Everything okay?' Adam asked, but she couldn't answer. 'Rose?' He pulled over and killed the engine. 'You're worrying me now,' he said. 'And I don't worry about anything except if I'm going to make it for last orders.'

Rose breathed hard. 'It's Joel Redman.'

'The bent copper?'

Rose nodded. 'He's killed himself in prison.'

She slid out of the car into the cold night air and pulled up a number she never used. She hesitated for a second before hitting the call button. Liberty Greenwood answered immediately.

'Redman's dead,' said Rose.

'How?' Greenwood asked.

The homeless man with the trolley came to a halt a few feet away and stared at her. Rose stared back and jabbed her thumb up the street for him to jog on. 'Suicide. Apparently.'

'Look, I can't speak now, I'm right in the middle of something.'

'Something more important than this?' asked Rose.

'I'm looking for someone. I'll meet you later,' Greenwood replied, and hung up.

Rose watched the man and his trolley move slowly away, dirty boots shuffling, wheels squeaking on the wet pavement.

The church hall was cold and smelt of disinfectant. The clinking of a metal spoon against a mug filled the air as Liberty stared at a picture of Jesus on the wall. His face was serene, like he was in soft focus, clearly not yet in the know about how he would end his days. She wondered for a second how Frankie had felt before he died. Did he know what was coming? Did it hurt? Or did he just float away into the blackness?

'Can I get you a brew?'

Liberty turned to a woman standing by a kettle, holding up a box of PG Tips. 'Actually, I'm looking for someone.'

'Aren't we all?' said the woman and popped a teabag into a cup. She had a name badge pinned to her cardigan: Jan.

'Her name's Daisy Clarke,' said Liberty. 'Sometimes goes by Daisy the Dog?'

Jan smiled and poured boiling water over the teabag. 'Milk and sugar?'

Liberty frowned. There was no way Jan hadn't heard her question. Jan fished out the teabag with a spoon, placed it on top of a mountain of others and shoved the still-wet spoon into a bag of sugar. She stirred three heaped spoonfuls into the cup and held it out to Liberty.

'Honestly, I'm just trying to find Daisy.'

Jan didn't lower her arm, face as placid as Jesus on the wall, so Liberty took the cup, not knowing what else to do.

'We don't use names except inside the group,' said Jan. 'Everything said there is in complete confidence, including the names of those who attend.' Liberty glanced at the name badge and Jan laughed. 'I run the group, so I'm an exception.' She nodded towards a side room already full of people. 'You're very welcome to join us.'

Liberty craned her neck to see if Daisy was in there, but she couldn't make out anyone's face. It was possible Daisy was there already or, more likely if she remembered Daisy right, she'd turn up late having missed her bus, lost her phone and managed to row with a randomer on the way. There was a reason Daisy had been mates with Frankie: peas in a pod. Or were they just two desperate crack heads finding a bit of comfort in each other? Was this search for Daisy something Liberty was doing to keep Frankie alive a bit longer? Everyone else seemed to think so. Frankie had been shot by a rival dealer from Manchester, who had sent kids down county lines to grab some Greenwood turf. You couldn't make that right by tracking down a working girl he occasionally shagged. Maybe, but Liberty hadn't come across town simply to walk away now.

Jan nodded at Liberty's cup. 'Bring it with you.'

Around twenty plastic chairs formed a circle in the middle of the side-room, and most were taken. Liberty slid into a free space and popped her handbag on the floor next to her feet.

Jan had followed her in and took a place near the door. 'For anyone new tonight, I'll repeat the rules of engagement. Say whatever you like. No one here is going to judge and no one will ever mention it outside these four walls.'

'What happens in Vegas,' said a man a few seats up from Liberty. He was vastly overweight, pink belly poking out from under his football top. White trainers splattered in red that might have been ketchup but could have been blood.

'Yes, indeed, Bradley,' said Jan. 'Now, how are we doing tonight?'

'Absolute shite, not gonna lie,' said Bradley. 'Coming off the gear is probably the worst idea I've ever had in my life.' A few people laughed. 'You think I'm joking?'

'Well, let's have a think about that, Bradley,' said Jan. 'What made you decide to try to get clean in the first place?'

Liberty scanned the room. There were two free chairs left, which meant Daisy could still turn up. Although it was clear they always put out a few extras for anyone wandering in, like Liberty had. She wondered if she could just stop the proceedings and ask them if Daisy was expected. But Jan would no doubt shut that right down. Liberty sighed. She'd been trying to track down Daisy for weeks with no joy. She'd asked every dealer on the estate, but no one had seen her. Which could only mean that by some miracle she'd actually managed to stay clean. Hence trying meetings like this one.

'I promised my mam,' said Bradley.

'And why did you do that?' asked Jan.

'Fucked if I know,' he replied. 'Must have been off my tits.'

The young girl directly opposite gave a huge cackle. A dirty duvet and three carrier bags of clothes sat behind her chair. 'I told me brother I'd pack it in if he did. That we'd do it together like.'

'And?' asked Bradley.

The girl shrugged. 'And I'm here and he's not.'

'Never trust a junkie,' said Bradley.

The door opened and heads bobbed up expectantly, including Liberty's. But it wasn't Daisy. Instead a young lad, no more than fifteen, skittered in and sat on the dirty duvet.

'All right?' the girl asked, and the boy seesawed his hand.

'You came, Ellis,' said Jan. 'That's the main thing.'

Ellis glanced around the room, overwhelmed and overloaded. Even though Liberty could smell the spice coming off him, it hadn't yet taken his beauty. He was like a porcelain doll, exquisite yet fragile, ready to shatter at any moment.

'We're just talking about why we're trying to get clean, Ellis,' said Jan.

Ellis looked down at his filthy nails. 'I want to look after my family.' The girl reached down and took his hand. 'The little ones got taken into care and . . .'

Liberty felt her throat contract. She tried to swallow but there was nowhere for the saliva to go. She lurched to her feet, cup of tea falling to the floor, Bradley swearing as his stained boots got soaked. Jan said something, but Liberty couldn't hear what as she ran to the door.

Sol took a long drag on his vape and checked his coffee flask. Empty. Probably for the best, he was already edgy. Behind him Gianni tapped away on his laptop.

When they'd arrived at the flat, the day had been fat with promise but, like with all surveillance ops, boredom had settled in quickly. Basically, watching street dealing was like ground-hog day with no plot. The youngers hung around until finally a customer turned up and handed over some money. A sign would be given, and another kid would pass across the drugs. Rinse and repeat. It baffled Sol that they could be arsed to do it day in day out when there'd be more variety working on the pizza counter in Asda. No wonder feuds took off over the least tiny issue – anything to break up the day.

Sol stretched. He'd been peeking around the side of the curtain, looking down onto the street for hours now, and was starting to feel trapped. Not as in clawing-the-walls trapped, but that feeling he got on an aeroplane when he needed to pee and the stewardess hadn't cleared away the trays. Hemmed in and frustrated by something seemingly unimportant, but left wondering why they needed to do an extra sweep of the cabin serving thimblefuls of tea, then another selling duty-free. (Did anyone ever buy that stuff? Who looked at the in-flight magazine and thought their life would be complete if only they had a set of three lipsticks that were cheaper back at the airport, or a model Boeing 747?)

At last a teenager in a denim jacket with a fur collar wandered into view. Yusef Isak, sixteen years old.

'He's here,' said Sol.

Gianni slammed shut his laptop and hovered behind Sol. 'Sure it's him?' Sol flashed Gianni a look. He'd picked out this kid himself weeks ago, after reading a million profiles, and had been tracking him ever since. Gianni put up his hands. 'Just asking.'

They watched the boy fist-pump a couple of others and lean in to tell them something. Yusef was the stash boy and he was telling the others where he'd left it. It wouldn't be too far away, but the location changed most days.

'Where d'you think it is?' Gianni asked.

'Doesn't matter,' Sol replied, and made the call to Hutch. 'Time to swoop, my friend.'

'On it,' Hutch replied.

Moments later, they heard the police before they saw them. The screech of tyres, the roll of van doors, boots on the ground. The youngers scattered, or tried to, but the officers knew who was the priority and one rugby-tackled Yusef to the ground. The kid struggled to get away but, after a faceful of CS spray, screamed and curled into a ball. Sol watched as Yusef was hauled into a van, eyes scrunched tightly shut.

'Right, then,' said Sol. 'We've got a fish on our hook. Time to reel him in.'

Sol and Gianni watched Yusef through the two-way mirror. The kid had been seen by the FME and had his eyes cleaned up. By now his body language said he was relaxed, elbow on the table, chin in his palm, bored expression across his face. Getting nicked was part and parcel of life on the streets for boys like him, and Yusef knew, like they all did, that at his age, with no weapon or serious amount of drugs on him, he'd walk soon enough. But, unlike the other lads, Yusef had more reasons to worry.

Sol leafed through Yusef's file. Born in Asmara, the capital of Eritrea, Yusef had fled across the border to Ethiopia with his sister Sofia. She'd been twelve, Yusef ten. There'd been a stay in a refugee camp, then a journey to Europe, and Yusef had rocked up in England alone with the name of an uncle who lived in Manchester. When the uncle didn't turn up for any appointments with the powers that be, Yusef was taken into care. Four years and eleven foster placements later, Yusef had set alight the bed in his care home and walked out for good. He'd called his key worker only when he got nicked.

Yusef was alone in the world – exactly what Sol was looking for.

'Do you think he'll go for it?' Gianni asked.

Sol stared. What the hell was up with Gianni? He knew full well how this would go.

Hutch entered the interview room with Yusef's appropriate adult. They hadn't been able to raise his key worker. Apparently, he was at a gender fluid awareness conference in London. So, here was some trainee who had never met Yusef before. She looked far more terrified than he did.

Hutch gestured for the frightened young woman to sit next to Yusef and took a seat opposite. Hutch looked great, hair cropped neatly to his scalp as always, skin and eyes clear. Sol raked his own hair with grubby fingers. He hadn't been to the barber's since he'd left Yorkshire.

Hutch smiled widely, exposing even white teeth. 'I'll just explain why you're here, Yusef.'

'You do that,' Yusef replied, in a strong Lancashire accent with no hint that he'd ever lived anywhere else.

Hutch tapped an expensive watch with the pad of his thumb. 'For some time now, we've been watching Latimer Street as part of an ongoing drugs operation.' Hutch paused, but Yusef just shrugged. Maybe he still thought he was in no real trouble.

'We've been filming. Obviously.' That was true. Gianni had set up a camera to tape what was happening. It probably covered about thirty feet of the road. Yusef didn't blink, but the movement of his Adam's apple told Sol that the news of a camera had hit a nerve. 'We know you're the stash man, Yusef.'

The kid rolled out a fake yawn and closed his eyes. Hutch gave a little what-now shrug at the trainee social worker. She licked already dry lips rapidly and put a hand on Yusef's shoulder. He jerked away from her without opening his eyes.

'Just to be clear,' said Hutch. 'We have the stash.'

Sol turned to Gianni. 'Here we go.'

'That's an awful lot of class As, my friend,' said Hutch. He waited to let the information land, then stood abruptly. 'I'll leave you to chat while your brief arrives.'

With Hutch out of the room, Yusef still didn't move or speak, no doubt processing what he'd just heard. Beside him the trainee pressed her palm against her chest as if at any second she expected her skin to split and her heart to fall out onto the table.

Gianni let out a long breath.

'What?' Sol snapped.

'Nothing.'

'For fuck's sake, just spit it out.'

Gianni rubbed his face and, for the first time, Sol noticed the bags under his eyes – purple and puffed up. 'Don't you wonder if all this is . . .' he searched for the right word '. . . normal?'

Sol laughed. Of course, none of this was normal. If it was then Gianni wouldn't even need to ask the question. But it was like Liberty had once told him: normal was vastly overrated. 'It's necessary,' he said at last.

'Lying? Making up a case against a kid?' Gianni asked. 'We haven't got the stash. Didn't even look for it.'

'We're not gonna charge him,' Sol replied.

'But we're using it to get what we want.'

17

Sol wanted to slap Gianni across his stupid tired face. Why was he feeling so sorry for some kid who at the end of the day was just a drug dealer? 'You came to me, Gianni. You and Hutch. You came to me to bring down Ricky Vine.'

'And you didn't think our methods were okay.' Gianni jabbed his finger at the boy in the interview room, who still hadn't opened his eyes. 'You had a lot of problems with how we worked, if I recall correctly. So, what's changed?'

Sol's cheeks were on fire as he pulled at the neck of his unironed T-shirt to reveal the edges of a scar on his shoulder. 'I got shot.'

Gianni stared at Sol and Sol stared back. Ricky Vine ruined lives and Sol was going to stop him, no matter what he had to do.

Yusef could hear the woman next to him breathing and it was seriously annoying. She hadn't said her name or anything. She hadn't even asked him if he was all right. What was the point of being an appropriate adult if you didn't do appropriate stuff?

He should tell her he was thinking about killing himself just to get a reaction out of her. But then he'd have to spend hours with a doctor, explaining it was just a piss-take. One time, he'd told one of his foster carers he was going to slit his wrists and they'd banged him up in hospital for weeks. It didn't matter how many times he explained that he'd known full well the cuts weren't deep enough and that he'd done them the wrong way, across, like you see on the telly, when everyone knows that to do proper damage you have to slice down your arm from the crook of your elbow to your wrist. It was during that hospital stay Yusef had worked out that when people said his behaviour 'worried' them they actually meant it scared them.

'Yusef,' she said at last. 'Are you okay?'

Yusef opened his eyes and looked at her. She had her nose pierced with one of those little silver rings. If he pulled it hard enough the skin of her nostril would split in two and she'd be left with the skin flapping for the rest of her life.

'Have you got any fags?' he asked.

'I don't smoke,' she said.

He sighed hard, his breath lifting her hair, like a breeze. 'Can you get me something to eat, then?'

She nodded and scurried out of the room, relieved to get away by the look of it. With her gone, Yusef stretched out his legs. He'd hardly slept last night, and his back ached. He never slept well anyway, but recently it was getting worse. For one thing the house he was staying in was like Piccadilly Gardens with the amount of comings and goings, half of the people crashing there off their heads or pure mental.

The door opened and he was expecting to see the social worker holding a cheese roll, but instead there was a scruffy man, the neck of his T-shirt stretched. He closed the door behind him, sat on the edge of the table and silently held out a packet of Marlboro.

Chapter 2

6 October 1990

I'm in the toy section of Woolie's looking at the price of a Mr Frosty for our Crystal and Frankie, when a mouth comes close to my ear. 'Not thinking of nicking that, are you?'

I spin round to tell the security guard to do one, but I'm shocked to find Tiny at my side. I haven't seen her in over six months, and we didn't part on good terms. I mean, we didn't fall out, but she made it plain that my problems were my own to sort out, which hurt, if I'm honest. But the big smile on her face makes it look as if she's forgotten about that.

I smile back or, at least, I try to.

'Bloody hell,' she says. 'I don't look that bad, do I?'

Actually, she looks a lot better than the last time I saw her when she was tired and stressed, trying to get her head around an unwanted pregnancy. Today she's almost back to her old self, bright red lippie to match a bright red baseball cap worn sideways.

Then there's a little cry, well, more like a miaow, and we look down into a buggy.

'This is Grace,' she says, and picks up the baby. 'Lady Gracious meet Pretty Lib.'

Tiny's baby is snug in a snowsuit so padded it makes her little arms stick out at right angles. She blows a spit bubble from perfect pink lips. I lean in so my nose is close to hers and she gives a syrupy hiccup.

'I'm gonna have to feed her before my tits go off,' says Tiny. 'Fancy a cuppa?'

And I nod because not so long ago Tiny was one of my closest friends and that's got to be worth something, hasn't it?

Tiny's flat is a mess. I mean, she was never one for keeping it spotless, but this is Fat Rob levels of muck. In the corner of the living room there's a pile of dirty nappies. They're tied up in them individual scented pink sacks, but the smell of shit still seeps through.

'Sorry about this place,' says Tiny, Grace slurping away on her boob. 'Can't seem to get on top of it.'

I hunt around for a bin bag, then fill it up with all the crap lying around. When it's full, I dump it in the kitchen and make us a coffee. The milk's gone off so we have to have it black. Grace has fallen asleep but Tiny doesn't move her.

'Shall I put her down for you?' I ask.

'Christ, no,' Tiny says. 'She'll sleep like this, but if she gets in sniffing distance of her cot, she'll scream the place down. I'm surprised next door haven't reported me to the social for child abuse.' She frowns. 'Sorry. I shouldn't have said that.'

I shake my head that I'm not offended and blow across the rim of my mug.

'Did your brother find you?' she asks. 'He came looking for you, so I gave him Rob's address.'

'Yeah,' I say. 'He came to stay with us in Manchester for a bit, but we had to come back.'

Tiny strokes Grace's head. She hasn't got much hair yet, just a bit of dark brown fur here and there. Our Frankie was the same when he was born.

'And Rob's doing all right?' she asks.

I tell her about his club nights at the Hacienda, where he has everyone bouncing off the ceiling with his sets, and her eyes sparkle. 'He's even got a girlfriend,' I say.

She throws her head back in a laugh. 'Is she on meds?'

I laugh as well because she's not being mean. She loved the bones of Rob and he felt the same about her. Maybe they still feel that way about each other. I mean, I haven't seen our Crystal and Jay in ages, but I still love them, don't I?

'Have you heard from Connor?' she asks. That wipes the smile from my face. 'He told me he was going to write to you.'

'I chucked his letter in the bin,' I say.

She bends down to kiss her baby. 'He probably deserves it.'

'He definitely deserves it.'

Tiny looks at me and suddenly she seems a lot older than me, even though we're only four years apart. I suppose having a kid will do that to you. 'We all make mistakes, Lib. It's what you do about them that matters.'

Present Day

Liberty pulled herself together on the way to meet Angel.

It had been a stupid idea to go into the group session. She should have left as soon as she'd seen Daisy wasn't in there. It was obviously going to be full of no-hopers pouring out their sad stories, like buckets of water from a sinking ship.

For years she'd been buttoned up so tight that the other lawyers in the firm where she worked had nicknamed her the Ice Queen and she hadn't felt remotely offended. Look at her now, dropping tea down herself in front of a bunch of junkies when someone mentioned they wanted to see their little brothers and sisters.

'Get yourself together, Lib,' she hissed, as she turned into a twenty-four-hour garage.

She locked the car, walked past the air pumps and entered the ladies' toilets. Only one of the three cubicles was shut and the sound of heaving bounced off the damp walls.

'Angel?' Liberty called.

'Mmm,' came the reply, closely followed by another bout of retching.

22

Liberty checked her reflection in the mirror, didn't like what she saw and turned away, leaning her back against the nearest basin. At last Angel emerged, sweat trickling down her forehead, a wad of toilet paper pressed against her mouth. Christ, the copper looked worse than Liberty.

'You up the duff?' Liberty asked.

'Very funny,' Angel replied, and ran the tap, slicing the stream with her finger until she was happy with the temperature. Then she bent forward from the waist to suck the water straight into her mouth.

'Is this performance for Redman?' Liberty asked. 'Because I'm not sure he was worth it.'

Angel lobbed the paper in the overflowing bin. 'We set him up.'

'Nope,' said Liberty. 'You did that.'

Redman had been Angel's partner, and when she'd found out he was bent, she'd planted evidence to bring him down. In fairness Liberty had given some assistance towards Redman's arrest, but there was absolutely nothing to link her to it. He was found fair and square colluding with Paul Hill, a well-known gangster, who in turn was found with a ton of drugs and weapons in the back of his car. That last bit might not have been square, but all was fair in love, war and dealing.

'He was corrupt,' Liberty added. 'Maybe that played on his conscience so he topped himself.'

Angel folded her arms across her chest. She was wearing one of those massive Day-glo jackets that made her look twice her normal size. 'I don't think he killed himself.'

'Because?'

'He was a survivor.'

'He was on the take,' said Liberty.

'It was never about the money for Joel,' Angel replied. 'He worked for Hill to keep his family safe.'

That could well be true. Coppers found themselves in the pockets of criminals through lots of different ways: blackmail, fear, money. Often a slippery mix of them all. Most people would do whatever it took to keep their family out of trouble. Liberty understood that better than most.

'Look, what has this got to do with me?' Liberty asked. 'Cos if you're thinking I had anything to do with his death, you're barking up the wrong tree.' Angel narrowed her eyes, which made Liberty laugh. 'He had dirt on you and Hill, not me. If I was looking to get rid of someone who could cause trouble for my family, it wouldn't be Redman.' She dropped the smile and stared hard at Angel.

'Are you threatening me?' Angel asked.

Liberty said nothing and marched out of the door.

The Cashino was busy. To be fair, it was always busy. It never ceased to amaze Liberty how eager people were to feed coins into machines that were designed to rip them off. The chink of metal as a jackpot paid out filled the air, along with whoops and laughter. Liberty smiled at the gang of women celebrating, knowing full well they'd have lost the lot and more in the next half an hour.

An alarm went off in the corner as a few kids tried to tilt the pinball machine and a side door flew open. All eyes turned to Jay, and the kids scarpered before he could batter any of them.

'Lib,' he shouted, when he caught sight of her and opened his arms for a hug. Liberty smiled back and let him squeeze her tightly. She flinched slightly at the cold metal of a gun tucked into the back of his waistband, but since Frankie had been killed, she knew it was a reasonable precaution.

When Jay had said he wanted to buy the arcade she'd been sceptical. But Mel had pointed out that it would at least keep him away from the dancers in the Black Cherry, which might convince his wife not to leave him. That hadn't worked as planned but the Cashino had turned out to be a great opportunity, both for generating cash and washing funds from other sources.

She followed Jay into the side-room. There was an ancient no-armed bandit in the corner, the metal limb on the floor in hope of a surgeon, a table covered with towers of one-pound coins.

Jay reached into a drawer in the table and brought out two glasses and a bottle of Jack Daniel's. 'This isn't the Cherry, so you'll have to slum it without ice.'

'Since when was there ever any ice at the Cherry?'

'How's things over there?' Jay asked.

Liberty took a sip of bourbon. 'The girls send their love.' He pulled a face and necked his drink in one. 'I need to know something, Jay. Absolutely no bullshit.'

'Go on.'

'Did you have Joel Redman killed?' Liberty asked.

He laughed. A big gorgeous gurgle of hilarity. 'Is he dead, then?'

'Tell me you didn't do it.'

Jay poured himself another drink. 'Why the hell would I do that?'

Liberty exhaled and held out her glass for a top-up. Jay was right: there had been no reason to kill Redman. But Jay had been a loose cannon recently. Well, actually he'd always been that, but since Frankie had died there was no talking sense to him sometimes. It wasn't helping that Becca had chucked him out. Liberty made a mental note to call her, just to see if there was any chance she'd hold off on starting divorce proceedings. She wasn't too proud to beg.

There was a knock at the door and a woman poked her head around. When she saw Liberty, her smile fell away. 'Sorry, Jay.'

He pushed a pile of coins from his side of the table towards her.

Her eyes, pretty, brown and nervous, darted towards Liberty. She scurried across the room, pulled the coins into her scooped left hand and took off.

'Who's that?' Liberty asked.

'Someone who helps me out from time to time.'

'With what?'

Jay chuckled. 'This and that.' Liberty whacked him on the arm. 'Ow.'

'Can you not keep it in your pants for one minute, Jay?'

'What can I tell you?' He kissed her head. 'I'm a catch and we both know it.'

All the way home, Rose's mobile pinged as she was tagged in post after post on Facebook. She'd given up checking them after the first two. One was an illustration of a woman beside a tree, a black heart beating in her chest. It would have been beautiful but for the noose hanging from a nearby branch. The second was a film clip of a little girl in plaits drawing her finger across her pale throat.

The news about Joel was out, then.

As soon as she let herself into the house, and punched in her alarm code, she knew something was wrong. The stench of rotting flesh permeated her hallway.

A couple of days after she'd arrested Joel, she'd come home to dog shit on her door mat and had fitted a brush guard to her letterbox. But letters could still be pushed through, and there in the hallway was a padded envelope, unsealed at the end. Her heart hammered, like the woman's on Facebook, as she peered inside.

A rat. Long dead. Maggots crawling in its ripped-open stomach.

Rose opened the door and threw the envelope and its contents out onto the street, then ran upstairs to the bathroom and threw up the last remnants of food left inside her. The unfairness of the

26

situation burned her. All she'd done was put away a bent copper. Was that so bad?

Later, as she sprayed an entire container of Febreze in the hallway, she checked the emails on her phone, tears stinging her eyes. The chief super wanted to see her first thing in the morning.

Sol watched Yusef light a fag with the dog-end of his last. He'd already chained most of the packet and must be feeling sick.

Hutch was making sure the trainee social worker didn't get back sharpish by insisting on getting her a cuppa in the canteen. No doubt she was smiling into his handsome face right this second as he charmed her with stories of bravery and derring-do.

'This one's going to stick, I'm afraid,' said Sol. Yusef blew a mouthful of smoke at the tip of his fag. 'Too many drugs involved. You know how it goes.'

Outside the interview room, someone screamed and there was a bang against the door. Sol slid off the edge of the table and peered through the window into the custody suite beyond. Some bloke was being dragged to a cell and he wasn't going quietly, spit flying as he bellowed in a language Sol didn't recognise.

When things calmed, he went back to Yusef but didn't sit. Instead he stood, back against the wall. 'Of course, your main problem isn't being sent down.' He wagged a finger at the boy. 'Your main problem is proving you're sixteen.' He nodded at Yusef's file still on the table. 'I read in there that there never was any proper evidence of how old you are. Be a shame if they decided you were eighteen, eh?'

Yusef laughed and flicked his ash, grey powder landing on his white trainers. (Of all the colours to pick for shoes, Sol could never fathom why anyone would go for white. It wasn't the chav-factor, which frankly went right over Sol's head, but the inconvenience. Given that it rained in Manchester virtually every day, how the hell did anyone keep them clean?)

27

'What? You think they can't look at that stuff again?' Sol asked.

'Like I give a shit?' Yusef shrugged. 'Rather be in a proper jail than YOI anyway.'

Sol nodded slowly, as if it were a fair point. 'If they decide you're eighteen, jail will be the least of your troubles.' Yusef ground out the fag with his heel. 'They'll just send you back to . . .' Sol reached for the file and pretended to leaf through it. 'Where is it you're from? Eritrea? Gotta be honest, mate, I've not got a Danny where that even is.'

'East Africa,' said Yusef.

'Every day's a learning day.' Sol slapped the file shut. 'Well, I suppose it could be worse.'

Yusef opened his mouth to tell him to fuck off, but Sol was already on his way out, giving the lad a cheery salute as he left.

Back on the other side of the mirror, Sol watched the kid as the social worker arrived with a paper plate of chicken nuggets and a sachet of ketchup.

'They're halal,' she said. 'I checked.'

Yusef sneered. 'What? You think I'm a Muslim?'

'I just . . .'

Yusef kissed his teeth and ripped open the ketchup. He squeezed out the sauce onto the side of the plate and dipped one of the nuggets into it. 'Thanks,' he muttered.

The door to the viewing room opened and Hutch entered.

'Enjoy a cosy cuppa, did you?' Sol asked, nodding at the social worker.

'Women love me,' said Hutch. 'Don't be salty about it.' They watched Yusef eat his food and lick his fingers clean. 'What's he got to say about his situation?'

'Nothing yet,' Sol replied. 'He's digesting things.'

Gianni returned as tight-lipped as when he'd left. Sol threw him a pointed look.

'There's got to be a better way than this,' said Gianni.

'Then why is Ricky Vine still on the streets?' Sol asked.

Gianni shook his head, defeated. 'This isn't police work.'

'Good job,' snapped Sol. 'Seeing as I'm not even a copper any more.'

Hutch put up both his hands, all ten nails neat and smooth. 'Let's just see where this leads us, shall we? For all we know the kid will tell us he's not interested in a deal.'

'Nah. Not with Child Catcher Connolly on the case,' said Gianni.

The Jade Garden was noisy with a group of school mums on a night out, three bottles of Pinot Grigio down. One lifted her jumper to show off a pair of big pants that went right up to her waist and the rest of the women hollered and hooted.

Jay eyed her up and chuckled.

'Have you no standards?' Liberty asked, and shoved a plate of spring rolls at him.

'Absolutely none.' He shook soy sauce over his food. 'You seen Becca?'

'Nope.'

'Bull.'

Liberty sighed and snapped open a pair of chopsticks. 'Can't you just go round there and plead with her to take you back? Give her the big gorgeous smile? It seems to work on every other woman on the planet.'

The woman with the big pants was now showing her bra. A flesh-coloured job with straps like they belonged on a rucksack.

'She won't listen,' said Jay. 'And, anyway, have you thought that maybe us splitting up is for the best?'

Liberty stopped in her tracks, a spicy prawn inches from her mouth. 'You two were great together, Jay. She made you happy.'

'Lib,' he said, crunching on the spring roll, 'I shagged the maid of honour at my own wedding.' Liberty stared. 'In between the leek and potato soup and the beef Wellington. Her name was Caroline and she was a friend of Becca from school.' He lifted a hand to the waitress to bring more beer. 'At least now I'm not lying all the time. Becca deserves better than that.' Liberty ate in silence, the salty taste of the sea on her tongue. It was true that she was so keen to get Jay back into a calm environment that she hadn't considered how horrible it was for Becca to be married to him. But, then, blood was thicker than water. Jay wiped his mouth. 'Look, I need to talk to you about something else, Lib.'

Liberty held up a chopstick, like a conductor's baton. 'If this is about going after Ricky Vine, forget it. I hate him as much as you, but we made a deal.'

'It's not about that shit-arse,' he said.

'Who, then?'

Song Chen, the owner of the Jade Garden, placed a cold beer in front of both Greenwoods, condensation running down the bottles. Then he put a third drink down and took a seat at the table. Liberty looked at Jay to find out what the hell was going on. Jay, in turn, nodded at Chen to speak.

'I hope you're enjoying your evening,' he said. 'The food is good?'

'Food's mint,' said Jay.

Liberty worried the edge of the label on the beer with her thumbnail until it began to peel. When the school mums began to sing 'All The Single Ladies', she frowned.

'Do you want me to tell them to leave?' asked Chen.

'Don't be daft,' Jay replied. 'They're just having a giggle. Why don't you tell Lib what the problem is?'

Chen gave a tiny bow of his head in thanks. 'I'm being squeezed for protection money, Miss Greenwood.'

Liberty shot Jay a look. How was this anything to do with them? The Greenwoods' business wasn't clean, far from it, but protection rackets were way off their radar. Getting into wars over who could grab a few quid from a tatty Chinese restaurant wasn't on her bucket list.

'Think about it, Lib,' said Jay. 'This is our local. Everybody knows that.'

Liberty took a long drink of beer and sighed. Jay was right. People could try to extort money anywhere they liked, but not from places that were considered part of the Greenwoods' patch. And the Jade Garden was definitely that. 'Have they done anything?' she asked.

'They put a hair dryer in my tank,' said Chen.

Liberty lifted her chin in the direction of the entrance. The tank, usually teeming with silver fish dodging in and out of a plastic shipwreck, was currently empty. She sighed again. 'Fine.' She reached into her handbag and pulled out a pen. 'Name and address of who's doing this.'

Chen took it with a smile and scribbled on the menu. Then he jumped from his seat and moved to the school-mum table. 'Ladies, I'm afraid we're closing. If you could finish your drinks.'

Big Pants glanced at Jay and Liberty, their table still laden with food.

'Two words.' Liberty smiled at the woman. 'Victoria's Secret.'

Tia was exactly where Liberty had seen her earlier, outside the all-night chemist, scowl plastered on her face, scratching her crotch when she thought no one was looking.

Jay pulled the car over and flashed his lights. Tia scuttled across,

31

and when she was in the back seat, Liberty handed her a thin white carrier of takeaway boxes.

'Chinese?' Tia asked, already peeling off one of the lids. 'I can't get enough of this seaweed stuff. They put sugar on it. Like sprinkle it all over.'

'We need you to do something, Tia,' said Liberty.

Tia shrugged and shovelled the crispy green shards of seaweed into her mouth with her fingers.

'Probably need to bring someone with you. Anyone you trust?' Liberty asked, jerking her thumb at the youngers.

'What can I tell you, Lib? They're all thick as pig shit.'

'Excellent.'

With the box of seaweed still in her hands, Tia jumped out of the car and shouted to a couple of lads who bounded over and got in.

'Is that a Chinese?' one asked, beaming.

'As if I'm sharing it with you pair of muppets,' said Tia.

The younger ignored her and reached into the bag for the box on the top, but Tia batted his hand away harder than necessary. He kissed his teeth.

'Let's get this done,' said Jay, and gunned the engine.

They pulled up close to the address Chen had given them. It was a minicab firm on the far side of the Crosshills. A lone taxi arrived for a passenger, then sped off into the drizzle. Liberty checked that the CCTV camera at the end of the street was still hanging off the wall and turned in her seat to face the three kids in the back. 'Nothing over the top, right?' she said. 'It's just a warning.'

All three nodded and got out. Liberty followed them to the boot and opened it. Jay had tossed in a couple of crowbars and a claw hammer.

'What if they're packing?' Tia asked.

'You're not on *The Wire*,' Liberty replied.

'The what?'

'*The Wire*.' Liberty met three blank faces. 'The best telly series of all time?'

'Never heard of it,' said Tia, and, by the look of it, neither had the other two.

'You're getting old, Lib,' said Jay, with a wink.

'Getting?' said Tia.

'Ha-ha,' said Liberty. 'Just do what needs to be done, smartarse. From now on the Jade Garden's off limits for this lot, okay?'

All three grabbed a weapon, pulled up their hoods and headed into the cab firm. The Kalkan family who owned it were Turkish bit players. There was a halal butcher and some small-time protection. Presumably they didn't know the Greenwoods used the Jade Garden as their local or they'd have stayed well clear. A smashed radio control and a slap around the head should put them right and sort things out.

Jay and Liberty got back into the car and waited. Liberty turned on the music. She knew what was going on inside, but she didn't want to have to hear it. Jay reached over for one of the food cartons and started tucking into some stir-fried noodles with his fingers, slurping them into his mouth like spaghetti.

'And we wonder why Becca doesn't want you,' said Liberty.

Jay wiped his greasy mouth with the back of his hand. 'You found Daisy yet?' Liberty shook her head. 'Maybe she moved away,' said Jay.

'Maybe.'

'Maybe she doesn't want to be found,' he said. Liberty raised an eyebrow at him. 'I just think that if she's still local she must know you're looking for her, so if she wanted to see you, she would have got in touch.' Liberty had considered that. Of course she had. Daisy might be trying to start a new life, and the last person she'd want to speak to would be Frankie Greenwood's sister. 'You can't fix everything, Lib.'

Liberty knew only too well what her limitations were in that department. No matter how hard she tried to keep everyone safe, there were too many mines buried in the road. But that didn't mean she should stop trying. When Tia stumbled out of the cab firm, Jay wound down his window.

'He's told us to fuck off,' Tia said. Jay and Liberty exchanged a look. 'He says he doesn't care who goes to the Jade Garden.'

'You told him it was us?' Jay asked. 'You told him it was the Greenwoods he's dealing with?'

Tia rolled her eyes. Like duh. 'He says he doesn't give a shit.'

Jay growled and Liberty sighed. Why wouldn't people see reason? The world would run far more smoothly if people just used common sense. They left the warmth of the car and headed into the cab firm.

Kalkan was on the floor in the corner, surrounded by bits of smashed plastic and shards of glass. His bottom lip was fat and bleeding and there was a gash above his eye. The youngers stood over him, crowbars held like baseball bats ready for the ball.

Jay's trainers crunched through the glass. He was still holding the tray of noodles as he leaned over the Turk.

'Oi.' Tia tried to grab the container. 'They're mine.'

Jay held it out of her reach.

'You're making a big mistake,' Kalkan muttered, and spat out a mouthful of blood.

A mobile rang and it took a second for anyone to realise it was in Kalkan's pocket. Liberty nodded at one of the youngers, who reached in for it and handed it to her.

'Someone called Pinar wants you,' she said to Kalkan. 'Who's that, then? The missus?'

'Fuck off,' said Kalkan.

'Rude,' said Tia, and kicked him in the stomach.

A scream erupted from the man and he curled into the foetal position. Tia kicked him again, this time at the base of his spine. The Turk writhed backwards, trying to catch his breath.

Liberty bent to a crouch next to the man's head. 'All we need is for you to stay clear of the Jade Garden. Do your thing wherever else you want, we really don't mind, but that restaurant is off limits. Understand?'

Kalkan looked up at Liberty, his mouth a twisted mess of ragged flesh. When he finally spoke, his voice crackled with wounded rage. 'Fuck. Off.'

Liberty stood, smoothed down the knees of her trousers and slid his mobile into her pocket. Jay handed her the noodles, grabbed a fistful of the Turk's hair and dragged him through the glass towards the door.

'Open the boot of the car,' Jay told Tia.

Chapter 3

18 October 1990

I'm sat across from Connor, hands jammed into my pockets. 'You look all right,' I tell him. And he does look loads better than the last time I saw him when he was white and thin, like a slice of cheap bread, begging me to tell the police that his drugs were mine. Actually, he looks more or less the same as before he got nicked except for a home-made tattoo on his neck that looks a bit like a mark in music but could just as easily be a b.

'You look beautiful,' he says. 'Well, you always do.'

I can feel I'm blushing, so I drop my head and stare at the table.

A trustee comes around with a trolley and winks at Connor. 'Girlfriend?'

Connor gives one of his cheeky grins. 'Ex.'

'Bummer.'

'All my own fault,' says Connor.

I look at the stuff on the trolley. I've only got a quid on me. 'How much is a Twix?'

'You don't have to bother, Lib,' says Connor.

The trustee frowns. The food in jail is so crap inmates will do anything for a bit of chocolate on a visit. When I used to go and see our Jay, he'd literally kiss me if I could afford to buy him a treat.

'It's fine,' I say, and give the trustee the pound coin.

He hands me the Twix and my change, then smiles at Connor. 'Must be love, eh, lad?' Then he pushes his trolley down the aisle to the next table where a woman with round glasses and a centre parting is talking ten to the dozen. She looks a bit like John Lennon with a double chin.

I rip open the chocolate with my teeth and hand a stick to Connor. If it was our Jay, he'd have crammed it straight into his mouth, but Connor lays it on the table in front of him, an index finger touching each end. When he looks at me, I can see he's all choked up. 'What's up? Did you want a Toffee Crisp?'

Connor laughs and wipes his eyes. 'How are you so amazing?'

'Practice,' I say.

We eat our bits of the Twix.

'I didn't think you'd come,' he says. I didn't either. I honestly thought if I never saw Connor again it would be too soon. I loved him. He loved me. And then he broke my heart. The end. 'I just want you to know how sorry I am, Lib.'

I chew the biscuit part of the Twix. He probably is sorry. He's probably been on one of them courses they make you take in prison about how you have to apologise to the people you've let down or whatever. But it doesn't change anything, does it? 'Sorry' – well, it's just a word.

'How're the kids?' he asks. I shrug. There's a hearing coming up, but I can't be bothered to think about it all, never mind explain it. 'What about college? Still the brain of Britain?'

'Look, Connor, what do you actually want?' I say.

'I told you, I wanted to say I'm sorry.'

'Right, well, you've said it.'

He pulls a rollie from the pocket of his jogging bottoms and puts it behind his ear. 'I want to tell you I've been thinking about things. I mean, there's bugger-all else to do in here, is there? And I've come to the conclusion that you're the best thing that ever happened to me. And I asked you to lie to the police cos I was scared shitless of being banged up but, to be honest, when I got used to being in here I realised I'm a lot more scared of not seeing you ever again.' He takes a breath and puts the rollie back in his pocket. 'I know you're not going to say it's all fine.'

'You're right. I'm not.'

37

*He smiles. The only boy I know with a more gorgeous smile is our Jay.
'I just want us to stay in touch, Lib.'*

'Why?'

'You're a one-off,' he says. 'And I miss you.'

*I miss you. Present tense. I did miss Connor when he first got arrested.
I felt like I'd been punched in the gut, constantly winded. But then I did
this thing where I pushed him out of my mind, and I felt better. There were
two ways of doing it. Think about him and feel like I was dying, or not
think about him at all. So I did the last one. I took a rubber and I got rid
of all traces of him. The laughing, the dancing, the kissing. The time he
drove me to court on his bike to see our Jay and we weren't even going out
then, so he was just being nice. The first time he told me he loved me after
we'd almost had sex twice but Rob kept interrupting. All erased like none
of it happened. Or it happened to someone else I know but not very well.*

'I've got to go,' I say.

*As I get to my feet, he grabs my hand. 'Will you come and see me
again?'*

'I don't know what I'm going to do,' I tell him.

Present Day

The New Kusadasi Halal butcher's smelt surprisingly fresh considering the amount of raw meat that surrounded them. To be
honest, Kalkan gave off a worse stench seeing as he'd peed himself
on the journey across the estate.

'That's minging,' said Tia, nodding at the dark stain across the
crotch of his trackie bottoms.

Liberty wrinkled her nose at the Turk hunched in the corner
next to a cold counter piled high with chicken legs. She pulled
out the phone she'd taken from him earlier. 'Say cheese.' The flash
briefly lit up the room. 'Got to be honest, you don't look great.'

'Better than your Tinder pic, Lib,' said Jay, peering over her
shoulder.

Tia hooted with laughter until Liberty flicked her upper arm. 'Ow.'

'What's through there?' Liberty asked, but she was already striding across the shop floor to a steel door, which she threw open.

'Whoah,' said Tia.

Beyond the doors was the cold store where animal carcasses hung from metal hooks, the skinned flesh covered with white fat.

'Are they pigs?' asked one of the young lads.

'It's a halal butcher's, you idiot,' snapped Tia, and turned to Liberty. 'Didn't I tell you they were thick? Though not as thick as him.' Tia gave the Turk another kick. 'I mean, why is he even making us do this?'

Some of the fight had left Kalkan and he didn't swear, but he still wasn't ready to capitulate. Instead he narrowed his eyes at Tia and slowly shook his head. What was wrong with him? All he had to do was agree to leave the Jade Garden alone.

'I'm going to send the photo to Pinar,' said Liberty. The Turk shrugged. 'No, actually, I'm going to send it to everyone in your contact list. Just so there's no misunderstanding about what's in store for the rest of your family if we can't reach an agreement tonight.'

'Make sure you get the piss stain in,' said Tia.

'Know what I think?' said Jay. 'A video is better. It'll give a more rounded picture of what's happening.'

'Good shout,' Liberty replied.

'We need some action, though,' said Jay. 'It's all a bit boring if he's just sitting there.'

'How about if I crack his kneecaps with this?' asked Tia, holding up the hammer. Kalkan glanced at the round metal head and breathed hard. 'If you get close enough, I bet you'll be able to record them popping. The sound quality's not bad on the iPhone eleven.'

Liberty had no doubt that Tia would cheerfully do what she was suggesting but wanted to avoid any serious injury, if possible. What she needed was something theatrical that would scare Kalkan into seeing sense but preferably without leaving him in a wheelchair. She looked around the butcher's and smiled at the slaughtered animals hanging in a row. 'Let's film our friend with all the other dead meat.'

Yusef's stomach churned and he wished he hadn't eaten the nuggets. Even the paper plate they came on was making him feel sick, with the big smear of sauce across it. He knocked it off the table and it flew across the interview room, landing upside down.

The social worker had disappeared again, saying she needed the toilet. He hadn't told her what the scruffy copper said. What would be the point? All these people were just the same. They were meant to look out for you, but they just watched their own backs.

When he'd first started talking about trying to leave home, his mum had cried and begged him not to go. She'd been convinced that only your own people would look out for you. It had transpired that she was right. But when his brother Kidane turned eighteen and was taken for his national service, she changed her tune. They heard he was at the border fighting the Sudanese, but it might have been a rumour because Kidane never called or wrote any letters. One time, Mum managed to get a yellow pass to travel to Keren so she could get some answers. There was a government man there who said he could get information. She paid him but he disappeared the next day. Maybe one of his neighbours informed on him, or maybe he just took the cash and ran away.

Yusef licked the tattoo on his thumb with the tip of his tongue. A tiny smiley face that his friend had scratched on for him the night before they left the Jungle in Calais.

The door opened and the scruffy cop reappeared. He noticed

the paper plate, picked it up and popped it into the bin in the corner. 'You don't want to go back home, do you?' he said.

Actually, Yusef would kill to do just that. He'd love to sit down with his mum, drink a cup of *shahi* while she complained about the cost of sunflower oil. But he couldn't do that, could he? Anyone who was sent home got detained.

He buried his chin in the collar of his jacket. It was white and furry, but something had got stuck in the fabric and it felt scratchy against his skin.

'So, how about we do each other a favour?' said the cop.

Yusef snorted. Men had asked him that a lot of times. Men at border patrols, men driving lorries, men offering clean clothes and deodorant in the Jungle. The favours always turned out to involve them sticking their cocks in some part of Yusef.

'Not that sort of favour,' said the cop, as if reading his mind. Yusef picked at the hard lump on his collar with his nail. 'I'm thinking that maybe I could make this charge go away.' The cop blew his fringe from his eyes. 'And no charge means no reason for the Home Office to look into your age.'

Yusef laughed. If the bloke didn't want anal, he wanted information. He wanted Yusef to grass up the suppliers. 'You think I know who brings in the drugs?'

'Nope.' The cop sat down at last. 'But I think you can find out.'

It took twenty minutes, two rolls of gaffer tape and a rope Tia found being used to tie up a sack of onions to attach the Turk feet first to a meat hook. He'd kicked and screamed for a bit, but when Jay punched him in the face, he'd shut up at last.

Jay was still flexing and unflexing his fingers. 'I think I've broken something.' Liberty glanced briefly at the knuckle on his middle finger swollen to twice its normal size. 'Thanks for the sympathy.'

Liberty grabbed his hand and kissed it, making her brother yelp. 'All better now?'

'So, what are we gonna do with him?' Tia asked.

Liberty had Kalkan's mobile in her hand and scrolled through his texts. They were mostly in Turkish but the emojis attached made her assume they were from family and friends. Pinar was fond of the winking smiley, the thumbs-up and, strangely enough, the mushroom. 'What's that about?' she asked Tia.

'Do I look like I speak Turkish?'

'Not the words, the bloody mushroom,' Liberty replied.

Tia grabbed the phone and scowled at the screen. 'Must be something to do with poison.'

'You reckon?' Liberty took back the phone. 'His missus sends it a lot.'

'Cos she wants to kill him.' Tia pointed to Kalkan dangling upside down between two headless lambs. 'Don't blame her if I'm honest.'

Liberty laughed and went into the camera setting, pressed for video and held it up so the Turk was in the middle of the frame. 'Right. Let's get this filmed and send it out to everyone he knows.'

'Bet it goes viral,' said Tia.

Liberty waved at the two youngers. 'Push him as far as you can to the left.'

The lads grabbed Kalkan and shoved him to the left. The hook he was hanging from slid along the pole a few inches but stopped when it ran out of momentum.

'You'll have to move the animals on either side of him first,' Liberty told them. 'Probably one at a time.'

The lads nodded and went to the lamb on the left side of Kalkan. But as soon as one of them touched the flesh he screamed and jumped away as if he'd been electrocuted.

'What's up with you?' Tia shouted.

'It's rank.' The lad shuddered. 'Really cold and horrible.'

Tia rolled her eyes. 'What did you expect? That it had been cooked?' The second lad reached out a tentative finger and touched the white fat, face pulled into a grimace. Tia lifted her claw hammer. 'Move the fucking meat.'

The first lad, sensing Tia would indeed cave in his skull, pulled his sleeves over his hands and pushed the carcass as far as he could. The other lad copied him, and soon they had all the dead lambs to the sides. Then they did the same with Kalkan, pulling him as far to the right as possible.

Jay blew on his finger. 'What the hell are you up to, Lib?'

'Okay, boys, I'm going to count to three and then I want you to push him the other way as hard as you can.' The lads got in place and nodded. 'One. Two. Three.'

The lads gave Kalkan a shove and his hook slid about a foot along its pole before coming to a halt.

Liberty lowered the phone. 'We need a bit more movement than that.'

The lads dragged Kalkan back to his starting position, then gave a harder shove. This time the Turk moved around two feet. Liberty sighed as they pulled him back again, ready for the next attempt, but Tia was already diving towards them, hammer raised. They jumped out of the way, hands on their heads for protection. But instead of battering anyone, Tia threw down the hammer and it landed on the tiled floor with a metallic clang. Then she grabbed Kalkan around the waist. 'Ready?' she shouted at Liberty.

Liberty held the camera aloft. 'Action.'

Tia pulled the Turk towards her, paused for a second, then pushed with all her might. The hook danced along the pole and Kalkan flew the length of it. As he went, he seemed to gather more and more speed until he disappeared just beyond the plastic curtain where he came to a halt with a thud.

Everyone cheered. Jay put his fingers into his mouth to whistle, remembered his injury and groaned. 'Did you get it?' he asked

Liberty, putting his hand between his thighs and jiggling his knees.

'Yup.' Liberty stopped filming. 'Now let's give our friend one more chance to see reason. If he agrees to our request, I'll wipe the video.'

The lads and Tia went behind the curtain to drag Kalkan back and Liberty could hear them grunting.

'He's stuck,' Tia called.

Liberty and Jay looked at one another. 'What the hell do you mean he's stuck?'

They joined the kids behind the plastic curtain and saw Tia trying to pull Kalkan back by the waistband of his trackies. She gestured for the youngers to take an arm each and between them they heaved Kalkan from the wall. At first his torso refused to budge, as if it was glued to the bricks of the wall. At last they prised it away and a squelching sound filled the cold store. Then they all saw the problem. The Turk had been skewered by a six-inch spike, and now he was free of it, blood spurted from the hole it had made. Kalkan's tongue rolled out of his lifeless mouth. Shit.

'Do you think he's dead?' Tia asked.

'Of course he's frigging dead,' said Liberty.

Jay licked his knuckle. 'Well, at least he won't be causing any more ructions at the Jade Garden.'

Fifteen minutes later Crystal arrived on the scene.

'What the hell are you doing here?' Liberty hissed at her sister. 'You're bloody pregnant.'

Crystal lifted her shirt to reveal her bulge. She point-blank refused to buy any maternity clothes so just wore long tops and her usual skinny jeans, zip undone. 'No shit, Sherlock.'

'You might go into labour with the shock,' said Liberty.

Crystal snorted. Clearly, she didn't think the sight of a dead man hanging from a meat hook constituted shocking and skirted around Liberty to take a look. A red stain had spread across Kalkan's hoodie and a pool of blood had collected below him.

'Where's Mel?' Jay asked.

'Making the necessary calls,' Crystal replied.

Liberty nodded. Mel could be relied upon to get rid of the body and sort out this mess. She'd break their heads in two for at least a year about what they'd done, but that was the price they'd have to pay.

'Where are the kids?' Crystal asked.

'Tia's taken them back to hers,' Liberty said.

'Can we trust them?'

Liberty let out a long breath. 'For now.' She didn't want to think about what might have to happen if that trust began to wane. 'Shall we get off?'

Crystal gave the Turk one last glance and closed the door to the cold store.

'I'll wait,' said Jay.

Liberty smiled weakly and gave him a hug, then left her brother to oversee the clean-up operation with Mel. 'Honestly, it would have been cheaper and easier to find a new Chinese.'

'No way.' Jay shook his head. 'Best spring rolls in Wakefield. And they don't charge us.'

Liberty laughed. For one thing, they could afford all the spring rolls in Yorkshire if they wanted them. And for another, there wouldn't be many restaurant owners who would ask the Greenwoods to pay. 'Tell Mel I'm sorry,' she said.

Now it was Jay's turn to laugh. 'We're gonna be apologising until the end of time for this fuck-up.'

Rose couldn't sleep. She'd stopped checking her phone, but knew it would be message after message, blaming her for Joel's death, so she lay on top of her duvet, eyes closed, mind turning the whole thing over and over. When she'd discovered what he was up to, she could have spoken to him, given him an ultimatum: clean up his act or Rose would expose him. But she hadn't done that. He probably wouldn't have listened to her, but she hadn't given him the chance.

When the bell rang, she ignored it. But then someone thumped hard on the door. She pulled back the corner of her bedroom curtain to see who was there, unsure what she'd do if it was one of Joel's mates. If it were a member of the public being harassed she'd advise them to call the police . . .

She looked down and saw Adam on her doorstep. He held up a hand in greeting and she replied in kind.

When she opened the door and Adam stepped over the threshold he gagged. 'What the actual?'

'Someone gave me a present,' she replied, and sprayed the hallway with more air freshener.

'You should report this to the boss,' said Adam.

'He probably sent it.'

Adam followed her through to the kitchen. They'd never been in each other's homes before. Never needed to. She didn't ask him if he wanted a beer, just went to the fridge and brought out two bottles of Bud.

'He didn't kill himself,' said Rose.

Adam nodded and took a sip. 'You got any food?'

'You had a burger like three hours ago.'

He shrugged and reached over to open a cupboard, found a tube of Smokey Bacon Pringles and let a stack of them slide out into his palm. Then he licked the top one with the tip of his tongue, lifted it and flicked it into his mouth. 'They'll have to look into it.' Adam crunched the Pringle. 'Death in custody and all that.'

Rose shook her head. 'He's an embarrassment to everybody. A bent copper. A suicide is a good result all round.'

'So what are you gonna do?' Adam asked.

'What I always do,' Rose replied. 'Give everyone even more reason to hate me.'

Adam laughed and shovelled the rest of the crisps into his mouth.

Sol and Hutch watched the screens. Yusef was back in his cell for the night and had bedded himself down, jacket covering his face.

'Gianni's losing his bottle,' said Sol.

'Yup,' Hutch replied.

'You don't seem surprised.'

Hutch shrugged. 'There's a time limit on how long any of us can stomach this.'

Sol pulled out his vape and wondered if he could get away with a cheeky toke while no one was around, but Hutch wagged a warning finger. Then his mobile rang, and he groaned when he saw who was calling. He put his finger to his lips for Sol to keep quiet and put his mobile on speaker.

'Gov.'

'Hutch.'

Sol's eyes widened. The boss kept pretty much out of their way, taking the view that what she didn't know couldn't hurt her.

'I hear from a little bird that you and your team are holed up in Longsight nick.'

'Ask me no questions and I'll tell you no lies, Gov,' Hutch replied.

Sol had met Chief Bella Kapur just a handful of times and had said almost nothing in her presence. She ran the Central Drugs Unit with a seemingly light touch, which left everyone in no doubt that when she did interject, she expected full attention and an immediate response. Although she was an Asian woman, Sol had never heard so much as a whisper about quotas or diversity. She was regarded by all as brilliant.

'They got me out of bed, Hutch,' she said. 'And I need all the beauty sleep I can get.'

'Sorry about that, Gov.'

'Apparently we have another kid.'

Hutch and Sol exchanged a glance. Their unorthodox recruitment policy had never been discussed openly at the CDU, but Kapur clearly knew all about it.

'He's got very close links with Ricky Vine,' Hutch replied.

Sol gave a snort. 'Close links' was probably overplaying it. Hutch scowled and ran a finger across his throat for Sol to shut up.

'Someone else there?' asked the boss.

Hutch mouthed, 'Well done.'

'Sol Connolly, Gov,' said Sol.

He was just one of the freelancers the CDU liked to have working for them, so had no need to call her his boss but, to be honest, he liked it. Top brass on the job were often a pain in the arse, but they were also the people who got you money and resources, and the best of the best would put their necks on the line for their teams. Bella Kapur was one of those.

'Well, Sol,' said the gov, 'tell me you've got something worth me getting all this earache about.'

'He feels like a decent spot, Gov,' Sol replied. 'He's already part of Vine's crew, so it's not like we're parachuting a newcomer into the fold. The fact that he's being used as the stash man means he's considered smarter than your average bear.'

'Can you turn him?' she asked.

Sol rubbed sweaty palms across his thighs. 'He's got a lot to lose.'

'Fine. You've got a month to make this work.'

Sol's mouth fell open. 'A month?'

'These things take a while,' said Hutch. 'We have to get our boy up the ranks. Make sure Vine trusts him. You can't put a time limit on that, Gov.'

'I can and I just have.'

Kapur hung up. The conversation was at an end. The clock had just started ticking.

The custody sergeant opened Yusef's cell and scowled at Sol. 'You've got ten minutes, then I'm bringing him up to the desk.' He nodded at the tea Sol was carrying. 'Stop messing about. Either charge or release.'

Sol saluted with his free hand, slid into the cell and kicked the door shut behind him with his heel.

Yusef hadn't moved, still flat on the bed, face obscured by his jacket. He wasn't asleep, though – Sol could tell by his breathing that the kid was wide awake.

'So, how did you get into dealing?' Sol asked, and put the tea on the floor by Yusef's bed. Not surprisingly the kid didn't move or reply. 'Let me take a wild guess. Ricky Vine or, more likely, one of his underlings got chatting with you when you were in a care home. Offered you somewhere to stay, and all you had to do was pass on a few baggies of gear. Fair's fair. I mean, you'd have been what? Thirteen, fourteen? Even if you did get caught, there's nothing the feds could do to you.'

'I ain't a snitch,' said Yusef, from under his coat.

'I'm not asking you to turn Queen's, mate.' Sol sat on the edge of the bed. 'You won't be in court facing Ricky. Just carry on doing your thing, but keep me in the loop. There's a tea there if you want it.'

Yusef didn't move and Sol stared straight ahead at the wall. At last Yusef pushed away his coat and leaned down to the floor for the cup. He took a gulp and sighed.

'Look, the truth is Ricky Vine doesn't give a shit about you,' said Sol. 'You're not stupid so you know this is true.'

Yusef laughed. 'Whereas you're just thinking about my welfare.'

'I can get these charges dropped.' Sol spoke to the wall. 'Or you can go to jail pending a Home Office investigation into your age.'

'I'm not a grass.'

Sol pulled out his phone, clicked on a link and played a YouTube video, all jaunty camera angles and jingly music as a presenter looked out over the rooftops of Asmara. 'Not gonna lie, it doesn't look too bad,' said Sol. There was a bang on the door. 'Fair dos.' Sol got to his feet and opened it to the custody sergeant. 'Let's charge him.'

The custody sergeant gestured for Sol to leave the cell. 'About time.'

'No bail,' said Sol.

'I think you'll find that's my decision,' said the custody sergeant.

'And you wouldn't want your decision to screw up a major drugs operation.'

'Fucking CDU,' the custody sergeant mumbled.

Sol chuckled and stepped out of the cell. He didn't turn around but could hear Yusef shuffling behind him. Hutch was waiting for them all at the custody desk, one eyebrow raised in a question mark.

Yusef sank onto the bench, shoulders hunched, and the custody sergeant skirted around to his side of the desk. 'Well, now, what are we charging him with?'

'Possession with intent to supply class A,' Hutch replied.

The custody sergeant tapped on his computer and Sol took a seat next to Yusef, who still had his cup in his hand. Sol played the YouTube video on his phone, though he muted the sound. 'Last-chance saloon, Yusef,' he whispered.

Yusef groaned. 'I'm not a grass.'

'You're also not in jail in Eritrea,' Sol replied.

'Fine.'

Sol tapped the kid's thigh and nodded at Hutch, who pulled out his own phone.

'Just a second,' said Hutch. 'Seems like there might be a problem with the evidence.'

The custody sergeant folded his arms across his chest. 'Funny that.'

Crystal drove through the estate, her hands barely able to reach the wheel.

'Drop me at the Cashino,' said Liberty. 'I left my car there.'

'How much have you had to drink?' Crystal asked.

Liberty shrugged. She'd had a couple in the Cherry and a couple with Jay in the arcade. And then some beers in the Jade Garden. 'I'll be fine.'

Crystal gave her the side-eye and drove to Empire Rise where Liberty rented a house. The road was empty and dark in the wet night, the streetlight outside her place on the blink. Good. The damn thing lit up her bedroom like Blackpool. She had enough trouble sleeping at the best of times without that shining in her eyes.

As Crystal pulled up, something darted across Liberty's eyeline. Crystal tensed: she'd clocked it too. A dark shape, no more than a shadow within a shadow. Crystal pointed at the glove compartment. Wordlessly, Liberty opened it and pulled out a gun. Crystal held out an open palm for it, but Liberty batted her away. She checked the gun was loaded, then carefully got out of the car.

She moved as quietly as she could towards her house, gun pointed in front of her, eyes checking for any sign of movement. The wind howled and her neighbours' hedges creaked. Maybe that was all it had been.

When she was at her front door, Liberty's heart was pounding. She put her hand on the wood and pushed, found that everything was locked up. She surveyed her windows – all shut, nothing broken – and breathed a sigh of relief.

51

'Anything?'

Liberty's jaw tightened at the sight of her sister by her side. 'Get back in the car.'

'Why?' Crystal asked.

'Because you're the size of a bus and I've got the bloody gun.'

Crystal waved a pistol. 'I double up these days.' She took a step to the right. 'We need to check the back.'

'At least let me go first,' said Liberty, as she held Crystal back by a handful of jacket.

They skirted the side of the house, both holding their weapons against their shoulders. When they were convinced the coast was clear, they relaxed their arms and Crystal laughed.

Liberty tucked her weapon into the back of her waistband. 'D'you wanna come in?'

'Nah,' Crystal replied, with a yawn. 'Knackered.'

They went back to the front door and Liberty unlocked it. With her key still in the lock and her hand still on the key, she said, 'We're getting as paranoid as Mel.'

Then they heard running footsteps and whipped their heads towards the road. Liberty grabbed the gun from her waistband and pointed into the black night. The sound came first, a whoosh of air, then the bright orange flare of a flame. The smell of petrol filled the air. Then the smash of breaking glass as something was thrown at Crystal's car.

Crystal took a step towards it, but again Liberty snatched at her jacket. 'No.'

And then the car was engulfed in a ball of fire, lighting up the street. Liberty dragged her sister into the house and threw the door shut just as the fuel tank exploded.

A few hours later when the fire brigade and the police had finally left, Jay and Mel arrived.

'Am I going to get any sleep tonight?' Mel demanded.

They stared at the charred remains of the BMW and Crystal moved a piece of scorched metal with the toe of her shoe. 'The Turks?'

Liberty shook her head. 'I doubt anyone's even missed Kalkan yet.'

The acrid smell of smoke filled their lungs. Liberty could taste soot at the back of her throat.

Jay coughed. 'Ricky Vine?'

In some ways it made sense. Not long ago, Liberty had threatened to firebomb his gym, so retaliation in kind would be on the cards. Except that peace had held between them since that threat. Despite Frankie's death and Vine losing his number two, both sides had accepted that a war across the Pennines would help no one. Why would Vine risk that now?

'Time for a trip to Manchester,' said Liberty.

'I absolutely hate Manchester,' said Jay.

'Yup,' Liberty agreed. 'Complete shithole.'

Chapter 4

22 October 1990

'Would you like a cup of tea?' Mrs Moser asks.

I'm about to say I'm all right, because I just want to crack on, when our Jay jumps in like Eddie the chuffing Eagle. 'Yes, please, Miss.' He grins from ear to ear. 'And some biscuits.'

Mrs Moser smiles and pops out of the office to get some, but as soon as she's gone, Jay roots around in the papers on her desk.

I hit him around the head. 'Pack it in.'

'Don't you want to know what she's saying about us, then?'

He's right. I do want to know. I grab a handful of papers and try to scan what's on them as quickly as possible.

'Christ,' says Jay. 'Her writing's worse than mine.'

It's not. Nobody's handwriting is worse than Jay's. Even our Frankie can do better with a crayon.

I spy Jay's name. 'Hey, this is about you.'

He snatches the sheet from me, almost ripping it, and squints at the words. 'What does this mean?'

I lean over his shoulder for a look: Jay would benefit from a family setting. Despite being older than Crystal and Frankie he is equally vulnerable. 'She's saying you're bloody childish,' I tell him.

'I am not.'

'Yes, you are.'

'Not, not, not.'

The door handle goes so we shove the papers back on the desk and pretend we're deep in conversation.

'So how's the school work going, Lib?' Jay asks, in a robotic voice.

'Very well, thank you,' I reply.

Mrs Moser looks puzzled as she puts a tray down. 'Help yourselves.'

Me and Jay both go for the Jammie Dodger, but obviously he beats me to it.

'I can get more of those,' she says.

I shake my head and take the pink wafer. 'It's fine. We're not kids, are we?'

She smiles at me, but it's a sad smile that I get a lot of. One of the things I always liked about Connor was that he didn't pity me. He knew I had a lot on my plate and wanted to help but at the same time acted like I was just normal. When I catch myself thinking about him, I'm annoyed. This meeting is important and I can't go getting distracted by a boy I don't care about.

Mrs Moser picks up a mug of tea and doesn't put in any milk or sugar. I know it would make me look more grown-up if I did the same, but although I can manage a black tea I can't do it unsweetened. I stick to one spoonful as a halfway house. Jay shovels in three and I have to swallow a sigh.

'So this morning I want to talk to you about the hearing,' says Mrs Moser.

'What hearing?' I ask.

'Didn't they tell you one's been set?'

'Nobody tells us owt,' says Jay, between slurps of tea.

'Well, it has only just been listed,' says Mrs Moser.

'What are you going to recommend?' I ask.

This is the crux of it. Me and Jay can ask to see Crystal and Frankie until we're blue in the face, but the judge will listen to the guardian ad litem. What she recommends usually goes.

'Obviously I'm in favour of sibling contact,' she says.

We wait. Everyone's 'in favour of sibling contact' but there's always some catch. Either Frankie's wetting the bed, or Jay's in YOI or I'm making matters worse by moving to Manchester.

'But, actually,' says Mrs Moser, 'I'm going to go further than that. I'm going to recommend a family placement.'

Jay and I exchange a look. There aren't any foster placements that will take all four of us.

'They've tried to sort that out no end of times,' I say.

'I know, but I might have secured a placement for three of you.'

She smiles at Jay but he's already shaking his head. 'I'm not going anywhere without Lib.'

'I understand it's not . . .'

Jay slams down his mug and tea sloshes onto Mrs Moser's paperwork. I grab his hands before he can throw the plate of biscuits across the room.

'Look at me,' I tell him. His chest goes up and down as he breathes hard. 'Look at me, Jay.' His eyes are wild when he finally turns my way. I squeeze his hands and drop my voice to a whisper. 'I've only got a few months left in care anyway. Then a year after that I'll be off to uni.' He grinds his teeth. 'But you've got a way to go, Jay.'

'I'd rather do my time in secure.'

'Bollocks would you,' I tell him. 'And what about the little ones? Who'll be keeping an eye on them while you're banging your head against a cell wall?'

We look at one another for a long moment and at last he gives a tiny nod.

I smile at Mrs Moser, but I'm still hanging on to Jay's hands for dear life.

Present Day

Mel prowled around the back of the bar in the Cherry, like a caged animal at the zoo, swiping at the surfaces with a wet cloth. At some point she'd changed into a pair of PVC leggings and a red satin blouse with pussy bow. Her gold chains were tangled in the knot of the bow.

Liberty sipped a Diet Coke. No one had had any sleep and tempers were frayed. Crystal tore a beer mat to shreds and Jay tapped out a rhythm on the bar with his thumbnail.

'Get it over with, Mel,' said Crystal.

'Me?' Mel sent the cloth into the bin with a wet slap. 'Why would I have anything to say?' Crystal smiled down at the pile of cardboard confetti. 'I suppose you lot think all this is funny?'

'No one's laughing, Mel,' said Liberty.

'Right,' she replied. 'Because from where I'm standing you've managed to kill one of the local Turks and get your car torched in the space of twelve hours. Which is good going even by your standards.' She grabbed Liberty's glass, though it was still half full, and rinsed it in the sink. 'And now you've decided to cause a scene with Ricky bloody Vine.'

'We just need to talk to him,' said Liberty.

'He'll see it as an act of war,' she shouted. 'Going onto his patch, demanding he account for himself. Can't you see how that looks?'

Jay stood up, the corners of his mouth twitching. 'If he set fire to Crystal's car, he made the first move.'

'We don't know he did that,' said Mel.

'Which is why we need to talk to him,' Liberty pointed out. 'No accusations, just a conversation.'

Mel snatched up her mobile and thrust it in Liberty's face. 'Ever heard of one of these?'

'What if it's bugged?' Crystal asked, and Liberty couldn't help but laugh.

But the humour was short-lived as Mel threw down the glass and it smashed on the floor. She turned her back to them as they looked at one another. Then Liberty went around to Mel's side of the bar and picked up a dustpan and brush.

'Leave that to me,' said Mel, her voice wobbling.

'It's fine,' said Liberty.

Mel balled her fists. 'Isn't it my job to clear up the mess the Greenwoods make?' She took the brush from Liberty. 'Go on, then, get off to Manchester.' She pointed the bristles at Crystal. 'But at least leave this one behind.'

'I can do some asking around at this end,' said Crystal. 'See if anyone's heard a whisper.'

'I meant you should just stay out of all this,' said Mel. 'You've a baby to think of.'

'Mel's right,' said Liberty.

'This is family business.' Crystal shrugged. 'So I can't just go home and put my feet up.'

By mid-morning, Liberty and Jay were halfway across Saddleworth Moor. The rain was lashing against the windscreen, the wipers on top speed. Mist swirled over the brown land, like a bad spell. Liberty couldn't recall any time she'd made this journey with the sun shining. It was as if the powers of the universe had a pact never to smile on the place until all the dead children buried there were laid properly to rest.

Jay reached into a carrier bag on the floor behind him and root-led around to produce a grab bag of Revels. He tore open the packet with his teeth, took out a chocolate, tossed it into the air and caught it in his mouth. 'Shit,' he said, as he chewed. 'Coffee.'

Liberty nodded in solidarity. The coffee-flavoured ones were pants, only marginally better than orange cream. She filtered through the bag with her finger, found a Galaxy counter, threw it into the air and caught it in her mouth. She cracked the shell with her teeth and sucked, letting the chocolate disc melt on her tongue.

They'd done nearly the whole bag and two cans of Lilt by the time they reached Moss Side. Narrow streets flanked on both sides by red-brick terrace houses. A deserted parade of shops offered an all-night newsagent, a discount wine shop and a Tasty Fried Chicken.

At last the satnav announced they'd arrived – they were outside what looked like an old school, a high wire fence on all sides.

'Is this it?' asked Jay, nose wrinkled.

Liberty shrugged as he circled the building until they found an entrance at the back and pulled over. 'Stay put,' said Liberty.

'If you're not out in ten, I'm tearing the place apart,' Jay replied.

Liberty pursed her lips. She hadn't seen what Jay had put in the boot, but she had no doubt that he was tooled up like he was expecting the Valentine's Day massacre. 'We're not here to start anything.'

'Are we not?' he asked.

'No,' said Liberty, and got out of the car. 'We're just here to get the lie of the land.'

There was no sign, but a handwritten note was attached to the buzzer – Shadowbox. So this was the right place. Liberty pressed the buzzer.

'Yeah,' a voice replied.

Liberty looked up directly into the camera above the door. 'I'm here to see Ricky.'

'Never heard of him,' said the voice.

'Yeah, you have,' Liberty replied. 'Tell him it's Liberty Greenwood paying a visit.'

Thirty seconds passed, and the door opened. Liberty stepped along a damp corridor and into the gym. Inside, the concrete floor was littered with black rubber mats, and punch bags hung from metal frames. A ring, which was actually square, stood in the centre. Two men sparred with one another, mostly dodging blows, hands covered not with boxing gloves but what looked like white bandages. They were being overseen by a huge bloke in a pair of tight Lycra shorts and a wife-beater vest.

'I'm looking for Ricky,' said Liberty.

The huge bloke nodded for the boxers to carry on and beckoned for Liberty to put her arms out to the sides. She did as instructed and he patted her down, like airport security.

'Follow me.'

It occurred to her that if he wanted to kill her now, he could. She swallowed at the thought. Jay might have a pump-action shotgun in his boot but it wouldn't help if this man mountain wanted to snap her neck. They plodded up bare steps, feet crunching on brick.

At the very top was a door with a silver plaque that read 'Treatment Room'. The sound of buzzing seeped out. Liberty tried not to think about electric saws as the huge bloke knocked with swollen knuckles.

'Yeah,' someone shouted from inside, and they entered.

There were two massage tables. On the nearest another huge bloke was having his shoulders pummelled by a masseuse who, although she was a tiny Asian woman, was kneading him like pizza dough. The bloke looked up at Liberty. The hole for his head in the table had left a red ring circling his pockmarked face. One of his ears appeared to be missing. He went back to his massage without a word.

On the second table Ricky Vine was naked from the waist up. But instead of another masseuse, a man with a bushy beard was hovering over him, a tattoo gun in his hand. He gave Liberty the once-over, pierced eyebrow raised. The gun vibrated in his hand. 'You've got company, Ricky,' he said.

Ricky didn't get up but waved at a plastic chair placed at the head of his bed. 'Take a pew, Liberty.'

She walked between the two beds, the smell of sweaty flesh choking her. As she passed Ricky, the tattooist wiped away ink and blood from his latest work.

'The girlfriend had a new baby last week,' Ricky told her.

She checked the tattoo. On his flabby shoulder blade there were four names and dates of birth. Jaden, Zach, Willow and Skylar. Today he was having a new name scratched into his skin. 'You need to get a telly, Rick,' she said.

He laughed but winced as the tattooist finished off. The new kid was called Caleb. Named after Vine's best friend and second in command. Liberty had put a bullet into his head.

She took a seat. Waited.

'I hear someone tried to turn your sister into toast,' he said.

'News travels fast.'

Ricky waited until the baby's birthday was done and the buzzing of the gun was turned off, then he looked her up and down. 'You're a very attractive woman, do you know that?'

Liberty rolled her eyes. 'So I'm told. Listen, if you had anything to do with last night's fire, there'll be repercussions.'

'If I'd come for you, you wouldn't be sitting here now.' He sat up and stretched. Peered over his shoulder to try to see the handiwork. 'Any road, all that stuff between us is in the past.' The tattoo on his back stated that that might not be the case.

Liberty watched as the tattooist applied ointment to Ricky's skin and covered the wound with a dressing. 'You ever hear of the Kalkans?'

Ricky shook his head and winced as he pulled a T-shirt over his head. 'Russian?'

'Turkish.'

Ricky laughed, ran a hand over a chubby pink cheek. 'They should stick to making kebabs.'

Liberty didn't laugh. Instead she just stared at him. Then she got to her feet and left. At the door, she turned. 'As long as we're both clear about what will happen if this peace between us breaks.'

'We've both got too much to lose for that,' he replied.

Liberty smiled. 'Well, I don't have any kids.'

She shut the door, her threat hanging in the air, and took the stairs two at a time. Back in the gym, the boxers were skipping and she left with the sound of rope whipping rubber ringing in her ears.

When she returned to the car, Jay was at the boot, frowning up at the gym.

'You can stand down the nuclear option,' she said.

Back inside, he tossed one of the last Revels into the air and caught it in his mouth. 'Toffee.'

'Result,' Liberty said.

Despite the chocolate he'd put away, Jay was starving, so they stopped at a pub called the Halfway House that served food, according to a sign by the door. The line of men sitting at the bar eyed them suspiciously, but the barmaid, all dark curls and eye-liner, pointed Jay in the direction of a free table. 'What can I get you?' she asked.

Jay licked his lips. 'Whatever you're offering, beautiful.'

She giggled and pointed to a blackboard that announced the specials as fish and chips, pie and chips, curry and chips.

'What do you think a man like me might fancy?' Jay asked.

'Oh, for the love of God.' Liberty cuffed him round the head. 'We'll have two pie and chips, please. And a couple of Peronis.'

The woman smiled and went back to the bar, wiggling her bum far more than was necessary. When she came back with their beers, she pushed a mat onto the table, and as Liberty went to put her bottle on it she spotted a phone number scribbled in biro. She turned it over and slammed down her beer before Jay caught wind of it.

'Do we believe Vine didn't do it?' asked Jay.

Liberty took a sip, the froth of the lager tickling her lips. She wiped them with the pad of her thumb as she thought about the question. 'I don't know.'

'So what shall we do?'

'I don't know,' she repeated.

The pub door opened and a young lad came in, all nylon cagoule and swagger. The barmaid's face fell, but he gave her the finger. Liberty nudged Jay for him to take a look. The lad leaned in to speak to one of the men at the bar, who nodded and reached into the inside pocket of his coat. He pulled out an envelope and passed it over.

'I've told you before, I don't want to bring trouble into my pub,' said the barmaid.

'Fuck off,' said the lad. 'You know what's what.'

Jay pressed his mouth together so tightly, his lips disappeared. A vein in his temple throbbed.

'Jay,' Liberty warned him. 'Don't even think about it.'

'Do you need to be so lippy?' Every face turned to Jay. Liberty gripped his knee under the table but it was too late. 'I asked you a question, gobshite,' Jay shouted.

The lad pulled out a switch knife and the click reverberated around the silent pub as he unleashed the blade.

'Pack it in,' said the barmaid. 'They're not even from round these parts.'

The lad was already crossing the pub towards Jay and Liberty, hand outstretched, the silver of the knife glinting at them. 'Shouldn't be in here, then, should they?'

When he was a couple of feet away, Jay and Liberty stood up, pulled out their guns and aimed them at his head. He stopped in his tracks as if turned to stone.

'I don't suppose you were expecting that,' said Liberty.

The man at the bar moved his hand to the pocket from which he'd drawn his envelope. Liberty turned her weapon to him. 'I wouldn't.'

He snarled at her, lip pulled up to one side to expose several missing teeth, but didn't make any moves towards his pocket.

Liberty walked over, delved her hand inside, pulled out the man's gun and laughed. It was a modified starting pistol. She held it up to Jay. 'On your marks.'

Jay took the few steps to the lad and pressed the barrel of his gun against his spotty temple. The lad closed his eyes and allowed Jay to take the knife from him.

'Apologise,' said Jay.

The lad's eyes opened. 'What?'

Jay dug the gun into the skin of the lad's face and forced his head to one side. 'Say sorry to . . .' He looked at the barmaid. 'What's your name, sweetheart?'

'Amy.'

'That's a gorgeous name,' said Jay.

'I think it means "love",' said Liberty.

'Well, I'm in love, that's for sure,' said Jay. Then he jabbed the gun even harder, making the lad squirm. 'Say sorry to Amy for bringing your trouble into her pub.'

The lad's Adam's apple bobbed furiously. 'Sorry, Amy.'

Jay smiled and pushed the lad over. He fell with a splat onto the floor.

Liberty smiled at Amy. 'Any chance of getting those pies to go?'

Adam didn't say a word on the way to the prison. He just kept his eyes on the road ahead, hands on the steering wheel at ten to two.

'You know you don't have to do this,' said Rose.

He signalled left and pulled into the prison car park, studiously ignoring the razor wire across the top of the walls.

'You can stay in the car, then if the shit hits the fan you can plead ignorance,' she told him.

Rose had operated alone for as long as she could remember. For years as an only child she'd sat by herself on the swings, watching

sets of brothers and sisters laugh and screech as they ran around
the playground. Or, more often than not, row over who got the
last biscuit and punch each other over who was the tallest.

Her stepfather had called her a loner. He always said it like it
was an insult, but Rose didn't see it that way. She was reliant on
no one's good opinion for her peace of mind, certainly not his.
She didn't even care much what her mother thought of her, especially since her choice in men displayed a level of judgement that,
even at ten, Rose could see was faulty.

Was that why she'd reacted to Joel's corruption as badly as she
had? Because she'd allowed him to become a friend? Because
she'd started to trust someone for the first time?

'I'm the oldest of four,' said Adam. 'Have I ever told you that?'

Rose shook her head, although he might have done. She liked
Adam but sometimes, well, quite often really, he just rattled on
about nothing important so she zoned out.

'Yeah. I've got two younger brothers and a sister.'

'That's nice,' Rose said.

He turned and looked her square in the face, eyes more serious
than she'd ever seen before. 'They're all doing well. Sean and
Callum run a business together, fitting kitchens and stuff. Both
married. Both got kids. And our Leanne moved away to Leicester,
runs some big warehouse over there.'

Rose frowned. None of it sounded terribly impressive to her.
'You're a copper, Adam.'

'Hardly.' His sleeve had ridden up and she could see the start
of the panther on his wrist. 'I mean, I didn't join up to mooch
around the estate nicking homeless folk.'

Rose didn't know what to say. To be honest, she'd no idea why
Adam might have joined the force. She thought maybe he just
wanted a steady number with a decent pension at the end of it. He
didn't seem too interested in catching criminals.

'I used to watch you lot in the canteen,' he said. 'Serious Crime

Squad. All with your heads together on some investigation or other.'

'No one on the team ever even spoke to me, Adam.'

'That's cos you always had your nose down, beavering away,' he said. It was actually because they hadn't liked or trusted her. And they'd turned out to be right. Adam nodded to himself. 'So now I just want to do some proper police work. If I can.'

The prison officer showed them into Joel's cell and, just as Rose had hoped, no one had yet cleared away his stuff.

'How did he do it?' Rose asked.

The screw scratched his chin, fingernail worrying a scab from a shaving cut. 'Ripped up his sheet.' He patted the metal frame of the top bunk. 'Tied it to this.'

It took a lot of effort and willpower to hang yourself in a prison. At home you could attach a rope to something high, then kick away the ladder. But in jail it was more like strangling yourself as you leaned into it, using your bodyweight until you passed out.

'Was he on suicide watch?' Adam asked. The screw shook his head. 'Did he report any problems?' The screw shook his head again. They all knew that any problems Joel had inevitably been experiencing would have been just as likely to come from staff as other inmates.

'I'll leave you to it,' said the screw. 'Just don't touch anything.'

After he'd stepped out, Rose moved around the cell, taking it all in. There was a photo pinned to the wall of a woman with a couple of kids. His sister, nieces or nephews? A roll-on deodorant with one underarm hair still stuck to the ball. A half-eaten Double Decker, the wrapper pulled back. What a waste of a life.

'No note?' Adam asked.

Rose shook her head, still not remotely convinced that Joel Redman had topped himself. 'We need to make a visit.'

'To who?'

'The people who will most definitely not want to see us.'

HARD AS NAILS

★★★

Sol watched Yusef slumped in the back of the van, chin buried in his jacket collar. After the charges had been dropped, he'd barely spoken a word, though he'd eaten the chips Sol had bought for him. (Teenage boys seemed able to put away food on industrial levels and not gain weight, although they also spent a disproportionate amount of time lying down. Even with high metabolisms, that made no sense.) Then he'd gone off to wherever he lived. He'd said a mate's house.

A night's sleep hadn't improved his mood. Then again, he was in the same clothes and smelt like he hadn't had a shower so maybe Yusef didn't live somewhere a good night's sleep could be had. Most of these kids who worked the road crashed with anyone who'd have them.

Sol tapped him on the leg. 'I need you to listen up.'

'I'm listening,' Yusef replied, without opening his eyes.

'Properly listen,' said Sol. Yusef sighed and opened his eyes, as if each lid was weighted with a brick. 'When you go back to your crew just tell them the charges got dropped cos we didn't get the stash.' Yusef nodded. 'Then report back to me if anyone higher up wants to talk to you about it.'

'They won't.'

'How can you be so sure?' Sol asked.

'It's like you told me, Ricky and dem don't give a shit about me.'

The van pulled up a good ten minutes' walk from Moss Side and someone banged on the partition between the driver's cab and the back. It could be Hutch or Gianni, although probably not the latter since he had a worse case of slapped-arse-face than Yusef this morning.

Sol threw open the door and nodded for the kid to make himself scarce.

Yusef jumped out into the rain, trainers splashing in a puddle. He scowled at Sol. 'You know you're gonna get me killed, right?'

Sol pulled the door shut, thumped the partition and they took off.

Yusef mumbled to himself as he walked to Latimer Road. Part swear, part prayer. He should have told Sol to do one, taken his chances in jail. But he could tell by the way the man rolled that he'd have got straight on the phone to the Home Office. Men like that always come good on their threats, or people get to realise they don't mean business. And though Yusef wasn't eighteen yet, there was no way he could prove it, which would just give them a reason to deport him.

He passed a flock of pigeons pecking at a sandwich someone had thrown in the street, taking it in turns to pull off some of the crust, trying to scare each other away even though there was no way one bird could eat the whole thing.

He kicked out at them and they flew off a few feet, then came straight back to their scavenging. See? They didn't believe he meant business.

When he got to the corner of Latimer Road, he leaned against the lamppost. Someone had tied a missing-kid poster to it. A boy with cornrows and a gap in his front teeth. Seemed like his family were properly worried for him. Yusef wondered if his own mum ever thought about him any longer, or if she'd just given up.

At last a lad on a BMX pulled up, a rucksack on his back. His name was Caden and they'd met before. Yusef bumped his fist.

'Heard you got pulled last night,' the lad said.

Yusef nodded as calmly as he could, pulled out a packet of fags and offered one to Caden. 'They sprayed me up proper,' he replied, lighting up.

'Nightmare.' They smoked their fags for a second, then Caden wagged the orange tip of his at Yusef. 'How come they let you out?'

Yusef felt his stomach turn over. He took a drag to steady his nerves. 'They didn't get the stash, so . . .'

Caden rubbed his beard as if he was weighing that up. Then he flicked away his fag and handed the rucksack to Yusef. 'Seven,' he said.

Yusef nodded. There were fifteen stash houses on rotation, each with a number. Sometimes a place was taken off the list and another added. The current number seven was a disused flat on the other side of the estate.

Caden stared at Yusef.

'What?' Yusef asked.

Caden shrugged. 'Nothing. You're the one acting weird as fuck.'

They bumped another fist and Caden rode away. Yusef watched him go, and when Caden turned the corner, he sighed in relief.

Liberty didn't speak as Jay drove back to Manchester. She didn't laugh when he tossed up the last Revel. And when he stuck out his tongue to display the crunched-up orange cream, she didn't even crack a smile.

'Look,' he said at last, 'the kid needed to learn some manners.'

Liberty stared at Jay. Manners! Manners? Her brother ate with his fingers and tried to turn his farts into a tune. 'Don't you think we've got enough enemies right now?'

'He was a nobody.'

'But he'll work for a somebody,' she said. 'And what if one of the punters had called the police while you were waving a gun around?'

'No one in a pub like that is calling the Old Bill.'

Jay was probably right about that but there was no way they

could be sure. And the last thing they needed right now was to get arrested.

'We need to be careful, Jay,' she said.

'Have you been listening to Mel?'

She crunched up the empty Revels packet in her fist, felt a hard lump in the corner. She poked in her finger, one remaining chocolate, and dropped it into her mouth. 'Malteser,' she said.

'Lucky cow,' Jay replied.

Liberty swallowed the honeycomb and watched the moors outside stretch into the mist. She didn't believe in luck. She believed in planning and analysing and holding her nerve. Other people could toss a coin, she'd rely on weighing up hard evidence.

'And, anyway, it wasn't just me waving a gun, was it?' Jay said. 'You had yours out like Omar in season three.' Liberty had to laugh at that. 'Admit it, Lib, you're hard as nails these days.'

Chapter 5

27 October 1990

Our Jay's going to meet the new foster family so I make him take an extra-long shower with a bottle of Matey I nicked from Boots.

'This is for kids,' he says, taking the sailor's little hat off and giving it a sniff.

'You are a kid,' I tell him, as I shove him under the water. 'Do your armpits and your arse. Properly.'

He sticks his head round the curtain. 'If they're gonna smell my bumhole I'm in trouble.'

When Mrs Moser comes to pick him up she smiles and says, 'Very nice, Jay,' which makes the other kids whistle. He gives them two fingers but I can tell he's pleased deep down. As he's getting in the car I warn him not to fart, swear or steal anything.

When they've gone, I feel a bit sad so I go over to Tiny's flat, but she's just leaving.

'Baby clinic,' she tells me. 'Come if you like.'

I've got nothing else to do and it'll take my mind off worrying about what Jay's doing, so I go with her.

When we get to the clinic, there are loads of other lasses all with their babies. Tiny nods at a couple and tells them their kids are bonny. But Lady Grace is the bonniest one there. I'm biased, cos Tiny's my mate, but I've got eyes.

When the nurse picks her up to weigh her, Grace pulls her legs up to her chest, like she's about to do a dive-bomb. 'Still on the breast?' the nurse asks.

'Can't get her off,' Tiny says. 'My nipples are like open sores.'

The nurse gives her some cream to help matters in that department and fills in the red book. As we wander down the road, Tiny gives the tube a squeeze and a bit of yellow stuff comes out. It looks like pus. 'Don't have kids, Lib,' she says.

'I've no intentions.'

She giggles, pushes her hand up her jumper and winces as she tries to rub in the cream. 'I swear they'll just fall off if they get any worse.'

'I went to see Connor,' I say.

She pulls at the neck of her jumper and blows down it. 'I know.'

'How?'

'He told me,' she says, and stops at a café on Carter Street, reaches over the pram to open the door.

I'm immediately embarrassed. 'I can't, Tiny. I haven't got any money.'

She somehow manages to manoeuvre her way in before the pram, then drags it up the step and inside. 'Some things never change, eh? Lucky for you I just got my Giro.'

There's a cloud of chip fat, fag smoke and steam from the kettle hanging in the air, as we take a table by the window and Tiny reads the plastic menu. When she passes it to me, I pretend to give it a once-over. 'Tea's fine. I ate just before I came out.'

When the owner comes over, he bends down to Grace and shakes the little plastic rattle Tiny has popped into the pram next to her. Grace gurgles and tries to grab it. 'What can I get you, ladies?' he asks, without taking his eyes off the baby.

'We'll both have egg and chips,' Tiny tells him. Then she puts up a finger before I argue. 'And a couple of Cokes.'

When our food arrives, Grace has nodded off and the owner smooths down her little blanket with a smile. I shake salt over my chips and shove one into my mouth. I lied: I'm absolutely famished.

Tiny squirts a blob of brown sauce onto the side of her plate, dips a chip in it and pierces the yolk of her egg. 'They get phone cards in prison.' She sucks the yellow-brown coating off the chip. 'And when Connor calls his mam, he calls me after.' She does another round of dipping and sucking, then bites off the end. A little bit of steam rises from the potato inside. 'That day you went to see him, he rang up so bloody excited.'

'I don't know why,' I say.

'Because he loves you,' she says, matter-of-fact. I spend a bit of time cutting up the white of my egg rather than answer that one. 'And I suppose he's hoping you might, you know, patch things up.'

I laugh. 'He's in jail. How could we do that?'

Lady Grace wakes up and starts creating, so Tiny lifts her out of her pram but that just makes her create even more. 'She can smell the milk,' says Tiny. 'Greedy little bugger. I only fed her two hours ago – she can't possibly be hungry again.'

'Give her here,' I say, and reach over the table. As soon as I've got her against my chest, she calms right down. I kiss her head and think about Frankie.

Tiny polishes off her food and guzzles her Coke. Then she lights a fag. 'He won't be in jail for ever, Lib.'

'At least another year,' I say.

Tiny blows the smoke up to the already-brown ceiling. 'Time off for good behaviour. And then there's rehabilitation visits.' I shake my head – I don't know what she's on about. 'It's for prisoners who aren't habitual reoffenders. They want them to be settled back in their communities before they're released so they get to go home on the regular.'

Dad never got anything like that. But then again he was a habitual reoffender. Same with our Jay.

'Anyway,' says Tiny, 'he sounded the best I'd heard him in a long time.'

Present Day

Back in her kitchen, Liberty leaned against the draining-board. She was bone-deep tired and not just because she hadn't slept in over thirty-six hours. Carrying the weight of the Greenwoods and their collective problems was a task of mythic proportions.

Years ago at university, she'd volunteered to do an extra module in classics. It had been a bit of a stretch on top of her law degree, but since everyone around her seemed to chuck around Latin like a second language, she'd felt the need to plug the gap. It had turned out to be a lot more interesting than the turgid lectures on contract law and negligence, and she'd especially loved the tales of torture and redemption that had rained down from the gods (though it turned out most of them were Greek). Like poor old Sisyphus, who had to spend eternity rolling a boulder up a hill only for it to fall down when he reached the summit.

These days, Liberty knew how he'd felt.

She leaned forward and let her cheek rest against the damp metal, the steel ridges cold on her skin. Back in her flat in London, the draining-board was built into the black granite her cleaner, Penelope, had squirted with special fluid to make it shine. On the other side of the sink there was always a chunky candle that smelt of rhubarb and roses. They lasted for ages, but when they were periodically replaced, Penelope would leave a receipt on the island and the next day, Liberty would leave the cash in the same spot.

Liberty straightened and looked around the kitchen of her rented house. How long had she been here? Ages. Yet, it still looked as if she had no intention of staying. She threw open a cupboard and surveyed the bare shelves. One (small) packet of Earl Grey teabags, a jar of coffee and three plain white mugs that she'd picked up in Tesco. Even when Sol had moved in they hadn't attempted to make it like a home. He'd arrived with a bag of clothes and left with the same. There was no real evidence that he'd ever actually lived there.

She went to her handbag, pulled out paper and pen and sat at her kitchen table. Then she wrote a list of the biggest issues she was facing right now. She stared at each item, turning it over and over in her mind, like a dirty penny, trying to uncover the best method of dealing with them all. Then she got out her phone.

'How did it go?' Crystal asked, as soon as she answered.

'Have you spoken to Jay?' Liberty knew that her brother and sister would have been in contact as soon as she was out of the way. Crystal snorted. 'Then you know how it went,' said Liberty.

'I'd have paid good money to be a fly on the wall in that pub,' said Crystal.

'You could have joined all the others,' Liberty replied. 'The place was a dump.'

Crystal didn't consider Jay's behaviour a liability. Part of how he'd made his way in the world was based on his unpredictability. Cross him and Jay might just give you an earful, but equally he might break your legs. But while that might have worked when he was building a messy little street gang, it was far from ideal when you were trying to run a proper business.

'What about Vine? D'you think he had anything to do with what happened to the car?' Crystal asked.

Liberty noticed the article. 'The' car, not 'my' car. Crystal had already mentally distanced herself from the danger. God, Liberty wished she could do that so easily. 'Not sure. Did you do any digging?'

'Yup. Everyone thinks it was Vine.'

'Based on what?'

'Based on the fact that no one round here would fucking dare cross us.'

The window of the chemist was having a make-over, the assistant peeling off the home-made ads for Radox and replacing them with posters for a new weight-loss supplement that apparently attracted fat like a magnet. Presumably there was small print as to where it went after that.

When Tia caught sight of the Porsche, she bounded over. 'What have I told you about coming round here?'

Liberty was too tired to have the same conversations on a loop so just jerked her head for Tia to get in. 'Anyone noticed the local butcher's missing?' Tia shook her head. 'What about your youngers? They okay?' Liberty asked.

They both knew she wasn't enquiring after their health.

'They're fine,' said Tia. 'They're not stupid. Well, they are, but they ain't got a death wish.'

They briefly watched the two lads, who indeed seemed fine, considering they'd been part of a murder, flicking chips at each other, laughing like kids, when a thought occurred to Liberty. 'What happened to your sofa?'

'My what?'

'Your sofa,' said Liberty. 'You had one back on the estate, remember. Some great big filthy brown thing. You used to be like the Queen on her throne.'

'Oh, that,' Tia replied. 'Well, sitting down's not good for business, is it?'

'Excuse me?'

Tia nodded enthusiastically. 'There's studies to prove it. Standing up makes you more productive and that. See them big warehouses where people have to like grab stuff off shelves and get it into boxes for delivery? Well, even when they're not busy, they ain't allowed to sit down. If anyone gets caught on their arse, they get disciplined. Makes total sense if you think about it.' It made no sense at all to Liberty. 'Because when they get back up, they're all relaxed and slow, so now, even though there's a ton of work to do, they're not firing on all cylinders.'

'Isn't everyone just knackered from being on their feet all day?' Liberty asked.

Tia tapped her temple. 'It's all about business psychology. People feel more tired when they get a rest. Honestly, there's books on it.'

Liberty closed her eyes. The thought of Tia reading management manuals was more than her exhausted brain could process.

'How's Crystal?' Tia asked.

Liberty opened her eyes. 'You know about that, then?'

Tia kissed her teeth. Of course she knew. Which was part of the reason Liberty had driven down there when, frankly, she needed a hot bath and a lie-down.

'Everybody's saying when you catch who did it, there's gonna be all-out war,' said Tia.

'There's not going to be any war,' Liberty replied. 'Not on my watch.' Tia laughed and opened the glove compartment. She moved the gun aside and fished around until she found a packet of Juicy Fruit that Crystal had left in there. She unwrapped a stick and shoved it into her mouth. 'Have you been hearing any whispers about who might have been responsible?' Liberty asked.

Tia chewed hard and wobbled her head. 'We all think they can't have been from round here. They must have arrived and done the job.' Tia mimed lighting a Molotov cocktail and lobbing it. 'Then got off straight after.' She pointed her thumb at the window. 'So that makes it fairly obvious.'

'But no one actually saw anything?'

'Some kid reckons he was on the next street when the car went up. But he talks a lot of shite at the best of times,' said Tia.

'Who is he?'

Tia grinned. 'He went to my school as it goes. But now he's in a right mess, always off his tits on spice.'

'Where can I find him?' Liberty asked.

'He's homeless, but I can ask around. Ellis something. Proper pretty boy back in the day – all the lasses fancied the arse off him. Want me to track him down?'

'Don't worry,' Liberty replied. 'I think I've got an idea where he'll be.'

Adam turned into the Peabody estate and pulled over at the address Rose had given him. 'You sure we should be doing this?'

Rose was certain they should not be doing this, but what was the alternative? She got out of the car without answering and headed to number twenty-six.

The small patch of grass at the front was covered with plastic toys – an orange pedal car, a deflated paddling pool with pictures of seahorses, half full of rainwater and leaves. By the door a bucket of sand was filled with windmills spinning in the wind.

Rose took a breath and rang the bell. When someone answered, Rose swallowed hard. Joel's sister was the spit of him, down to the DIY hair colour.

'Charli?' Rose asked.

Charli Redman didn't answer, just looked from Rose to Adam and back again. She was still in pyjamas, though it was mid-afternoon, but had pulled on a zip-up hoodie and a pair of fluffy socks. In the house behind her the telly blared, a kids' cartoon by the sound of it.

'Can we talk to you?' Rose asked.

Charli blinked, eyes red and sore from crying. 'Aren't you . . .'

She let the words trail off, but they both knew the punchline. Aren't you the one who put my brother away? Charli rubbed her nose with the sleeve of her hoodie.

'I don't think Joel killed himself,' said Rose.

Charli looked down at the bucket of windmills, the little plastic arms whirring. At last she turned and went back inside, but she hadn't shut the door behind her.

In the sitting room, Charli didn't ask them to sit and she didn't sit either. Instead, she bent down to ruffle the hair of the kid watching the telly. In the alcove above there were lots of framed photos of two other children. A girl with a heart-shaped face and French plaits. A boy in an Arsenal kit, sitting on Joel's knee. Peas in a pod. Dead peas. These were the children who had been killed in a smash on the motorway when Joel had first turned down an offer to work for a local face, Paul Hill. He didn't turn down the second.

Adam beamed at the kid on the floor, nose an inch from the screen. 'I love *Frozen*.' The kid looked up at him and Adam broke into song.

Charli snapped off the television with the remote and scooped up her daughter. 'I don't think you should be here.'

'We don't want to make matters any worse,' said Rose. 'I just wanted to ask you if Joel had said anything to you recently that might make you think something wasn't right.'

Charli buried her mouth and nose in the little girl's hair and breathed in. It made Rose's stomach churn. Her own mother had done that to her all the time when her dad died. Like she wanted to suck in a trace of him from his DNA. It had been painfully sad, but it had also given Rose previously unavailable access to her mother, the physical intimacy a thrill despite the circumstances. Sometimes her mother would sneak into her bed in the middle of the night and just breathe Rose in. Rose would stay as still as she could, pretending she was asleep, until her mother finally nodded off. It had all gone back to normal when her stepdad came onto the scene, of course.

'He used to ring once a week if he had credit,' said Charli. 'He'd have liked me to visit, but it's not that easy with this one.' She nodded at the toddler, who was now wriggling to be set free. 'And the buses.'

'But when you did manage to speak to him, did he seem okay?' Rose asked.

Charli frowned. 'Well, he were in jail.'

The little girl began to buck, throwing back her head and

kicking. Adam held his hands open and, as if on autopilot, Charli passed over her child. Adam pulled a face and the toddler immediately laughed and grabbed his mouth with sticky fingers.

'Obviously it would have been hard for Joel,' Rose said. She paused as Charli reached into her hoodie pocket and retrieved a pouch of Golden Virginia. 'But did he mention anything unusual?'

Charli spread a pinch of tobacco into a paper and rolled. It was difficult to tell if she was listening. Rose forced herself to be patient as Charli poked at a few strands of tobacco escaping from the end of her fag with a match.

'Anything at all come to mind?' Rose asked.

Charli stared at the blank television screen, unlit cigarette in one hand, unlit match in the other. 'He told me he was worried.'

'About what?'

'A lot of things,' Charli said.

Rose nodded in what she hoped was encouragement. She'd always been crap at the visits with victims' families. Naturally as a woman she'd been tasked with the job more often than not, but her superior officers quickly got wind of the fact that she was not what you'd call empathetic.

The kid was squirming now, so Adam placed her gently on the carpet and picked up a half-eaten packet of Skips. He rustled the packet and pretended to eat one, making noises like a ravenous wolf.

'He was getting the blame for a ton of stuff that had nothing to do with him,' Charli volunteered at last.

'From who?' Rose asked.

'Faces round the place . . .'

Charli tailed off at the sound of a key in the lock and turned to the door. As it opened, her eyes filled with fat tears. 'Dean.' She moved towards him, arms outstretched, but he had eyes only for Rose.

'Get out.' He pointed at the still open door. 'I said get out.'

Then he pointed at Adam. 'And you get away from my kid.'

Adam stood. He was taller than Dean, stockier too, but Dean had that look in his eye every copper knew all too well.

'I said get out.'

Rose let out a breath and said, 'I know you're upset . . .'

Dean took a step towards Rose, fist balled, but Adam was quicker, between them in a nanosecond. The two men stood inches apart, staring into each other's faces.

'We're leaving,' said Adam, and grabbed Rose. He pushed her through the door and out onto the patch of grass in front.

The woman next door was on her step, scowling at them. 'Why don't you just leave them alone?' She wrapped her arms around herself. 'You lot have caused nothing but misery round here.'

'Joel didn't kill himself,' Rose called.

'It doesn't matter one way or the other, does it?' the woman shouted back. 'Dead is still dead.'

Sol plonked a pint in front of Gianni. He hated places like this, all glass tables and blond wood, with a menu of organic gin cocktails chalked on a blackboard. Twelve quid for something flavoured with elderflower. (Who'd decided that flowers had a nice taste? What next? Beer with extract of daffodil?) But Gianni was uncomfortable enough without sticking him in an old-fashioned boozer.

Sol lifted his glass. 'Cheers.' Gianni clinked and took a sip of his lager. 'So, do you want to tell me what's up?'

'The wife's pregnant,' said Gianni.

So that was it. Gianni wasn't worried about Yusef. No, he was rethinking the whole job. Sol had seen it time and time again. Decent coppers who loved the game suddenly went all squeamish as soon as their missus was up the duff and started applying for desk jobs.

'Congratulations,' said Sol. 'Boy or girl?'

'We're not actually telling anyone until the gender reveal,' said Gianni, sheepishly.

'The what?'

'It's a party,' Gianni explained. 'Where you tell people what sex it is.' Sol took a long drink and tried not to laugh. 'All the wife's mates have had one.'

'And what happens at these parties?' Sol asked. 'Is it like the Oscars? Someone gets up onstage and reads it off a card?'

Gianni put his head into his hands and laughed. 'I went to one a couple of weeks ago where they had this big balloon and the bloke and his missus popped it with a pin and a ton of pink confetti went everywhere.'

'And what did you do?' Sol asked.

'I clapped and went, "Ooh, lovely, a baby girl," and then I had another drink,' said Gianni.

Both men laughed now. The thought that anyone would give a shit that someone else who wasn't immediate family was having a baby, let alone if it was a boy or a girl, was a fundamental mistake. Or maybe that was just blokes. Maybe women were really excited for their friends. An image of Liberty flashed through Sol's mind. She didn't have friends to care about. Just Jay and Crystal, now Frankie was gone. He could only imagine what she'd make of a gender-reveal party.

'Are you leaving CDU?' Sol asked.

'Probably.' Gianni finished his pint. 'It makes you think about kids in a different light. I mean, what if Yusef was mine or yours?'

'He's no bloody baby, is he?'

Gianni was on his feet, feeling for his wallet to get his round in. 'He's somebody's baby, Sol.'

After the next drink, Gianni made his excuses and left. Sol didn't care: the guy wasn't great company and neither was Sol. He headed into the smoking area and stood under the portable heater while he had a fag and called Hutch.

'Everything all right?' Hutch asked.

'Gianni's leaving us,' Sol replied.

'We could do without that mid-job,' said Hutch.

'It's for the best.' The barmaid who'd served him came outside, a cigarette between lips painted almost black. She flicked her thumb at him in a request for a light and he handed over a box of matches. 'Bloke's lost his bottle.'

Liberty watched the church hall from the safety of her car. There was a group on the steps to the entrance, having a quick ciggie before the meeting. Bradley was among them in the same footie top and blood-splattered trainers, laughing with a bloke who seemed unsteady on his feet, tottering backwards and forwards as if he were on a ship out at sea.

The girl from the previous meeting arrived with her shopping bags, though her duvet had been replaced by a blue sleeping-bag that she wore like a cape.

Then Liberty spotted who she'd been hoping for. Ellis. Ten paces behind his sister, he dragged his feet as if this was the last place in the world he wanted to be. At the door, she turned and shouted at him. He mumbled something back and slipped in after her, head down.

Liberty double-checked her car was locked and walked over to the church hall. She nodded at Bradley, who looked her up and down.

'You owe me for a trip to the launderette after last time,' he said.

'Send your invoice to Head Office,' Liberty replied, and pushed past him.

Once inside, she looked everywhere for Ellis, but there was no sign. Just Jan at her tea station. She beamed when she caught sight of Liberty. 'Welcome back.'

Liberty nodded at the side-room where the group met. 'Has everyone gone inside?'

'Yeah.' Jan popped a teabag into a mug. 'Take a brew with you.'

Liberty waited while she poured boiling water over the teabag, then fished it out. She smiled as Jan stirred in industrial quantities of milk and sugar. Then she took it and headed into the meeting. The chairs on either side of Ellis were taken by his sister and a woman maybe in her thirties – though it was tough to tell – a thick layer of foundation on her face, including her lips, and the hood of her Puffa up.

Liberty sat in a free seat opposite.

Eventually Bradley joined them. No sign of the drunk guy from outside – he'd clearly had second thoughts.

Jan fiddled with her name badge, undoing the pin, wiping it, then re-threading it through the wool of her cardi. 'No one new here tonight so we all know the drill. Whatever gets said between these four walls remains here.' Everyone muttered their agreement. 'So, we haven't seen you for a while, Lauren.' Jan smiled at the woman with her hood up. 'Everything okay?'

'Up and down, you know?' she said.

'And how are the ups?' Bradley said. 'Asking for a friend.'

Everyone laughed, including Lauren.

'I was doing all right and then I met this bloke,' Lauren said. 'He seemed pretty decent. Job and all that. But it turned out he was on the Vallies.' There was a room-wide groan. 'And you know how it goes.'

'The rattle from those things is the worst,' said Bradley.

Lauren nodded and pushed away her hood, revealing a scraped-back ponytail, her foundation right up to her hairline like a mask.

Suddenly Jan turned to Liberty. 'And what about you? Would you like to share anything with the group?'

'No.' Liberty's voice was sharp. She coughed and tried again. 'Thank you.'

'Is it sex addiction?' Bradley asked. 'Because I can help with that.'

Even Liberty had to chuckle at that one. 'It's not sex addiction, I promise you.'

'Drinking?' Ellis asked, his voice soft and almost girlish.

Liberty appraised him. Tia was right: he was a very pretty boy. 'I like a drink,' she told him, 'but I'm not an alcoholic.' Everyone hooted at that one. 'I'm not,' Liberty said.

'How much have you had to drink today?' Lauren asked.

Liberty frowned. 'Nothing.'

'Yesterday?'

'I don't know. I didn't count,' Liberty snapped.

Jan smiled. 'No one's judging you . . . Sorry, what shall we call you? Real name or alias, we don't care.'

'Lib.'

'Right then, Lib. In this group we're all addicts, some of us recovering, some of us in the eye of the storm. But we all want the same thing.'

'And what's that?' Liberty asked.

'To be free,' Jan said. 'And we can only do that if we're at least truthful.'

'Honesty is the best policy,' said Bradley. 'Though I've been in jail for theft, armed robbery and fraud, so I'm no expert.'

Liberty looked around the group. A pathetic handful of junkies with missing teeth and clothes that smelt of pee. She'd only come in to ask Ellis about last night. And here she was under cross-examination. It was a bloody joke.

'How about you ignore the addiction for now?' said Jan. 'Share something else.'

'Like what?' Liberty asked.

'My mother brought up my little girl and I haven't seen either of them in ten years,' said Jan.

Liberty gulped down a lump in her throat but it was lodged fast like a fishbone. Everyone looked at her expectantly. Well, they could wait for ever if they thought she was going to join in this charade.

'I nicked my next-door neighbour's pension book,' said Lauren. 'She still doesn't know it was me and she's terrified of burglars now.'

Liberty bit her lip.

'I'm not allowed to see my brothers and sisters,' said Ellis. 'I turned up at a contact session on the spice and scared them.'

His sister puffed out her cheeks. 'You scared everybody, screeching and clawing at your face. I thought you were having a fit.' Her tone was matter-of-fact, not an ounce of anger at Ellis or self-pity for herself. 'The social worker was telling me to calm you down and I was like "Bitch, I'm not going near him, he'll have my eye out."'

Ellis held the bridge of his nose with his thumb and forefinger, the nails black and bitten to the quick. He was too young to be in this state, blaming himself for what was happening to his siblings.

'When I was seventeen, I left my little brothers and sister.' Liberty stared straight at Ellis. 'I ran away and I didn't look back. And now the baby of the family's dead.'

There was a silence in the room, but it wasn't uncomfortable. Just calm. Something physically lifted from Liberty and her spine no longer bowed and ached.

'I shat myself in Leeds Crown Court,' said Bradley. 'That didn't make me popular, I can tell you.'

Yusef was still in the stash house, playing Mortal Kombat, checking his mobile every few minutes. When he got word that he needed to move the food to the streets, it wouldn't go well for him if he was late. But it wasn't just that making him edgy: he was worried that Sol was going to get in touch.

The lad behind him on the sofa kissed his teeth loudly. 'What is wrong with you, man? You're like some little girl tonight.'

Yusef threw down his controller.

'Was it me or you got sprayed and banged up last night, pussy?' The lad laughed loudly so Yusef took the disk from the PS4 and lobbed it at him. 'Whoah. You'll get that scratched up.'

At last a text came in that Yusef needed to ship out so he grabbed his rucksack and dropped most of the baggies next to the TV. He counted he had the right amount and left, giving the lad a kick as he went. Not hard enough to cause beef, but hard enough to make his point. Yusef's rep meant the lad expected it and just shook his head with a smile, already sliding onto the floor and rifling through the games.

He was on his way to Latimer Road, when a text he didn't want arrived: *Can you call about the outstanding paperwork please.*

Yusef squeezed his eyes tight shut, but when he opened them the message was still there. He punched 'call back'.

'Evening,' said Sol, in that annoying accent.

The bloke needed a slap and Yusef would have given him one if it wasn't for the whole mess he was in. 'I'm on my way to work,' said Yusef.

'I can see that,' Sol replied. Yusef looked over his shoulder and all around. He sighed when he saw the white van parked up ahead. 'Don't make it obvious, lad.'

'What do you want?' Yusef hissed. 'I can't stop now, can I?'

'Just wanted to check in, let you know I'm thinking about you,' said Sol, with a chuckle.

Yusef rounded the corner and almost smacked into Caden. He hung up and dashed his phone into his pocket.

'Problem?' Caden asked.

'Nah. Just my fool brief saying I need to sign some forms and that so's he can get the legal aid.'

Caden pushed out his lips. 'At this time?'

'They're greedy, innit?'

Yusef pushed the rucksack at Caden, who immediately went to hide it, then Yusef strolled over to the other dealers and fist-bumped everyone, answering their questions about his night in the cells, all the while his heart hammered in his chest.

When the meeting finished, Liberty followed Ellis and his sister at a safe distance. She could have grabbed them in the hall, but decided she needed to have the conversation away from any prying eyes or ears.

Eventually, they turned into a small park and headed to the slide. The girl laid out the sleeping-bag and dumped down her carrier bags. Ellis lit a candle stub, dripped some wax onto the tarmac and pressed the end of the candle into the puddle to secure it. Then he sat cross-legged in front of it.

Liberty knew she had to grab him before he got any spice inside him. After that, he'd be fit for nothing. She crossed the park and stood over them. They didn't seem surprised and carried on with their tasks, Ellis building a blunt, his sister making a pillow out of some dirty jumpers.

'Do you know who I am?' Liberty asked. The kids nodded. 'I just need to ask a few questions.'

Ellis twisted the end of his blunt and bent to the candle to light it, pushing his hair back from his face. Liberty's mam had done the same, lighting a fag on the gas hob, many a time. Liberty reached over and plucked the spliff from Ellis.

He gave a mournful face. 'I'm rattling.'

'You can have it in a second, I promise,' Liberty told him.

'You'll have to be quick,' said his sister, 'or he'll throw up.'

'What's your name?' Liberty asked the girl.

'Real or my street name?'

Liberty smiled. 'Up to you?'

'Everybody calls me Mouse.'

'Nice to meet you, Mouse.'

Ellis gagged, caught a string of mucus in the palm of his hand, wiped it on the thigh of his jeans. Liberty needed to crack on.

'Were you near Empire Rise last night?' Liberty asked. Ellis nodded. 'Why?'

Ellis glanced at his sister, who shrugged. 'There's a bloke who lives on Beaton Street. It's one up from Empire. Anyway, this bloke's in a wheelchair and that . . .' He looked again at Mouse but she was suddenly very busy with her bedding. 'Look, he pays me to suck him off, all right?' He looked at the spice blunt with love in his eyes. 'He's fine as it goes. Doesn't want anything else. And he's quick.'

'Did you see the car on fire?' Liberty asked.

Ellis sniffed. 'I'd just left his house and was on my way back here so I cut across the streets and that's when I saw it.' He threw up his hands. 'Whoosh.'

'Did you see who did it?' Liberty asked. Ellis shook his head. 'Seriously?'

'It was dark,' said Ellis, eyes wide. 'They were in black.'

'They?'

'Three of them. Black hoods, black jackets, black everything. They ran straight past me and I still couldn't see their faces or nothing.'

Mouse stopped kneading the jumpers and said, 'Maybe not their faces.' Ellis punched her leg. 'What?' Mouse punched him back. 'If she finds out you know something and you don't tell her, you're in deep shit.'

'True,' said Liberty. 'But I'll be honest, I really don't want to hurt anyone.'

'Fine,' said Ellis. 'I saw them run towards a car. I didn't see if they definitely got in it because there was all this fire and noise and heat. But when I ran off, it'd gone.'

Liberty crouched down so she was at eye level with Ellis. She could smell the bile on his jeans. 'What sort of car?'

'Black Merc. I didn't see all the reg but there was a K and a D in it.' He drew his fingers across the tarmac. 'KD then something. Then maybe a six.'

Liberty tossed the blunt to Ellis, then fished in her bag, pulled out a wedge of notes and pressed them into Mouse's cold fingers. 'Get yourself some new clothes and some decent food.'

As she moved across the park towards the gate, Mouse called after her, 'Was that true what you said at the meeting? About leaving your family behind?'

Liberty waved over her shoulder, but didn't reply.

Chapter 6

30 October 1990

I'm watching This Morning in the telly room, and I'm laid out on one of the settees because I've got the place to myself for once. Everyone else is at school or PRU. Or pretending that's where they've gone. Even our Jay got off this morning without any whining, still in a top mood since he got back from meeting the new foster family last Friday. They're called the Petersons and he says they're dead nice. They took him to McDonald's and bought him a Happy Meal. I mean, he's obviously too old for all that, but he promises he didn't let on. They even told him they were sorry they couldn't consider having me as well, but they know how important it is that everybody still gets to see me.

There's this doctor on the telly who's getting folk to have a puff on a fag, then blow into a machine. A couple of seconds later, the machine gives a reading of how much carbon monoxide they've got in their breath. Everybody's making out like they're surprised. I doubt anybody ever packed in smoking cos a machine said it was bad for them. It does make me think about all the millions of fags I've inhaled second-hand, though. I'll probably die of lung cancer before I get to thirty. Which will be chuffing unfair.

The pay phone in the corridor rings. Usually someone will pick it up in two seconds, but there's no one around, so I drag myself away from the telly and answer.

'Is Lib Greenwood there?'

'Speaking,' I say.

'It's Tiny,' she says, with a laugh. 'Listen, I was wondering if you want to go out tonight. And before you start banging on about money, I can get us in for free.'

'Where?' I ask her.

'Paradise,' she says.

It's a new club night over at the Roxy in Leeds that everybody's been talking about. 'I'm not meant to be out after ten.'

'Since when did that ever stop you?' she says. 'C'mon, Lib, I've hardly left the house since Grace was born and my nan's offered to have her for the night. Though God knows how they'll get on, seeing as Grace can't be off the boob for five minutes without bringing the house down.' She laughs again. 'Be a mate.'

I smile. I mean, I do want to go out. 'Go on, then.'

'I'll ring you tonight when I'm setting off.'

After tea, I pitch myself in the kitchen so I'll be close by when the phone rings. Our Jay sits opposite, shovelling down an extra slice of toast. Sausage, mash and beans and he's still hungry! Michaela's squashed up next to him, her chin on his shoulder. She sneaks a hand under the table and our Jay gives a sly grin.

'Seriously?' I say.

'Well, you go off on one every time we go upstairs,' says Jay.

'Because I'm in the room next door.'

Jay pulls up Michaela's hand and drops it next to his plate, like a dead fish. 'It's like living in a monkery.'

'What the hell's a monkery?' I ask.

'Where monks live,' he replies.

'You mean a monastery?'

Jay shakes his head. 'Don't be fucking daft. Nuns live in nunneries. Monks live in monkeries. Everybody knows that.'

I'm literally saved by the bell: the phone rings. I jump up and make for the door.

'It's probably for me,' says Michaela. 'My dad's been trying to get hold of me.' She's been saying that since she got here. Yet somehow she keeps managing to miss all his calls. 'He'll be livid when he hears I haven't been getting his messages.'

I nod and answer the phone. It isn't Michaela's dad, obviously.

'I'm off,' says Tiny. 'See you in five minutes.'

As I pass the kitchen door our Jay and Michaela are snogging, the slurps louder than the telly in the other room.

'The phone was for me,' I tell Michaela.

Our Jay pulls away from her, his mouth still wet. 'Who called you?'

'Tiny.'

He's on his feet. 'How come?'

'Just a chat,' I say, with a shrug.

'A chat that lasted two seconds?'

I have to walk away because I'm a good liar but our Jay's like a bloody copper. He knows when stuff doesn't add up and he's trailing me up the stairs, Michaela trailing him.

'Are you off out?' he shouts. I glance down in case Hemma's hovering around. 'Well, are you, Lib?'

I stalk to my room and dive inside. Jay scoots in behind me. 'Do you want to let everybody know?' I hiss.

'You're off out and not taking me with you?' Jay yells.

Michaela's in my room as well now, so I push them both down onto the bed and slam my door. 'Can you stop bloody shouting before I get gated?'

There's a clunk on my window and I groan. It'll be Tiny chucking a stone. Our Jay knows that too and he's got it open before I can tell him to stop. He leans out and waves at Tiny.

'Hiya,' she shouts, and waves back.

'You look gorgeous,' he tells her.

She does. She's got a pair of velvet shorts over thick black tights. Her thighs are a bit chunkier than before she had Grace, but she's still well sexy, especially in her floppy velvet hat with a massive silver pin in it, like the ones you get in a kilt. I look down at my faded jeans. God, I need some new clothes.

'You ready?' Tiny calls up at me.

'I'll just get my trainers on.'

As I shove my feet in without undoing the laces, Jay shouts to Tiny, 'How many spare tickets have you got?'

She holds up a handful and Jay rubs his hands together. He sticks one leg out, fingers gripping the top of the frame.

I grab his chin and make him look at me. 'Absolutely no chance. If you get caught, what will them new foster carers think?'

'We won't get caught,' he says, and then he's gone, shimmying down the drainpipe.

I slide my finger down the flattened backs of my trainers to pull them on properly, then make my way down to Tiny. She must see I'm not happy about Jay tagging along and mouths, 'Sorry.'

He shouts up at Michaela, 'You coming?'

'I can't,' she says. 'My dad's gonna ring me.'

He looks at me, biting his lip, and I have to turn my back so Michaela won't see me laughing. Then we're off, Tiny in the middle, linking arms with me and our Jay. 'That your girlfriend?' she asks him.

'Not tonight.'

Present Day

Liberty rubbed her eyes as she drove across the Pennines for the third time in two days. After missing an entire night's sleep when Crystal's car went up, she'd hoped for a decent few hours last night, but it had been hard to stop the thoughts rattling round her brain. For one thing, she felt uncomfortable making this trip without telling Jay or Crystal. After Frankie died they'd agreed that from then on it was all for one and one for all, that they'd stick together, even when they pissed one another off. But Liberty reasoned that this was different. Back at the Halfway House, she hoped to God she was doing the right thing.

Amy the barmaid looked up, clocked who Liberty was

immediately and held up the pint glass she was drying. 'I don't want any trouble.'

'You won't get any from me,' Liberty said, and pointed at the man on a stool at the bar in exactly the same spot he'd been in the previous day. 'Here to see Mr Kelly.'

The man still had his back to Liberty, eyes down on something. At last, he nodded at Amy, who darted her own eyes at the spare stool next to Kelly. Liberty took a pew.

'What can I get you?' Amy asked.

Liberty fancied a beer or a cold glass of wine. 'Orange juice. Ice, if you've got it.'

While she waited for her drink, Kelly didn't speak or turn to her, glued to a website on his phone, flicking through articles and news items. Amy extracted two ice cubes from a bucket with a pair of silver tongs and emptied a bottle of Britvic over them. Liberty reached into her bag for her purse.

'On the house,' said Amy.

'Thank you.'

Kelly was still engrossed in what looked to be an old piece about a house fire in Moss Side. Liberty couldn't read the detail but there were photographs of two little boys, next to a charred building.

'Thanks for agreeing to see me.' Liberty spoke straight ahead.

'Your brother owes me an apology,' said Kelly, voice low and menacing.

'He was out of order,' Liberty agreed. 'But you've got to admit the younger was being a right dick to Amy.'

Kelly gave a half-grunt half-laugh. 'Kids these days have no manners.'

'I swear most of the time it's all I can do not to kill half of my lot,' Liberty agreed.

Kelly turned to her. His hair was dark, but his beard was flecked with grey. Under his black Puffa he wore a black jumper and his jeans were black too. 'You've quite a few on the payroll then?'

'I'm sure you've done your homework on me, Mr Kelly.' Liberty took a swig of juice. 'So you know what sort of operation we're running back in Yorkshire.'

Liberty had certainly checked out Kelly. Ten years back he'd been one of the biggest noises in Manchester. The oldest of six brothers, he'd run it all: drugs, girls, guns. Then Ricky Vine had arrived.

Kelly flicked a finger at his empty pint glass and Amy went to refill it.

'So what is it you want, Ms Greenwood?'

'Call me Liberty.' She picked out one of the ice cubes, licked off the juice, dropped it back into her glass. 'And I'm here to make you an offer.' Kelly gave a full grunt and went back to his screen. 'We work together and rebuild what you've lost,' said Liberty.

'I'm doing just fine.'

This was going to be the hard bit. Getting a man like Kelly to admit he no longer had the standing he once enjoyed. Yet she guessed he must hate Ricky Vine with every cell in his body.

'We've got a lot of people,' she told him. 'You know how these streets work. Together, we hit Vine hard, take his turf.'

'You think you've got what it takes to come at Ricky Vine?'

Liberty reached over and grabbed Kelly's phone, turned it screen down on the bar. She ignored Kelly's growl. 'I shot Caleb Clarke in the head.' Liberty made a gun with two fingers. 'And Ricky didn't do a thing. Why do you think that is?' Kelly stared at her. He had hooded eyes, more mournful then angry. 'We can bring him down.'

'And why do you want to do that?' Kelly asked. 'Why do you care about Ricky?'

'He's a threat to my family and I'm not having that,' she replied. 'So what do you say?'

'Fifty-fifty?' Kelly asked.

In truth, Liberty didn't give a monkey's about the money. But extra turf was never a bad thing. She held out her hand to Kelly. 'Except the gym. I want his gym for myself, if that's okay?'

Kelly spat on his hand and they shook. 'Consider it yours.'

Behind them the pub door opened and cold air swept in. Liberty took the opportunity to wipe her palm down the front of her trousers. There was a mini bottle of hand sanitiser in her bag, which would be emptied when she was out of there.

'You?'

A lad's voice raged across the bar. By the time Liberty turned to the sound, he was almost upon her. It was the younger Jay had attacked.

'Back off, Macca,' warned Kelly.

But the lad was already pulling a knife. Liberty reached around for the gun in her waistband. Too late. Macca sliced the air and Liberty's sleeve with the blade.

'I said no,' Kelly roared.

As Macca went for another go at Liberty, Kelly hopped from his stool, picked it up in both hands and smashed the lad across the back with it. Macca flew forward into the bar, the knife dropping from his hand. Kelly brought the stool down again, this time across Macca's shoulder blades.

Liberty bent and scooped up the knife. 'Problem sorted,' she told Kelly.

'People round here need to start listening to what I say.' The sad eyes blazed now. 'It's time everyone remembered what's what.'

Macca curled up in a ball, hands over his head, and Liberty took in the sight of her new business partner, beard flecked with spit, holding a stool over his head.

Amy sighed loudly at Liberty. 'Is it going to be like this every time you come in here?'

Some joker had Sellotaped a picture to Rose's locker. A woman at least in her eighties wearing only a thong and heels, boobs flat and long, like a spaniel's ears. Rose's face superimposed.

Rose ripped it off, balled it and shoved it into her pocket.

'You should tell someone about all this harassment,' said Adam, tossing his hoodie into his locker.

'At least they've moved on from death threats,' Rose replied.

Adam raised an eyebrow so she busied herself with storing her stuff. She took the top off a tube of lip balm, squeezed and rubbed the ointment across her lips, feeling the ridges of cracked skin under the pad of her finger. Then she popped the tube inside the locker with her shoes.

'Got any deodorant?' Adam asked.

'Just this,' Rose replied and handed over a rose-scented roll-on. She'd started using rose-scented toiletries when she was in school and a classmate had given her some M&S talc as a birthday gift. That Christmas she'd asked her mum for bubble bath and hand lotion to match. Her step dad had said it was 'self-absorbed', and when the big day came she found a dressing gown under the tree. But Granny Lions had sent a gift token for Boots so Rose had hunted down a rose-scented toiletries set in the sales and stored it under her bed.

Adam whipped off his T-shirt and rolled the deodorant under each arm. He bent his head and tried to smell his pits.

'Getting in touch with your feminine side?' Rose said.

Adam wafted his arms up and down in an attempt to dry the deodorant and laughed. Rose joined in, something about Adam's laugh was infectious, and pulled on her hi-vis jacket. Her mobile bleeped, and when she saw who had emailed her, she groaned.

'Not more bad news?' asked Adam.

'You could say that.'

The chief super didn't invite Rose to sit. Neither did he offer her a coffee as he poured himself a cup from his cafetière. She watched him stir with a small silver spoon, her feet apart, hands behind her back, army style.

'You've heard about Redman?' he said at last. Rose nodded. 'Terrible, terrible business. As if the poor family haven't suffered enough.'

Rose stared at the wall just above the chief's head. There was nothing she could say that wouldn't make matters worse.

'Are you experiencing any difficulties about it?' the chief asked. 'From other officers?'

'No, sir,' she said. The chief nodded and sipped his black coffee. They both knew she was lying. 'But thank you for asking.'

She wished she'd taken off the jacket before she came in. The chief had the heating on and she was sweating. She moved her neck to the right to reveal a bit of skin to the air. The jacket creaked.

'I could have got rid of you after the business with the Greenwoods,' said the chief. 'But I decided to give you another chance.'

Another lie. He'd have chucked her out as soon as look at her, but after she nicked Joel and exposed corruption on the unit, questions would have been asked if she'd disappeared. Instead, he buried her on foot patrol, in the hope she'd leave of her own accord. She probably would have done if she could have thought of a single other thing to do with her life.

'However, there'll be no second chances if you cause any problems over Redman's death.'

'What sort of problems, sir?'

The chief put down his cup with care, steepled his hands under his chin. 'Joel Redman committed suicide. It's very sad but there we are.' He stared at her. 'Are we clear, Officer Angel?'

'As crystal, sir.'

★★★

Sol picked up two McMuffins in a drive-through and went to meet Yusef. The kid was skulking on a corner, face like a wet bank holiday Monday.

'Get in,' Sol told him.

Yusef was yakking as soon as his backside hit the seat. 'You don't need to follow me.'

'What?'

'Last night.' Yusef kissed his teeth. 'Hanging around, watching me. What did you think I was gonna do?'

Sol chucked the greasy brown bag of food at him and gunned the engine. It was easy to lose an informer in the early days. They panicked and ran. Or sometimes they told people up the chain, who nodded in sympathy, then tossed them into a canal. Letting them know you had eyeballs on them was part of the game in the opening laps.

'Is one of these for you?' Yusef asked.

'Do I look like I'd eat that stuff?' said Sol, and drove to the office.

Back in Wakefield, Hutch had managed to get the use of a room behind a nail bar. It had stunk of polish and whatever the Vietnamese girls were cooking that day. Here in Manchester, the office wasn't any more luxurious.

'Is this it?' Yusef gazed through the car window at the disused MoT garage. 'I thought it'd be like MI5 or some shit.'

'Just the shit part,' Sol replied, and pulled up next to the ramp.

He got out of the car, unlocked the door to what had once been Reception and nodded for Yusef to join him. The kid was still shaking his head in disbelief as they walked past a Fiat calendar for 2015, the page open at December, a blue Punto gleaming in the sort of snowdrift you never saw.

In the workshop behind there was an abandoned car. A ten-year-old Beemer, which the police must have considered worthless when they'd raided the place. The owner had rented out some storage at the back and swore he had no idea that kilos of charlie were nestled among the tyre wrenches, but the jury hadn't believed him.

Sol had set up a whiteboard and now he tacked three pictures to it. 'Pull up a chair.'

Yusef found one in the far corner and dragged it over, the metal legs grating against the concrete floor. He wiped off the dust with the sleeve of his jacket, then took a seat.

'So, which of these charmers do you know?' Sol asked. Yusef pointed at the top picture of Ricky Vine, face like a sweaty cheese. 'What about him?' Sol patted the photograph of Vine's second in command, leaving Vine's gym in Moss Side.

'Seen him but never spoke to him or anything,' said Yusef.

'He's called Cameron Bolton,' said Sol, 'a.k.a Baller.'

Yusef nodded that he knew. 'Took over from Clarkey, when he got popped.'

Sol felt a jag of adrenalin shoot through him. Liberty had killed Clarke. He'd known she was hard, but he'd never dreamed she would shoot someone in cold blood. Then again, here he was, sending kids out to do his dirty work.

'What about this one?' Sol asked, about the photograph of Ricky Vine's third in line. Probably the most vicious of the whole crew.

Yusef tossed his head. 'It's Coops, innit?' Sol narrowed his eyes at the picture. 'Nobody messes with Coops.' Yusef laughed. 'I heard that there was this bloke up in Hulme, used to be some big-time face, and he wouldn't give up whatever it was Ricky wanted, you get me? So Coops burned down his house with like his whole family inside.' Yusef sniffed. 'Could be a load of crap, but you never know with Coops.'

Sol rubbed the scar under his eye. He'd heard a lot of stories about Coops, none of them good.

'So what's the point of all this?' Yusef asked.

'Just checking you know the players.' Sol pulled off the pictures and tossed them into a plastic wallet. Then he pulled out three more and tacked them up. Yusef sighed. 'Sorry to bore you,' said Sol.

Yusef got to his feet and approached the board. He bent forward and bashed the first photograph with his forehead. 'Gishy.' He smacked the second. 'Tyson.' Finally he head–butted number three. 'Can't remember his name right now.'

'Oren Martinez,' said Sol, as Yusef's head still kissed the picture. 'And I'm giving you his job.'

Yusef snatched his face away from the board. 'What?'

'Oren's going to be leaving the game,' Sol explained. 'And you're having his spot on the team.'

As Liberty arrived back in Wakefield, she wondered if she'd made the right call in getting Kelly involved. Jay and Crystal would not be happy when they discovered she'd gone behind their backs. Plus the guy seemed a loose cannon. The way he'd battered the younger with the stool had been over the top, the glint in his eye manic. Keeping her siblings under control was tough enough, without inviting nutters into the fold.

But she had to do something about Vine. If Ellis was right, Vine's people had torched Crystal's car and there was no way Liberty was going to let that stand. And she couldn't just start a war in Manchester, not without local help.

As she mulled it over, she spotted something out of the corner of her eye; a BMW garage. She slammed on her brakes, flipped the finger to the driver behind when he pressed the horn and did a U turn. Once on the garage forecourt she pulled up next to a red M5. The price tag flapped in the wind: £54,999.

A salesman appeared, all skinny tie and hair gel. 'You looking to trade up?' He patted the top of the Porsche. 'I love a nine eleven, but she's getting on.'

Liberty felt a sting of protectiveness over her car. 'I'm not getting rid of this.'

The salesman's face fell as he saw a possible part-exchange disappear. 'You're just looking, then?' No doubt a thousand people admired the M5 every day.

'I want to buy it for my sister,' said Liberty. The salesman laughed, realised Liberty wasn't joking and his eyes widened. 'Can you do that?' Liberty asked him. 'Buy a car for someone else as a surprise?'

An hour and two vending-machine cappuccinos later, Liberty had signed for the car. It would take a few days for the paperwork and money to clear, and then the showroom would let her pick it up.

'You must really love your sister,' said the salesman.

Liberty chugged down the last bit of froth in the plastic cup. 'Something like that.'

Back at Empire Rise, Liberty nodded at a couple of Jay's blokes stationed in a car opposite her house.

'Anything?' she asked.

'All quiet,' one replied.

Once inside, she checked all the doors and windows anyway. She needed to move to somewhere with better security and an entry-phone system, like Crystal's flat. Jay's old house, where he'd lived with Becca and the boys, had walls all around, an electric gate and state-of-the-art alarms. Liberty used to tease them about living like the Mafia but could now see it made sense.

She didn't much like this house anyway and had initially rented it on a six-month let just to move out of the Radisson Hotel. The shower was always too hot and there was a damp patch in the living room under the window that Sol had kept threatening to paint over.

Liberty kicked off her shoes and ferreted in the fridge. There were a couple of pre-packaged salads that had been there over a week. She peeled the cellophane off one and sniffed. It seemed okay so she squirted some salad cream over it and grabbed a fork. When Sol had quit the force he'd appointed himself head cook and taken to looking up recipes with unusual ingredients. There'd been a phase of buying heirloom carrots. Of course he'd never actually used them and would periodically dump them in the bin when they turned slimy. He'd once researched how to turn them into soup and that had made her laugh for hours. She missed how much he'd made her laugh.

She stabbed a cherry tomato with her fork and pushed it into her mouth. She wished she could stop thinking about Sol.

She'd deleted his number from her contacts ages ago. And all his texts, except one. He'd sent it before anything had happened between them. When he was still a good copper who knew which side of the law he was on, married to a woman who loved him and attached notes to his packed lunch telling him just how much.

Liberty reread the text for the millionth time: *You once told me that control is an illusion. That we're all just a bunch of needs, wants and urges.*

Yeah, she'd told him that. Her finger hovered over the delete button. But instead, she closed her eyes and wished he was there right now. Her mobile rang, making her jump. 'What?'

'You need to come,' said Tia.

Tia's place was one room above a kebab shop on the Crosshills. Liberty had offered to help her move a dozen times, but Tia always said she was 'settled'.

A grey elephant's trunk slowly rotated on its vertical spit and the kebab-shop owner peeled it like a meat apple. When he saw Liberty he waved his huge knife and smiled. As she made her way upstairs she could already hear the ructions going off in Tia's room. Banging, high-pitched screaming, Tia's voice telling someone to 'calm the fuck down'.

Liberty knocked on the door with her knuckles. 'It's me.'

The door swung open and Tia stood on the threshold, sweating like a greasy kebab. 'I'm gonna kill him.'

Behind her a lad lay on her bed writhing as if in agony, wearing only socks. He clawed his hands in front of his face as if fighting off a monster. Then his stomach began to convulse and his chest heaved.

'Don't you dare puke,' Tia raged.

Too late, the lad opened his mouth wider than seemed possible and green liquid projected into the air, only for gravity to do its thing, and land back on his face in a second, much of it back into his still open mouth. He threw his head from side to side and shrieked, sick running down either side of his neck onto Tia's duvet.

She roared in anger and raced over. 'You filthy twat.'

'Stop it, Tia,' Liberty shouted, but Tia had already punched him on the nose.

There was the sound of bone crunching, then blood mixed with the vomit. But the lad seemed to calm and, instead of screaming, sobbed quietly to himself. Liberty could see now that it was one of the youngers who had been there the night Kalkan had met his accident.

'What's going on, Tia?' Liberty asked.

'He's on the bloody spice,' she replied.

'You let your crew take spice?'

Tia looked mortally offended. 'No, I do not. But last night he kept having nightmares about that thing in the butcher's, so I gave him a couple of hours off to get his head together.' She gritted her teeth at the crying boy. 'When he didn't turn up at all I came to give him what for and found him like this.' She bent right over his face and shouted, 'Stark bollock naked and screeching the place down.'

The younger began to shake as if suddenly freezing, teeth chattering. 'M-m-meat,' he muttered. 'Meat-hook.'

Liberty and Tia exchanged a look. This wasn't good.

'What's his name?' Liberty asked.

'JB.'

'I mean his real name,' said Liberty.

'How should I know?' Tia shrugged. 'I'm not his mother, am I?'

Liberty took a deep breath. How had her life come to this? She took a step closer to the bed, wrinkled her nose at the stench of sick. 'JB?' She spoke calmly. 'JB, can you hear me?'

He looked at her, but there was no way of knowing whether he could see her or whether she was like a vampire to him. There was a Puffa coat chucked in the corner. Liberty picked it up and placed it gently over JB. Tia pulled it down a touch to cover his flaccid cock and balls.

'I need you to stay nice and quiet, JB. Understand?' Liberty said.

JB stared deeply into Liberty's eyes. She smiled, but tears still ran down his cheeks. 'He's dead,' the boy whispered.

'Jesus,' said Tia.

Liberty turned. 'I need you to stay with him, Tia. He goes nowhere until this is out of his system, then we need a proper talk.'

Adam hummed quietly as they crossed the estate. 'Eye Of The Tiger'. Duh. Duh-duh-duh. Duh-duh-duuhhh. And again.

'Can you not?' Rose said.

This time Adam added hand gestures – a drum beat for every 'duh'. He leaned over and elbowed her in the ribs, still smelling faintly of the roll-on deodorant. 'Gonna tell me what he said?'

'Who?'

Adam pointed to the sky. 'He who must be obeyed. The chief.'

'He warned me off doing anything about Joel's death,' Rose replied.

'And how's that working out?'

Rose narrowed her eyes and thumped the garage door. She listened and heard something that might have been a cough, but could easily have been a retch. 'Don't make me call the Drugs Squad.'

At last the door opened and Salty poked out his head. He looked even worse than the last time Rose had seen him, if that was possible. Skinnier, paler, open sores under each nostril weeping greenish liquid. Rose had used him for information when she'd been on Serious Crime. He might look like a rotting corpse, but his eyes and ears were always open.

'Thought they'd sacked you,' said Salty.

'You wish,' Rose replied.

He stuck out his upturned palm. 'Is it raining? I need to find my shoes if it is.'

'It's not,' said Rose.

Salty stepped out, a pair of football socks pulled over his jeans. He looked Adam up and down, then turned back to Rose. 'New boyfriend?'

Rose pulled him away from the garage door to the nearest wall and plonked herself down. She patted for Salty to join her. Adam hovered nearby.

'Did you hear Joel Redman's dead?' Rose asked.

Salty nodded, reached into his sock and pulled out a roll-up. 'Don't suppose you've got a light, handsome?' he asked Adam. Rose dug a lighter from her pocket and pushed it at Salty. 'Spoilsport,' said Salty.

'Redman? Anything?' Rose asked. Salty took a drag and shook his head. 'Anyone poking around?'

'Not about that,' Salty answered.

Rose waited for more. Salty waited for some money. She sighed. Detectives could claim for snout money, but patrol officers barely got paid themselves. She'd waited so long for new boots when the last lot fell apart that she'd bought her own pair.

Salty held out his hand until she dropped a fiver into it. Then he held out a hand to Adam.

'I haven't asked any questions, mate,' he told Salty.

'Your girlfriend here has and if you want to get any tonight I suggest you come across with the royal blue.' Adam shook his head in disbelief but took out a fold of banknotes. Salty tried to reach for a tenner, but Adam slapped away his hand, eventually finding a five-pound note. Salty stuffed both down the other football sock. It was clearly one for fags, one for cash. Presumably his gear was in his bloodstream.

'Talk to me,' said Rose.

'Us,' said Adam.

'What?' said Rose.

'Talk to us,' said Adam. 'I put money in.'

Salty chuckled. 'Where did you find this one? I like him.'

'Just tell us what you've heard,' snapped Rose.

Salty finished his roll-up. Pocketed the lighter. 'Couple of Turks asking around after the bloke that runs the minicab firm.' He pointed vaguely across the estate. 'They said he'd been missing a day or two. But I reckon it's three cos Big Candy went in there on Tuesday night and the place was smashed up.'

'A robbery?' Rose asked.

Salty shook his head. 'They wouldn't have taken him if they just wanted to nick the cash, would they? Plus Candy said there was still money in the till when she went in there.'

'Just checking, was she?' Adam asked. 'Before she called the police?'

Salty winked. 'Ask me no questions, I'll tell you no lies.'

Rose frowned. She knew the man Salty was talking about.

From a family of small-fry criminals, who were hardly likely to be able to cough up a decent ransom. So who would have grabbed him and why? 'Any idea if there's been bad blood?'

'The Turks haven't been dealing if that's what you're asking,' Salty replied. 'But there was a row down the Jade Garden. I heard some fish got electrocuted.'

Salty jumped off the wall and stood very close to Adam. He breathed deeply and gave a tiny moan of pleasure. 'You smell lush.' Then he was off, shuffling away in his filthy socks, back to his needle-infested garage.

Chapter 7

30 October 1990

We skip straight to the front of the queue, because the bouncer knows Tiny.

'Hey up,' he says to her. 'How's that baby of yours doing?'

Tiny kisses his cheek. 'Constantly hungry.'

He laughs and lets us in without even checking our tickets. 'Are you still not saying who the dad is, then?'

'Don't know and I don't care,' Tiny replies, with a wink.

I don't think that's true. I think she does know but she's just not telling. I've racked my brains for who she might have been seeing, but can't think of any blokes in particular. And, anyway, if she doesn't want folk to know, that's her business.

We pass through into the club and the music engulfs us: a banging Chicago house re-mix I haven't heard before. I turn to Tiny and she's already grinning from ear to ear, shoulders dipping. I wish Fat Rob was here.

Tiny leads us through the crowd, and I push past all the people dancing, feeling the sweat seeping through their clothes. A laser cuts the air just above my head and our Jay lifts his hand and wiggles his fingers in the flashing beam of light. When we reach the bottom of a podium, I'm smiling and letting the bass wash through me. Ever since we got back from Manchester I've been wound up so tightly, my stomach on a constant churn cycle. At last my muscles start to relax.

Someone jumps from the podium, nearly knocking me off my feet. 'Oi,' I shout. Then I'm in the air as the jumper lifts me off my feet. 'Oi,' I shout again.

Then I see who it is and my eyes open wide. He smiles his big goofy grin and kisses me on the mouth.

'Danny?'

'Lib,' he says, still holding me up in the air. 'You look fucking great.'

He kisses me again and I don't even mind that his lips are frothy with spit and sweat because I haven't seen him in ages. When he puts me down, he's already got his hand in his pocket and pulls out a baggie of pills. Jay and I exchange a glance. As usual we've not got a pot to piss in.

'Can I pay you later in the week?' Tiny asks him.

'Whenever,' Danny says, with a shrug.

Tiny takes three pills from the bag. She holds one up for Jay and he sticks out his tongue. When she drops the pill on it, he closes his mouth and sucks her finger. 'I'm old enough to be your mother,' she tells him. Then she turns to me and I poke out my tongue. She gives me my pill and leans to whisper in my ear, 'I'm really glad you came home, Lib.' Last of all, she swallows one herself and gives the bag back to Danny. He looks like he's already had a couple, but he snaps one in half and takes that. Back when we used to go clubbing all the time, too much was never enough for Danny. Looks like nothing's changed.

Twenty minutes later and we're all on the podium, along with some bloke wearing a kilt. He puts his hands on Tiny's hips and they dance in time, jerking with each beat. Jay tries to do the same with me but we're rubbish and end up creasing over with laughter.

I'm still cracking up when I see someone mooch through the sea of people, his head bobbing, and my face falls. Jay notices and squints to see what's spoiled the fun. Connor. Jay leaps from the podium and, before I can stop him, punches Connor square in the face. Connor flies backwards and lands on his arse. I jump down and grab hold of Jay's top before he can hit Connor again.

The bouncer appears with a frown. There's almost never any fighting in

111

clubs like this, so he's more surprised than anything. Connor's back on his feet, hands up to say it's all okay. 'Misunderstanding,' he tells the bouncer.

'No, it was not,' says Jay.

Tiny's off the podium now, an arm around the bouncer's waist. 'We're all good, Baz. Honest.'

'Maybe go outside and cool off,' he says.

Tiny nods and drags all of us to the door. Out in the night air, we're suddenly freezing as the wind hits our sweaty skin.

'For God's sake, Jay.' Tiny checks Connor's lip and wipes it with a tissue she's found in the pocket of her shorts. It doesn't look clean, but I don't mention it. 'You can't go around attacking people.'

'I deserve it,' says Connor. He steps towards Jay. 'Smack me again, mate, if it'll make you feel better.'

'You tried to get Lib sent down,' Jay says, but he sounds more bewildered than angry. 'Our Lib, who's never hurt a fly.'

'Absolutely no excuse,' says Connor.

I'm shivering now and wrap my arms across my chest. 'When did you get out?'

Connor spits a stray flake of tissue from his mouth. 'Overnight release. Gotta be back tomorrow.' He glances at a cop car parked on the other side of the road. 'Shouldn't be here, really, but I wanted to see you.'

Danny appears. Somewhere between the podium and the fight, he's lost his T-shirt, but if his bare chest is freezing, he doesn't show it. Instead, he drapes one arm around my neck and one around Tiny's. 'C'mon,' he says. 'I thought we were all supposed to be mates.'

I nod at our Jay that everything's fine. We all stand there like lemons for a second, then Jay grabs Tiny's hand and licks it.

'Animal,' she shouts at him, but she's laughing and lets Danny drag the three of them back inside, leaving me and Connor staring at each other.

I jerk my head at the police car. 'You should go home.'

'I know,' he replies, but doesn't move.

'Or at least come and dance,' I tell him. 'Like Danny says, we're all supposed to be mates.'

Connor shakes his head. 'You're not my mate, Lib. You're the love of my bloody life.'

Present Day

Liberty woke up with a headache and a tight chest. She dry-swallowed a couple of paracetamol and headed over to Tia's.

When she reached the flat above the kebab shop, things were calmer than the day before although Tia had a face like a flat pint. The younger who had been raving on spice was dressed, kneeling on the floor, swiping at dried vomit with a packet of face wipes for sensitive skin. When he looked up at Liberty, he gulped. 'Sorry.'

'So you bloody well should be,' Tia snapped, and gave him a kick.

Liberty grabbed the wipes from the lad and threw them into the corner. 'I can't have you behaving like you did last night, JB.' She perched on the edge of the bare mattress and patted it for the kid to join her. 'If I can't trust you . . .'

'You can,' the boy said. 'Course you can.'

'Well, you were chatting all sorts of rubbish last night,' said Liberty. 'What if the wrong ears had been listening?'

'I'm not touching that stuff again,' he said.

'No, you're not.' Liberty patted his knee. 'And you're shipping out later today so get your stuff together.'

The lad's forehead furrowed. 'Where to?'

'Manchester,' said Liberty. 'A friend of mine needs some troops.'

'Manchester?' Tia burst out laughing. 'Absolute shithole.' She flicked the lad's cheek. 'Serves you right.'

Liberty smiled. 'You're coming too, lady.'

Liberty met Jay and Crystal in the Cherry. She wasn't looking forward to filling them in on the latest state of affairs, but it had to be done. They glanced at one another as she took a couple of Diet Cokes from Mel and placed them on the table.

'Spit it out, Lib,' said Jay.

Liberty pointed to the seats at the table and didn't say a word until her brother and sister plonked themselves down.

'I think Vine torched the car,' she said.

Crystal let out a long breath, and Jay closed his eyes. Then he picked up his glass and threw it across the bar. It smashed a mirror on the wall, which exploded into hundreds of sharp shards of glass.

'For the love of God,' muttered Mel, and reached down for the dustpan and brush.

'Are you a hundred per cent?' Crystal asked.

'Nope. But I can't think of anyone else who'd risk it, can you?' Liberty replied.

Crystal shook her head.

'Right,' said Jay. 'Let's tool up and head over there.'

Liberty put up her hands. 'Wait a second, I think I've got a better plan than that.' Crystal nodded that she should carry on. 'I went to see a face over the Pennines, someone who hates Vine even more than we do, and he's agreed to partner up with us to get rid.'

'We can get rid of him on our own,' shouted Jay, and made a gun gesture with his fingers.

'Then Vine's new number two will come for us and there'll be more and more blood,' said Liberty.

'Bring it on,' Jay replied.

Liberty grabbed his hand. 'Your brother's dead. Do you want to lose one of us as well? With Crystal pregnant into the bargain?' Jay didn't answer, and the only sound was the swoosh of a brush and the chink of glass landing in Mel's dustpan. 'We partner up, Jay, and we decimate the whole Vine business. We take the areas, the money and the people.' She squeezed his hand tightly. 'Vine will be gone and there'll be no one left with enough clout to come for us.'

'Plus we get a share of the Manchester deal, I assume,' said Crystal. 'It's actually a smart move.'

'Fifty-fifty,' said Liberty. 'Except Vine's gym. That's mine.'

'So who is this new partner?' Jay asked.

Liberty forced a smile. What the hell would they make of Kelly? 'I'm taking a few youngers over later, why don't you come and meet him?'

'You'll have to drive.' Crystal elbowed Jay in the belly. 'My car's out of action.'

Sol and Hutch waited to go through security at the CDU headquarters in Birmingham. They placed the contents of their pockets in a tray that went through an X-ray machine, and stood in a queue to go through airport-style scanners.

Hutch swanned through, but Sol managed to set off the alarms three times. At last he made it, minus belt, shoes and watch, with Hutch trying not to laugh.

They descended the stairs two at a time, Sol re-threading his belt in his jeans, until they arrived at the basement, or 'the store', as it was colloquially called. Here was kept all manner of items that could not normally be procured in the general run of police investigations.

Hutch handed a letter to the store master and waited for three kilos of best-quality heroin to be handed over. Not an industrial amount, but enough to ensure that their target didn't get bail.

'What if Vine doesn't replace Oren with Yusef?' Sol asked.

'Then we get rid of the replacement,' Hutch replied.

'The boss gave us three weeks.' Sol turned over the cling-film-wrapped bag of smack in his hands. 'Vine will know something's off if he loses two soldiers in that space of time.'

'Let's just travel hopefully,' said Hutch, and signed for the gear.
Sol couldn't recall when he'd last done that. Maybe when he'd
got married to Natasha. He must at least have hoped it would work
out long term. With Liberty it had been a case of not thinking or
hoping at all, just an acceptance that they wanted each other.

They made the journey back to Manchester with Hutch playing country music all the way, some sad stuff about being dirt
poor and unable to feed the kids. Depressing as the rain smacking
the windscreen. Sol cracked the window and lit a fag.

The warehouse was cold, dark and wet, droplets of water falling
from the ceiling into puddles on the floor. The sign outside said
it used to house carpets, but now there were just boxes stacked
against a wall.

Jay flicked the cardboard with his thumb, deeply unimpressed.
'So what sort of business did you say this partner of ours runs?'

'Don't act like we've got a string of swanky hotels, Jay,' said
Crystal.

Liberty laughed, and splashed dirty water with the toe of her
boot. 'We've all gotta make a pound or two where we can.'

At last the back door opened and Kelly strode towards them,
still dressed from head to toe in black, still scowling. Liberty
introduced everyone but there was no shaking of hands.

'Did you bring me some lads?' Kelly asked.

'In the van,' Liberty replied.

'Let's have a look at them, shall we?' said Kelly, then nodded at
Crystal's belly. 'Family's a wonderful thing.'

Jay put an arm around his sister. 'Yes, it is.'

In the van, the Greenwood youngers were nearly all asleep, had
headphones plugged in or both. Only Tia raised her head when
the van door opened.

'Are you having a laugh?' Kelly asked. 'They look half dead.'

'What do you want them to do? A dance routine?' asked Liberty.

Kelly reached into his Puffa coat, pulled out an iron bar, then banged on the outside of the van, denting the metal. That woke the youngers up. Kelly dragged the first kid out by his jacket and threw him onto the concrete.

'What the fuck?' the lad shouted, but Kelly was already onto the next and then the next, until they were all out of the van and muttering about what they were going to do to him.

'Listen to me,' said Kelly. 'I only want people I can trust to get the job done.'

The lad who had face-planted on the ground brushed off his jeans. 'We don't want to be here in the first place. Absolute shithole.'

Without even looking at him, Kelly backhanded the lad across the face, sending him onto his arse. Jay growled, but Liberty pressed her fingers into his forearm. The youngers needed to know what was what with Kelly. A few looked at her for guidance on how to react and her silence spoke volumes.

'Anyone else want to get lippy?' Kelly roared. 'Because I'm way past the point of dealing with lippy kids. Understand?' He finally cast his eyes on the lad he'd hit. 'You'd better show me what you're made of or I'm sending you home with more than a flea in your ear.' He held out his hand to the kid and pulled him to his feet. 'Get back in the van, all of you, we're going on a job.'

When the last one was back inside, he slammed the door.

'What's going on?' Liberty asked.

'You'll see.'

Kelly drove the van like he was stock-car racing, with Jay, Crystal and Liberty sliding around in the passenger seats. The way Kelly took corners would probably send Crystal into early labour. When they seemed to go on two wheels, Tia cheered.

At last, Kelly screeched to a halt outside a pedicure bar. It was one of those places with tanks full of little fish that were meant to nibble the hard skin off your feet, before some poor woman painted your nails while she tried to pay back her fare over here from Vietnam.

'Who's packing?' Kelly howled at the kids.

Tia dragged out a flick knife, a small hammer and a screwdriver. The lad who had hit the deck revealed a crowbar. The rest had between them enough tools to keep B&Q in business. And last, but by no means least, JB displayed a baseball bat that he'd somehow hidden down the leg of his trackies.

Kelly nodded in approval. 'Maybe you're all a bit sharper than you look.' He pointed to the foot bar. 'Now, this place here used to be mine.'

'You did pedicures?' asked Tia, and all the youngers laughed.

'Shut up, Tia,' said Liberty.

'I owned it,' said Kelly. 'Good place to wash the cash, it was. But the manager decided to sell me out to a new face in town. I think now is a good time to show her that was a mistake.'

'CCTV?' Tia asked.

Kelly nodded to the camera above the shop, already knocked off its perch. 'And just in case, cover your faces, all right?' The youngers all pulled up their hoods and zipped their jackets up to their noses. Tia even had a bandanna that she wrapped around her mouth and nose. These kids knew how not to get caught. 'Five minutes,' said Kelly, dragging a balaclava over his head. 'In and out, maximum noise. Right?' He chucked a GoPro at Tia. 'You're the cameraman.' Then he threw his mobile at Liberty. 'Enjoy.'

When he had jumped out of the van to open the back door, Liberty hissed at the youngers, 'Do what he says,' and they didn't need more encouragement, tumbling out, laughing and hollering. Dealing drugs was pretty dull in the scheme of things. Lots of waiting, lots of loitering. The idea of causing some merry hell was exciting, even if only for five minutes.

'Come on, then.' Kelly raised his own iron bar above his head. 'Let's kick off.'

They ran like a pack of dogs to the shop, Tia cracking the window with her hammer before she dived inside.

'This is all kinds of wrong,' said Jay.

Liberty nodded and watched the screen, Crystal peering over her shoulder.

Inside, the shop was carnage. Tia smashed one of the tanks and the place was swimming in water, tiny fish flapping around. JB ran his baseball bat along a shelf of bottles of varnish, sending them flying through the air. The two women working in the place ran to the back door, screaming, but Kelly barred their way, baring his teeth.

As the lad with the crowbar brought it crashing down on top of the cash register, one of the women pulled out her mobile phone, but before she could make a call, Kelly batted it from her hand and dragged her towards the last remaining fish tank that hadn't been smashed or overturned. He pushed down on the back of her neck and forced her face into the water. Through the glass, Liberty could see the woman's mouth and eyes wide open as they filled with water and fish. She thrashed but Kelly was far too strong and held her under. The other woman began shouting something in a language none of them could understand, then sank to her knees, hands pushed together in prayer above her head. Liberty could work that one out.

The woman with her head in the tank had all but stopped flailing. Another few seconds and it would be too late.

'Is he going to kill her?' asked Jay.

'Good question,' Liberty muttered.

Crystal sniffed. 'He's not exactly a quiet type, is he?'

At the final moment, Kelly heaved the woman from the water

and left her gasping on the floor. Her friend crawled over to her, crying. Kelly bent to them both. 'Tell your boss she needs to clean up. Understand?'

'Yes,' the woman gabbled, in accented English. 'Yes, I understand.'

Kelly stood, looked around at the mayhem he'd caused and, for the first time, laughed.

'He's off his head,' Jay whispered to Liberty.

'Yep,' she replied, and turned off the phone as Kelly and the youngers raced back to the van.

Rose had spent all day reading up on the Kalkans, their social services records, arrest records, immigration records. Any bit of paper that mentioned them, she scoured for some hint of what was going on.

Adam yawned. 'What has any of this got to do with Joel Redman?'

'Maybe nothing,' Rose replied. 'But twenty-four hours after Joel dies, a small-time gangster goes missing, and the Greenwoods' car gets fire-bombed. Something's going on.'

Adam waved a photo of Pinar Kalkan, the missing man's wife. Even in her mugshot she was a good-looking woman, with thick black hair and high cheekbones. She hadn't reported her husband missing, and when Adam called her, she had muttered that he'd probably gone to visit family in London.

'Got any food?' Adam asked.

They were camped out in Rose's kitchen, because it would have drawn too much attention to do the work at the nick, and he'd already finished off every biscuit and packet of crisps in her cupboards. He'd even polished off a Moon Cake she'd picked up last Chinese New Year and never eaten.

'If you read another file, I'll buy us both dinner,' said Rose.

120

'Where?'

'Your choice,' she said.

'I like Chinese,' Adam said. 'And your snout mentioned one, didn't he? We can kill two birds with one stone.'

A couple of hours later, they were in the Jade Garden looking at the dessert menu. Rose didn't want another mouthful but Adam was torn between the lychee ice cream and a deep-fried pineapple fritter. He'd already seen off chicken and sweetcorn soup, sticky spare ribs, beef in black bean sauce, egg fried rice and a side of stir-fried veg.

'Why don't you just have both?' Rose asked.

'I'm not a dustbin,' he replied. When Rose raised an eyebrow, he pouted. 'How about we share them?'

Rose attracted the attention of the waitress and ordered both puddings. 'And two spoons.'

When they arrived, Adam gave the waitress a wide grin, which she returned. He had that effect on people.

'You've replaced your fish, then?' he said, and nodded at the tank in Reception.

The waitress laughed. 'The boss loves them.' She bent conspiratorially. 'I think they're horrible. If one of them has babies, they eat them, you know?'

'Oh, my days,' said Adam. 'You'll put me off my afters. Maybe whoever killed them was trying to do you a favour.' Adam nudged her playfully. 'Probably a customer with the hots for you.'

The waitress giggled. She was pretty and it was entirely plausible that customers fancied her. Rose wondered if Adam did.

'It wasn't a customer that killed the fish,' the waitress told them. 'Nasty people who should know better.'

'Better than what?' Adam asked.

'They should know that we have customers who like it here.' She winked at Adam. 'Customers who look out for us.'

Rose was surprised by how much more food she could squeeze

down. Adam laughed and tapped her spoon with his. 'What do you think she was talking about?' he asked.

'I'd say Mr Kalkan messed with the wrong restaurant.'

Adam frowned. 'Do people start doing kidnap over some catfish, though?'

When the bill arrived, Rose took out her credit card.

'Hold up,' said Adam. 'I don't expect you to pay for mine.'

'That was the deal,' Rose replied.

He peeled some notes from his wallet. 'Behave. We both earn the same, which as we know is bugger-all.'

Suddenly Rose was filled with the urge to tell Adam the truth about something she never mentioned to anyone. It was like his superpower, making people comfortable. 'I have a private income,' she said.

'Like savings?' Adam whistled. 'Nice.'

'Not savings. Properties I rent out.' She wiped her mouth on a napkin. 'When my dad died he left me some flats.' Adam stared wide-eyed. 'And some offices.'

'You're rich, then?'

Rose's cheeks burned. Her stepdad always called her that and she'd argue with him that there wasn't as much money coming in as he thought. He didn't believe her and called her mean for not sharing any of it with her mother. Rose reasoned that if Dad had wanted her mother to have any of the properties, he'd have said so in his will.

'Why so serious?' Adam asked. 'I wish I was bloody rich.'

Rose smiled sadly. 'They've caused me a lot of upset over the years.'

'Hand them over to me, then,' said Adam. 'Problem solved.'

They agreed that, Rose's millions in the bank or not, they should still go Dutch, and a huge wet burp from Adam, as he stood to leave, closed the conversation. On the way out he patted the tank, now full of new inhabitants, but it was something else that caught Rose's attention. A reflection from behind: fresh customers arriving.

Outside, Rose turned to Adam. 'There are definitely people who will kidnap and worse over something seemingly small.'

'Round here?'

Rose put her hand on Adam's cheek and pushed his face back in the direction of the restaurant reception where Liberty, Jay and Crystal Greenwood were being introduced to the new fish on the block.

Jay dipped a prawn cracker in sweet chilli sauce and eyed Liberty. 'You sure about getting into bed with Kelly?'

'Since when were you fussy about who you got into bed with?' Liberty asked.

Jay pushed out his tongue, the top covered with white cracker slowly dissolving, like communion wafer.

'Can we control him?' Crystal asked. 'That's the question.'

Liberty drained her bottle of beer and waved for another. 'I doubt it.' She laughed and her siblings stared at her. 'What? He's our attack dog.'

'And the youngers we've handed over?' Jay asked.

'He needs a pack. His own youngers are just a bunch of scallies and they need to see how it's done properly. And as soon as local kids over there notice how the new pack rolls, it will grow even bigger. When we get enough firepower, we can take on Vine.'

Jay pointed a fresh cracker at Liberty. 'I was shocked you left Tia with him.'

Liberty accepted a fresh beer from the waitress with a smile. She was indeed worried about leaving Tia with Kelly. For one thing, Tia was needed here to keep the drug supply moving. And for another, people around Kelly got hurt. They always had in the past and there was no reason to think it would go differently this time. Liberty felt protective of Tia, but she needed eyes and ears she could trust in Moss Side.

'I still don't get why Vine torched the car,' said Crystal. 'He must know that we won't just leave it.'

'You ever hear the tale of the scorpion?' Liberty asked. Crystal shook her head. 'A scorpion needs to cross a river but he can't swim. He sees a fish and asks for a lift to the other side. The fish says, "How do I know you won't sting me?" and the scorpion replies, "If I sting you, you'll die and then I'll drown." The fish thinks about it and agrees to take the scorpion across the river. Halfway across, the scorpion stings the fish and, with his dying breath, the fish asks, "Why did you do that, knowing you'll drown?" And the scorpion replies, "I'm a scorpion. It's what I do."'

Chapter 8

31 October 1990

It's half five in the morning and me and Connor are at the table in his kitchen. Apparently his mam is in Ireland at a funeral.

'I didn't tell the prison that,' he says. 'Obviously.'

He stirs sugar into a cup of tea and pushes it at me. His mam would go crackers if she could see he isn't using a coaster. Our Jay and some lass he pulled in the kebab shop on the way home have gone upstairs to crash out and Tiny's got off home, so it's just the two of us.

'When have you got to go back?' I ask.

'Half eleven,' he says.

'Don't you want to get some kip?'

'We're banged up twenty hours a day, Lib, and there's not much to do except sleep.'

I warm my hands around the mug. His mam's painted the walls since I was last in here: a sort of bright yellow that's probably meant to be cheery, but looks a bit sickly in this light.

'Do you keep in touch with Rob?' Connor asks.

'Of course I do.'

Connor nods and looks down into his own cuppa. 'He wrote to me, you know, telling me what a twat I was for trying to get you to take the blame.' *I didn't know that. Rob told me he'd never been in contact with Connor.* 'He always did have a thing for you, though.'

'He does not,' *I say.* 'We're just mates. And, anyway, he's got a girlfriend.'

'*Do you love him?*' Connor asks.

'*Yes,*' I tell him. '*When my life went to shit, he saved me.*'

'*What about me? Do you still love me?*' he asks, and I don't know how to answer that. '*Because I still love you,*' he says.

'*You're in jail, Connor,*' I reply, though it's not really an answer to his question.

'*Right this second, I'm not in jail.*' He looks around the kitchen. '*But I can see how you made that mistake.*' I laugh and it turns into a yawn. '*Do you want to crash for a bit?*' he asks.

'*I'm not going to shag you, Connor.*'

'*Fair enough.*' He gets to his feet and grabs both our teas. '*You're not as fit as my cellmate any road.*'

Up in his room, nothing's changed. Flyers for club nights taped to the wall and bits of motorbike all over the floor. I've been to live in Manchester and Connor's been to jail, but this bedroom is like time has stood still since we were last together. He makes space for the cups on his bedside table and lies on his back on top of the continental quilt, arms crossed over his chest. I kick off my trainers.

'*Don't you ever undo the laces first?*'

'*No, Dad,*' I say, and shuffle down next to him.

We lie like that for a while until he shifts onto his side so he's facing me. Then he reaches over and pushes a piece of my hair off my face. I should stop him because I know he's going to kiss me next. And then I'll kiss him back. And then I'll shag him.

'*I've missed you so much, Lib.*'

I wait, and eventually he moves closer until I can feel his breath on my mouth. But before our lips can touch, the unmistakable sound of squeaking bed springs comes through the wall. Connor snorts, but I jump up and bang it with my fist.

'*Bloody hell, Lib,*' Jay shouts. '*Have you got bionic hearing?*'

Connor walks back to Orchard Lodge with me and Jay. I told him he didn't have to but he said he needs to get off back to the prison straight after

126

because it's two buses and takes ages. When we arrive, Michaela lets us in and she throws her arms around our Jay's neck. He kisses her hard on the mouth and pushes her against the wall.

'He's got some stamina, I'll give him that,' says Connor. When he turns to leave he gives me a wink. 'Stay in touch, pretty Lib.'

I watch him walk away in the direction of the bus stop, but before he gets out of sight I chase after him. 'Do you want some company?' He nods at me. 'You'll have to pay my fares, though, cos I'm skint,' I say.

We don't talk much on the way, watching the world wake up through the bus windows. A bloke gets on, and sits in the seat in front of us, then immediately falls asleep, snoring so loud he could be a drill. Me and Connor exchange a glance and try not to laugh.

When we're almost there, Connor's shoulders sag. 'Tell me something nice, Lib.'

'They've found a place for Crystal, Jay and Frankie,' I say. 'A proper foster family that's going to be permanent.'

Connor frowns. 'What about you?'

'There's not enough room for me.'

We stand to get off the bus and Connor leans across me to press the bell. 'They can't leave you on your own. That's not right.'

'It's fine,' I say. 'I'll be finished in care soon anyway.' Once off the bus, we stand in front of the prison, cold in the shadows. 'I just want the kids to be settled so I can sort myself out.' He checks his watch, face serious, and I feel bad: this was meant to be good news. 'Honestly, it's all going to work out this time.'

'It had bloody better,' he says. 'Because nobody deserves a break more than you.' Then he kisses my cheek and presses some more coins into my hand for the ride back.

Present Day

'Are you some kind of nonce?' Yusef shouted.

Sol sighed and sank into his chair. 'Don't be an idiot.'

'You just asked to check my crack.'

'I asked to check your wire,' Sol replied.

'Which is taped to my arse crack.'

Sol looked at Hutch for assistance. It came as no great shock that he was busy checking the tools left rusting by the MoT garage owner. 'If it's in the wrong place, it won't pick up the conversation, and if it's not secure and ends up escaping out of your trouser legs, you can say goodbye to your ears.'

'Fine.' Yusef dropped his jeans. 'But don't get too close.'

Sure that the wire was where it needed to be, Sol lit a fag and took a deep drag while the kid pulled up his trousers. Then he handed the fag to Yusef, who accepted it with a nod.

'Remember, you're not supposed to know that Oren's been nicked,' said Sol. 'And if anyone talks to you about it, just say it's a load of crap or whatever.'

'What if no one brings it up?' Yusef asked.

Hutch wandered over, a pair of pliers in his hand. 'Depends. Do you see much of Oren usually?' Yusef shrugged. 'Well, would you notice if he was missing? If no, don't say anything. If yes, then maybe ask where he's at. Play it by ear.'

Yusef walked through the market, trying not rub his backside but, man, the tape was scratchy. There was a public toilet not far from the pedestrian crossing: maybe he should go in there and re-strap the wire to his thigh. He stopped outside, the smell of pee filling his nostrils. But Sol was right: if anyone caught him wearing this thing, he'd be begging them to let him die. He kept walking.

Once he got to the stash house, he made the call.

'Yeah?' It was Coops. 'Who's this?'

Yusef's mouth went dry. Coops was a pure nutter. He coughed to clear his throat. 'Yusef.'

The phone went dead, and the steel door opened. When he

was inside, Coops bolted it behind him. He waited to be asked to move through the hallway to the kitchen, but Coops didn't speak. He glanced towards it, but the kitchen door was closed.

'You all right?' Coops asked.

'I'm okay,' Yusef replied.

'Heard you got nicked.'

'Brief got me out cos the feds didn't find the stash.'

Coops stared at him. 'Lucky.'

'For real.'

Neither moved – well, Yusef couldn't because Coops was blocking the way into the hall and behind him there was only the front door. His scalp prickled with fear and he rubbed his hairline with his thumb.

At last Coops nodded and walked to the kitchen. Yusef stayed put. If there was any way to leg it, then he would, but Coops would have a shank in him before he could undo the second bolt.

'Come,' she said.

Yusef tried not to breathe too loudly and forced his legs to carry him to the kitchen. He paused at the door, hands shoved into his pockets. Coops opened the fridge and grabbed a carton of Ribena. 'You want one?' she asked.

Yusef watched her shove the little straw into the hole. Should he say yes or no? He'd never once been offered anything. He arrived, they gave him the food, he left. This was all wrong.

'What – are you deaf now?' Coops snapped.

'Yeah, I'll take one,' he muttered, immediately regretting it when she threw one at him and he didn't catch it. When it bounced along the floor under the table, he knew he was going to have to crawl and get it.

Coops sucked down her drink. 'Are you on something?'

'Nah, nah. My eyes are still killing me from where I got pepper sprayed.'

Yusef bent for the Ribena, and the tape that held the wire in place pinched a hair. When he was back on his feet, Coops was laughing. 'Stings like a mother fucker, eh?'

Yusef's eyes widened. How did she know about the wire? Was this thing a set-up and Coops was just playing with him until she opened him up? Everyone knew she carried the same knife with her everywhere and that the list of people she'd cut with it ran into the hundreds. Caden reckoned he'd seen her chiv some bloke in the top of his leg. There was some special vein there that meant you could lose a ton of blood real fast. Caden said there was buckets of it and the man was screaming, but Coops just knelt next to him and watched until he was quiet.

'They say it wears off after a couple of hours, but I swear my eyes were blurry for days after I last got sprayed,' said Coops.

She meant the spray, not the wire. Yusef almost laughed at his mistake.

'For real,' he muttered, hands sweating so much he nearly dropped the carton again. There was no way he'd be able to drink it without throwing up, so he just held it and hoped Coops wouldn't notice or care.

'You heard about Oren?' Coops asked. Yusef shook his head. 'Got done last night.'

. 'Shit.'

Coops nodded and slung her empty carton into the bin in the corner. There was never a lid on it and the whole place stank. 'Complete fit-up.'

'No way.'

'They're saying he had like three K of brown on him and there's no chance of that.' Coops licked her bottom lip. 'So they must have planted it.'

'Why'd they do that?' Yusef managed to say.

'Could just be trying to massage their figures. They gotta get enough cases and that. Or could be they're gunning for us.' She wagged her finger at him. Weirdly, Coops always had long

130

fingernails, painted all kinds of mad colours. Today's was like Day-glo yellow with black zebra stripes. Bet all the girls she went with weren't too keen on them. 'Either way you'll have to be careful, yeah?'

'I never take the same route two days running,' said Yusef. 'Always mix it up. And I'm good with my hiding places.'

'I know,' Coops replied. 'That's why you didn't get charged.' She tapped her temple. 'You're smart. So we need you to do a few more bits for us, okay?'

'Course.'

'Just do the usual today, then find me later and we'll talk.'

Yusef nodded and Coops led him back to the front door. When he was outside, she shut it without saying goodbye. He heard the bolts slide into place and nearly cried.

On the other side of the road in their van, Sol and Hutch turned off the audio feed, looked at one another and smiled.

'Pint?' Sol asked.

'It's half ten,' Hutch replied.

'Whisky, then.'

Liberty woke up much later than normal and scrabbled around in the kitchen for something to eat. There were three satsumas in the fruit bowl, all well past their best, but she ate them segment by segment in turn. She tore up the peel, rubbing each piece between finger and thumb and smelling it.

She thought about going back to bed but there was a bang on the door. She checked she had her gun in her dressing-gown pocket and looked through the spy-hole. It was Crystal.

'Everything all right?' Liberty asked, as she opened the door.

Crystal nodded and held up a takeaway coffee. 'Thought you

might need this, seeing how many beers you put away last night.'

'Not that many.'

Crystal laughed and flapped a hand at Liberty's bed hair. 'So this is you fresh as a daisy?'

'I haven't been sleeping well,' said Liberty, and took the coffee from her sister. It had a shot of caramel and was sickly sweet. Just what the doctor ordered. 'Come on, then, what's up?'

'Can't I just visit you?'

Liberty snorted, trudged into the sitting room and plonked herself down on the sofa. Crystal lowered herself carefully into the armchair opposite. She lifted a cushion and picked at the seam. It was ugly, in brown velour. Sol had bought four. What had happened to the other three?

'Spit it out,' said Liberty.

'I'm worried about Kelly,' said Crystal.

Liberty took a gulp of her drink. Mam had called it 'milky coffee' in the days before anyone had ever heard of lattes.

'I know he's not an ideal colleague,' said Liberty. 'But the choices were few. Most people in Moss Side are too scared of Ricky Vine to take him on. Kelly's the only one mental enough to have a go.'

'It's not that,' said Crystal. 'I think we need someone with a death wish. I'm just wondering how we keep tabs on what he's actually doing.'

'Tia will keep us in the loop.'

Crystal raised an eyebrow. 'The youngers are not loyal to Tia. I mean, they're not really loyal to us. If they think they're getting a better deal with Kelly, they'll soon see him as the new boss.'

'Tia's got help. A kid definitely tied to us,' said Liberty. 'The two of them will keep the rest in line.'

'What do you mean, tied to us?'

Liberty went to the chest of drawers in the corner of the room, the top so thick with dust that the last time she'd passed she'd drawn a smiley face in it. She opened the top drawer and pulled out Kalkan's mobile. She scrolled through until she found what she wanted and handed it to Crystal. 'Press play.'

Crystal stabbed the screen with her thumb and the film rolled. It started with JB helping Tia heave Kalkan onto a meat hook and ended with him standing beside the dead body as it bled out onto the cold-store floor.

'This kid was there yesterday, when Kelly attacked the foot spa,' said Crystal.

'And he's there now,' Liberty replied. 'With Tia. He's going nowhere, trust me.'

Crystal shook her head and smiled. 'You've changed.'

'Maybe I've just reverted to type.'

'By the way.' Crystal struggled to her feet. 'Pinar Kalkan wants to talk to us.'

The curtains were closed at the Kalkans' and no one answered the door, even though Rose kept her finger on the buzzer for half a minute.

She opened the letterbox and shouted, 'Mrs Kalkan, can we have a word, please?' Nothing. 'It's about your husband.' Still nothing.

Adam emerged from the side of the house and shook his head: he'd had no joy at the back door.

Twenty minutes later they stood in front of the halal butcher's and read the handwritten sign pinned to the inside of the door – 'Closed Until Further Notice'.

'If your husband had just gone to London to see his family, how come you're not answering your door and you've shut up shop?' Adam asked.

'Because she knows full well that he's messed with the wrong people.'

★★★

Pinar Kalkan wore a dark green pashmina draped loosely over her glossy hair and just the lightest slick of lip gloss. Her husband had been punching like Tyson Fury. Liberty didn't need to look at Jay to know that he was giving her his most beautiful smile. She closed the door to the back room of the Cashino and leaned against it. Crystal was already in the chair at the desk covered with towers of pound coins.

'Is my husband dead?' Pinar asked Jay.

His smile didn't slip. 'What makes you think that?'

'Because he was a fool,' said Pinar. Liberty hadn't been expecting that. She'd anticipated screaming, threats to go to the police, or maybe tears, but not that. 'When my father introduced us I knew straight away that he was not a clever man, but I did what I had to do.' She looked deeply into Jay's eyes. 'I still never would have dreamed he'd get himself killed over a tank of fish.'

Crystal chinked together two pound coins. 'It wasn't about the fish.'

Liberty skirted around Pinar to stand next to Crystal. She didn't want her sister to say anything more about what had taken place and why. The Turkish woman's perfume greeted her as she moved past, sweet like vanilla essence. The latte churned in Liberty's stomach.

'What can we do for you, Mrs Kalkan?' she asked.

'I need you to buy the shop.'

Jay roared with laughter. 'Do I look like a butcher?'

Pinar tapped her full lips with her nail in answer to that one. 'The taxi firm is rented and so is the house, but we own the butcher's.'

'Is it in your name?' Liberty asked.

'Of course.'

Jay laughed again, as he dragged his greedy eyes away from the

134

grieving widow. 'What the hell will we do with a butcher's shop, Lib?'

'Do customers pay in cash?' Liberty asked Pinar.

'Half and half,' Pinar replied.

'There's your answer, Jay,' said Liberty, and Crystal knocked over a tower of coins.

'Where will you go, Mrs Kalkan?' Liberty asked. 'If you get your money?'

'Maybe back to Turkey.' Pinar pulled the scarf slightly forward over the crown of her head, though plenty of glorious hair was still on display. 'My boys would have a good life there.'

'What about Mr Kalkan's brothers?' Liberty asked.

'Two are in prison and the youngest one can come with me,' said Pinar. 'Ahmet's only sixteen and his mother died last year.'

So that was the Kalkans out of Liberty's hair for a couple of hundred grand. And the Greenwoods would get themselves somewhere extra to wash their money. The Cashino and the Cherry were already at maximum. Any more activity would risk attracting suspicion. Liberty breathed a sigh of relief.

Rose checked up and down the street for anyone watching Liberty's house. There might have been some security after her sister's car was burned, but either they hadn't bothered or they'd gone for a break.

Adam tried the front door and the windows.

'This is Liberty Greenwood,' said Rose. 'She's not going to leave them open.'

'You'd be surprised,' said Adam, and hurried around to the back of the house. 'There's no alarm.'

Rose looked up. He was right: there was no box on the side of the house. 'So are we doing this, then?' he asked.

Rose nodded and Adam grabbed the bin. He wheeled it to the

back window, jumped onto it and smashed a smaller pane with his torch, pushing all the sharp pieces around the edge through. Then he reached inside and unlocked it.

'You're on,' he told Rose, and leaped down.

'Why me?'

'Well, I'm not about to fit through that gap, am I?' He patted the top of the bin. 'Get a wiggle on.'

Rose scrambled up, wobbling on the lid, and opened the window. As she heaved herself through, she wished she hadn't eaten the fritters at the Jade Garden. It was a tight fit, but she did manage to squeeze her torso through. Then she grabbed the handle of the larger window below and pulled herself all the way, landing with a bang on the windowsill before crashing to the floor.

'All right?' Adam called, from outside.

Rose dragged herself to her feet and gave him a thumbs-up. Then she made her way to the back door and opened it for him.

'What are we looking for?' he asked.

'Not a clue.'

They worked their way methodically through kitchen drawers, finding only cutlery and a pile of tea-towels. Adam opened a cupboard to reveal a couple of cheap mugs and a box of teabags.

'Christ, she doesn't like clutter, does she?'

Rose cast an eye around the kitchen, every surface clear except for an empty fruit bowl that needed a scrub. She jerked her head that they should move to the sitting room and found it equally sparse. A coffee table housing no newspapers or books, just an empty takeaway cup.

Adam lifted the cushions on the sofa but there was only dust and crumbs underneath. Rose opened a chest of drawers, beginning to suspect that the risk they were taking would be in vain. Then, bingo, a mobile. 'Oi-oi,' she said to Adam.

'Is it locked?' he asked. She tried the key pad and couldn't believe her eyes. 'You're kidding me?' he said.

Rose went into texts and found most of them in a foreign language.

Adam looked over her shoulder. 'What the hell is that?'

'What?'

He pointed to an emoji used frequently. 'A mushroom?'

'Never mind that, look who it's from.'

They both looked at the contact name – Pinar. Rose went into photos and found the usual raft of selfies and pictures of kids playing with a dog. The phone obviously belonged to Pinar's missing husband. Rose clicked on the last video and they watched in silence.

'Holy shit,' said Adam, when it finished.

Chapter 9

3 November 1990

When Mrs Moser picks us up, me and our Jay can't stop grinning. We've finally got a contact session with the little ones. Only a couple of hours but we don't care.

Her car is a red Fiat and she pushes back her seat so Jay can get in the back. I go in the front, which I'm expecting our Jay to whinge about, but he's on his best behaviour. And, anyway, he's asleep by the time we've hit the main road.

There's a sticker on the glove compartment that's got a quotation on it: 'Be yourself: everyone else is already taken.'

Mrs Moser sees me reading it. 'Oscar Wilde.'

'I've read The Picture of Dorian Gray,' I say.

'What did you think?'

'I suppose leading a double life is a bit shit.'

Mrs Moser laughs. 'That's what being in care is like, though, a double life.' She winds down her window to let in a bit of fresh air. 'Always trying to second-guess what everyone wants you to say?' She glances at me when I don't reply. 'Am I right?'

Of course she is, but I don't want to say so in case she starts thinking that what I tell her isn't true and that I'm only telling her what she wants to hear. Which is completely the case. 'I hadn't really thought about it in any detail,' I say.

She laughs again. 'You'll make a very good solicitor with answers like that.'

'How do you know that's what I want to do?'

'I've read all your files.' She looks at me. 'Is it what you want to do or is it just something you say to give a good impression?'

I shake my head. 'No, I definitely want to be a solicitor. It's a really good job.'

'It is.'

When we reach the contact centre, she pulls on the handbrake with a creak and turns around to Jay. 'Hey, sleepy head, we're here.'

He wipes away some dribble on his chin and grins as Mrs Moser gets out to push back her seat.

'Don't rile the kids up,' I hiss at him. 'Keep it all really calm.'

He nods and we both get out of the car. The last thing we need is our Frankie going doo-lally and shitting his pants.

Inside the centre, it's the usual layout: toys, craft tables and that. Social workers spying on your every move. Me and Jay sit in the corner while we wait. When he starts to pick his ear, I bat his hand away.

At long last the kids arrive and our Jay bursts out laughing. Someone's parted Frankie's hair in the middle and smoothed it down at either side. With both front teeth missing as well, he looks like he's not the full ticket. When he sees us, he does a little jig on tiptoe and nudges Crystal, who spots us, flies over and throws herself at Jay. He picks her up and twirls her around. I lean over and kiss her cheek and she bursts into tears. I try to take her from Jay, but Frankie jumps on my back, half strangling me.

'Let's all sit down,' I say, praying things don't get out of hand.

Mrs Moser smiles and nods. 'Good idea, Lib. And how about I get everyone a glass of squash?'

When she's popped away to the kitchen, I plonk Frankie down in a chair and prise Crystal out of Jay's arms. 'Come on,' I whisper. 'We don't want them to see you making a fuss.' It's a bit harsh on her, but when everybody compares notes on how this session went, I don't need anyone saying there were tears. I hand Crystal a tissue and she swipes at her eyes with it. I give her forehead a quick rub and tell her she's to be brave.

'Here you go,' says Mrs Moser, carrying a tray full of plastic cups of orange pop. She hands the first to Crystal. 'It can all get a bit much, can't it?'

'Can I have one?' our Frankie shouts.

'I should think so,' she says, with a wink.

He grabs a cup, necks the squash in one and burps. Our Jay roars with laughter.

'Frankie.' I give a tut. 'What do you say?'

He frowns at me, like he's no idea what the answer is, then he goes, 'I need a wee.'

Jay takes him off to the toilet, and Crystal leaps onto my knee. She's far too big for this sort of thing, but what am I going to do?

'How about we do a picture?' I suggest.

Crystal shakes her head. Nervously, I risk a glance at Mrs Moser, expecting her to be unimpressed with how the kids are behaving. Instead she puts a hand on my arm. 'Stop worrying,' she tells me. 'It's all perfectly understandable.'

After that, things get easier. Frankie comes back from the toilet and convinces Crystal that we should all play with the Lego. So we sit on a mat and make a whole village. Our Jay builds a tower that he says is full of princesses. Frankie dots single pieces around the place for houses, and Crystal puts together an amazing palace that has windows and everything. We find some little trees and make a forest for the village children to play in.

'What's it called?' Mrs Moser asks.

'The Crosshills,' Frankie replies.

And even I'm laughing at that one.

Present Day

Liberty sauntered along the chilled aisle with a spring in her step. Bringing Kelly on board meant that they could soon demolish

Ricky Vine, and a few hundred grand had sorted the Kalkan problem. She dropped a medium-sized chicken into her basket, then swapped it for an extra-large. Proper cooking had been lacking in recent months, but she was planning a roast dinner and had already texted Crystal and Jay, inviting them to come over to hers later. Jay had suggested the Jade Garden, but Liberty was determined to make them all some decent food.

She went to the freezer section and grabbed some Yorkshire puddings, then headed to the till.

'Good as home-made, they are,' said the cashier, nodding at the packet of Aunt Bessie's.

'Just as well,' said Liberty. 'I wouldn't know where to start.'

She'd never really learned to cook. Mam had been a sausage and chips fan, with peas, if she felt the urge to throw in a vitamin, spaghetti hoops when she didn't much care. Liberty recalled a lot of spaghetti hoops.

Some of the foster carers she'd been with would get annoyed that she found their wholegrain bread and fresh vegetables hard to stomach, even though she'd always tried her best. There'd been one woman she'd really liked who used to bake loads of cakes, all of them dry and rock hard. Liberty had wanted to stay there, but it hadn't worked out.

Once she'd started her job in London, she had generally bought pre-prepared stuff.

'My gran used to make massive ones,' said the cashier. 'As big as a tea plate. Then she'd fill them with gravy. All from scratch as well.' She pushed a bag of potatoes through the scanner. 'We bring her to ours on Sundays and tell her that the frozen ones aren't as good as the ones she made.' She pushed the key pad towards Liberty for payment. 'But I'm not convinced.'

When she was back at home, Liberty checked the street. She'd told Jay's men to stop camping out because they were making the neighbours suspicious. The old woman next door had just about swallowed Liberty's story that the car going up had been an awful accident, but when she'd asked about the two great lumps sitting opposite, what could Liberty say?

The answer, as she knew full well, was to move to a more secure property. She'd get her brother and sister to help her choose somewhere when they came round later.

With her key still in the door, Liberty knew something was wrong as soon as she stepped into the house. Cold air was moving towards her as opposed to coming from the open door behind, and there was outside noise that didn't belong: wind, birds, kids playing on a trampoline. She took one step backwards and left the house, only to bump into Jay.

'Hey up,' he said. 'What's happening?' He clocked her serious face and narrowed his eyes. 'Lib?'

'I don't know,' she replied. Jay pushed past her, gun already in his hand. 'We should wait. Call some people,' Liberty shouted after him.

'No.' Jay strode down the hall. 'If someone's in here, I'm not giving them the chance to run off.'

Liberty followed him to the kitchen, which was empty and just as she had left it. Then they moved to the sitting room and found the window smashed, the top drawer of the chest open.

'Shit,' Liberty yelled, and rushed to the drawer, rifling for the phone.

Jay made them both a coffee, mumbling about the lack of sugar and milk. Then he forced Liberty into a chair at the kitchen table.

'Who do we think did this?' he asked. 'Kalkan's missus?'

Liberty shook her head. 'She wouldn't risk it when she hasn't even got her money yet.'

'Then who?'

★★★

142

Rose's heart was still racing, not helped by the fact that Adam was pacing her kitchen, his broad steps covering the space from wall to wall in seconds, before he turned and marched back the other way. 'Can you stop that, Adam?'

He stared at her, then pointed to the mobile Rose still clutched in her hand. 'That's evidence of a murder.' Rose could feel her fingers sweating against the case. 'A woman has lost her husband and her kids have lost their dad,' Adam said.

As soon as they'd rushed from Liberty Greenwood's house, Adam had demanded they hand the phone in to the chief super. And he wasn't stopping now.

'And how will we explain where we found it?' Rose asked.

'We'll tell them we suspected the Greenwoods of being involved, so we entered the property,' Adam replied.

'We burgled the house,' said Rose.

'We entered in the course of an investigation.'

'What investigation?' Rose snapped. 'No one has reported Kalkan missing, let alone dead. And if they had, we wouldn't be on the case, would we, a couple of beat monkeys like us?' She held out the mobile to Adam. 'But go on, be my guest and drop us both in it.'

For a second, it looked like Adam might take up her offer, but instead he flopped into a chair. 'So what now?'

'We take it to the Greenwoods.'

Adam's mouth made a perfect O. 'They'll kill us.'

'Not with this as insurance,' said Rose, and waggled the phone at him.

Yusef's heart hammered in his chest as he jogged back through the market. One of the stalls was selling fried noodles, a woman in a beanie stirring them in a big wok with peppers and mushrooms and bits of chicken. Usually, he'd have gone for a carton of that like a shot, but right now he couldn't have kept them down.

Coops had called him half an hour ago, telling him to meet her at a different stash house. He'd said yes, but then hadn't set off. For fifteen minutes he'd just stood there trying to breathe. Then he'd counted up all the cash he had on him and tried to work out if he could get a bus to somewhere. Maybe London. London was massive and he could probably just get lost there. Coops, Ricky Vine, Sol and Hutch, none of them would be able to find him, if he kept his head down.

Trouble was Yusef only had eleven quid and he was pretty sure the bus fare would be more than that. He could try jumping the train without a ticket, but if he got caught, they'd bring him back to Manchester and everyone would know he'd tried to escape.

Now he was late for Coops.

When he finally got to the stash house, he was out of breath. He called Coops's number and she let him in.

'Who you running from?' she asked, slamming the door behind him.

'Just keeping fit,' Yusef replied. 'Never know when you've gotta get away on your toes.'

Coops laughed. 'You're weird as, you know that?'

Yusef tried to laugh but he was panting so hard he just started coughing. 'I need a drink.'

Coops led him into the kitchen, if you could call it that. Someone had smashed all the cupboards and most of the tiles on the wall. There wasn't a fridge or anything. She turned on the tap and let it run into the cracked sink. 'There's no glasses,' she told him.

Yusef nodded and bent to the stream of water, taking a gulp before wiping his chin. 'Thanks.'

'I need you to do something, yeah?' Coops said. Yusef kept rubbing his chin for something to do. 'You know Ricky's gym?'

'Never been there but I know where it is,' Yusef replied.

Coops scratched her head. The long nails made a horrible sound as they raked the bristles of her hair. She wore it low, like a lot of black boys. Probably needed to buzz it every couple of days.

'There's some shit I need you to collect,' she said. 'Bring it back here.'

'Okay.'

Sol and Hutch watched Yusef leave the stash house. The kid had only got round the corner when he threw up. Two women in burqa, arms full of shopping, stopped.

'You all right, love?' said one.

Considering the position of the mic, the sound quality was excellent.

Yusef staggered away from the women without replying.

'Manners, Yusef,' muttered Sol.

'You think he's going to bottle it?' Hutch asked.

Sol shook his head. 'He'll be just fine.'

They let him take the bus across to the gym. Picking him up would be too risky. Right now on his first job for Coops, she might have someone watching him. Everyone would be extra cautious after Oren had been nicked.

When Yusef got off the bus, a few streets from Vine's gym, he lit a fag with shaking hands, blowing smoke on the tip. He stood for a moment, smoking, shoulders hunched.

'Give him a call?' Hutch suggested. 'Tell him to get a shift on.'

'Just a sec,' said Sol. 'It's better if he starts to make the right choices himself.'

They waited, and just as Sol was beginning to wonder if Hutch was right, Yusef set off. They followed him to the gym, watched him ring the buzzer and heard him speak into the entry-phone.

'Yeah, it's Yusef,' he said. 'Coops sent me.'

There was no mistaking the terror in Yusef's eyes as the door opened and he stepped inside.

★★★

The bloke who showed Yusef in didn't say a word, just held his arms out to the side as a sign that Yusef should do the same.

Yusef didn't know what to do. If he let the man frisk him there was a chance he'd find the wire, but if he refused, they'd search him anyway. A muscle near his eye twitched. It had happened a lot in the Jungle in Calais, so much that some of the boys had taken the piss, saying he was queer and winking at them. They'd only stopped when Yusef bit the earlobe off the biggest one.

He pushed out his arms and let the bloke run his hands up and down the length, then inside his jacket.

'Lift your top up,' the bloke said.

Yusef lifted it up and the man ran a finger around the waistband of Yusef's jeans. Thank God Sol hadn't let him tape the wire to his stomach. When the man patted down Yusef's legs, he scrunched his eyes tight shut. Sometimes that stopped the twitching.

'Ricky's upstairs,' said the man.

Yusef didn't reply, but followed him up the concrete stairs, until they got to a corridor at the top. The man knocked on a door and someone shouted, 'Come in.'

There were three men inside. All on chairs, playing cards around a bed. Not a bed you slept in, with sheets and that. It was the sort they used for massages. The money was in the middle of the bed, on the plastic cover. None of them looked at Yusef. There was a black bloke with a broken front tooth that he ran his tongue over constantly, and a white bloke with a roll-up tucked behind his ear. Then there was Ricky Vine.

A bright light above the bed was making Ricky sweat. Yusef had never met him but he knew what he looked like. A bit fat and pink, sausage fingers dealing out the deck.

'You Coops's boy?' Ricky asked.

The white bloke extracted his rollie and put it between his lips.

'Be the first time Coops went near a cock.'

'She needed me to collect something,' Yusef muttered, over the men's laughter.

'What was that?' Ricky asked. 'Don't whisper at me, I haven't got bionic hearing.'

Yusef cleared his throat. 'Coops said I should pick something up for her.'

Ricky rubbed his nose with his thumb, making his nostrils go wide so Yusef could see all the hairs. There was a bit of bogey stuck to one that Vine managed not to flick off. Yusef felt puke rise up his throat. It burned as he swallowed it back down.

'Get the packet, Moody,' said Vine.

The white bloke, who still had the unlit rollie in his mouth, reached under the bed to a cardboard box. Then he pulled out a gun from the box, showed it to Ricky, who nodded.

'Tell Coops not to fucking kill anyone,' said Ricky, and the other two laughed again.

The white bloke held out the gun to Yusef so he was forced to step forward and get it. When he was close enough to smell Ricky, he reached for the gun, but Ricky put a hand on his. 'What's that?' Ricky asked. Yusef panicked and tried to pull his hand away, but Ricky held it tightly. 'Asked you a question,' said Ricky.

'What's what?' Yusef asked. Ricky dug his thumbnail into Yusef's tiny tattoo of a smiley face. 'Oh, that. Just messing about when I was a kid,' Yusef said.

'And you're all grown-up now, eh?' Ricky said, with a sneer.

Ricky was hurting Yusef, but he knew it would be stupid to resist. If Ricky carried on there was a chance he would break Yusef's thumb. Yusef breathed out as slowly as possible, like a deflating balloon. When all the air was gone, he could feel the squeeze in his chest. The tightness getting harder and harder to control, so that he couldn't even remember what Ricky was doing to him.

At last Ricky let go and so did the white bloke, leaving Yusef holding the gun. For a second, he imagined shooting them. Bang, bang, bang. All three heads blown off. At this range, he'd be covered with blood and bones and bits of hair, but it'd be worth it. Instead, he slid the gun down the back of his jeans. Shit. The tape pulled hard and he felt the wire slip from his skin.

'I should take this to Coops,' he said, and backed from the room.

'I'm not the chuffing Queen,' said Ricky.

Yusef knew that if he turned, there was a chance they'd see the loose wire through his jeans. People like Ricky could sniff out a snitch, like dogs could find a fox turd. Suddenly Yusef smiled, bowed and continued backing from the room.

'Cheeky little sod,' said Ricky.

The other two joined in, bowing and pretending to take off their hats.

'Your honour,' said the black bloke.

'That's a judge, you muppet,' said Ricky.

When Yusef was out of the door and ready to run, Ricky called over to him. 'Need you to ask about, lad. There's a salon that got trashed up near Gooch. Find out who did it, yeah? Then come back and let me know.'

Yusef nodded and closed the door.

Liberty didn't tell Jay about Angel's phone call, arranging to meet in the same garage toilets where they'd last seen one another. If she had, there'd have been no way she could have prevented her brother murdering the copper.

When she pulled into the forecourt, Liberty still couldn't quite believe that Angel had been the one to break into her house, but how else had she got hold of the footage in the butcher's?

There was another cop outside the toilet door. He wasn't

in uniform but Liberty could taste police in the air. He was a good-looking bloke, who obviously liked lifting weights, his arms muscular and covered with ink sleeves.

'You know if my brother finds out about this, he's going to cut off your head and post it to your mam,' she said. 'I'm at least prepared to hear you out.'

Fair play to the cop, who just opened the door silently.

Unlike last time, Angel wasn't pouring the contents of her stomach into the toilet bowl. Instead, she leaned casually against the frame of the cubicle door, arms crossed.

'Here we are again,' said Liberty.

Angel smiled, didn't speak. Liberty knew what the other woman was expecting, what she wanted: a demand to know what exactly Angel thought she was doing, what she planned to do with the film. Then Angel could calmly make her demands. Nah. It wasn't going to happen like that. Instead, Liberty smiled back, didn't speak.

Time ticked by, so Liberty pulled out her mobile and scrolled through her emails. Crystal's car would be ready for pick-up in a few days and the dealership would like to take Liberty through the paperwork. The only sound was the drip, drip, drip of a tap into a dirty basin. In the end, it was the sidekick who lost his nerve.

'We have enough to put you away for murder,' he said.

Liberty raised an eyebrow at him. 'If that was true, my friend, we'd be having this conversation down the station.'

'We've seen the film,' he said.

'Then you know I'm not in it.'

He bridled at that. 'You can be heard in the background, orchestrating events.'

'Had voice recognition done on it, have you?' Liberty snapped her fingers. 'Oh, wait, that would involve making this official rather than asking to meet me on the quiet in some filthy bogs.'

She turned to Angel. 'Where the hell did you find this one? I mean, I'm only flesh and blood so I can see the attraction, but he's not the sharpest tool, is he?'

Liberty heard the door close behind her. Angel's lapdog must have stormed off. 'Why don't we just get this over with?' she suggested. 'Obviously we can do the dance, if you'd prefer. You say you can get me put away. I point out that you broke into my house. You say a jury won't care how you got the phone. I point out that a jury will think you planted it. You say you're willing to risk it. I point out that if that was the case you'd already have taken the phone to top brass.' Liberty laughed. 'The truth is, you daren't spin the wheel, Rose.'

Angel laughed back. 'Nor you, Liberty. If you were feeling half as cocky about this as you're making out, you wouldn't be standing in these filthy bogs with me, would you?'

They stared at one another, knowing full well that the other had a point.

Angel moved to the sink and tried to stop the dripping tap, by banging it with her fist. It didn't work. 'I want to know what happened to Joel Redman.'

'We didn't kill him.'

'Then find out who did,' said Angel.

So that was it. The police weren't investigating Redman's death. It probably suited them that he'd gone quietly. But Angel couldn't let it go. Why? Did she feel guilty for putting him away in the first place?

'And if I do that for you?' Liberty asked. 'You'll just forget all about what you saw on that phone?'

'I don't care about Kalkan. He was just a two-bit criminal,' said Angel. 'Even his own wife doesn't care that he's dead.' Liberty couldn't argue with that. 'Once you give me an answer about Joel, I'm done.'

Liberty frowned. 'Fine.'

★★★

Adam drove Rose back to her house in complete silence. When he pulled up outside, he stared straight ahead. She thought about just getting out and leaving things, because she was exhausted and didn't know if she could face another round of arguments.

'Why don't you just spit it out, Adam?' she said at last.

For a second, he didn't move, but when he did finally turn to her, he looked more hurt than angry, his big eyes full of disbelief. 'You're just going to let the Greenwoods get away with murder because you don't care about their victim?' Adam shook his head. 'Since when do we get to decide who's worth our time and who's not?'

Rose put a hand on Adam's knee and he jumped as if scalded. She whipped it away quickly. 'I'm not going to let them get away with anything.'

'But you told . . .'

Suddenly the light bulb went on in Adam's brain.

'She needs to think that once she's got me what I want, I'll walk away, or why wouldn't she just tell me to get lost? But once I know what happened to Joel, I'm obviously not just going to shake hands and move along.' She extracted Kalkan's mobile from her pocket and dropped it into Adam's lap. 'And you're going to hang on to the leverage.'

'Me?'

Rose opened the car door. 'We're going to find out what happened to Joel and then we're going to get the Greenwoods.' She slid out, glad to feel some cool air on her face. 'And if they get rid of me first, you can nail them to the wall.'

She slammed the car door and went inside.

Sol went to pick up a takeaway. He'd fancied an Indian, but couldn't face his bowels falling out the next day. It didn't matter what he ordered, they seemed to mix it with a slow-release lax-ative. So he'd settled on a Chinese. The one on the corner of the street where he lived was half decent. Well, a quarter decent anyway.

It wasn't ready when he arrived, so he stepped outside for a fag and called Yusef.

'What?' The lad sounded angry and stressed.

'Just checking in about what happened with Vine,' said Sol.

'You were listening to every word, so you know what happened.'

'And what about the info he asked you to get for him?' Sol asked. 'Some salon that got done over?'

Yusef growled. 'Word is it was kids from outside the area.'

'You need to get something more solid so you can go back to the gym and tell Ricky,' said Sol.

'I'm not stupid,' Yusef shouted.

'Hey, calm down.'

'How can I when you're going to get me killed?' Yusef panted down the phone, like he couldn't catch his breath. 'The wire came loose, man. They could have easily seen it. Then what? I'm not wearing it no more, okay?'

'We'll talk about it tomorrow morning,' said Sol.

'No, we won't. I've told you I'm not wearing it again, and I'm not. You put it on me and I'll rip it off. If you want to send me back to jail for that, then go on and do it.'

Sol could tell that there'd be no reasoning with Yusef tonight so he hung up. Sometimes the informants needed to get it out of their system. They got claustrophobic, knowing they had no choices, so they lashed out.

The young woman behind the counter held up five fingers to indicate how long he needed to wait. Sol waved back at her and finished his smoke. When his mobile rang again, he assumed it would be Yusef ready to give another round of abuse, but it was the boss, Bella Kapur.

'Gov?'

'Sorry to call you at this time, Sol,' said Kapur, though she didn't sound it.

'It's fine. Everything okay?'

'No idea if I'm honest,' she said. 'But your wife has turned up at HQ.'

It took Sol a couple of hours to get to Birmingham and find Natasha flicking through an old copy of *TV Choice* in the reception area. She looked great with her hair cut a little shorter so it touched her shoulders.

'You look like hell,' she told him. Sol raked a hand through greasy untrimmed hair. 'When did you last wash those jeans?' she demanded.

He sat down in the chair next to her and glanced at the reviews for soaps at least a month out of date. Danny Dyer stared back at him from the centre pages.

Natasha sniffed. 'You've started smoking again.'

'Good to see you too, Tash.'

She dropped the magazine back on the table. 'No one at the station had your new number, but the old desk sergeant said he thought you'd taken a job here.'

'I'm freelance,' Sol replied. A cleaner scuttled across the foyer, a hoover in hand, one of those ones with a face on the front. They had a name, but Sol couldn't remember what it was. (Why would anyone need to put a face on a hoover and name it? Was that not just weird?) 'Look, Tash, is everything okay?'

She had a bag at her feet and she reached into it, pulling out a brown envelope. So that was it: she wanted a divorce. Well, he certainly couldn't argue with that.

'What grounds?' he asked. 'Please don't tell me you've cited adultery and named Lib.'

153

Natasha slapped the envelope against her thigh. 'And why shouldn't I do that, Sol? Why should I spare that woman's feelings?'

Sol couldn't think of one good reason, other than his leaving Natasha wasn't Liberty's fault. He'd been a crap husband in every way possible before Liberty had come along. And she'd never once asked him to leave his wife. In fact, more than a few times, Liberty had told him to stop risking his marriage. He took the envelope and opened it, scanning the paperwork inside. It was some sort of legal document, but not a petition for divorce. 'What's this?'

Natasha sat up straight in her chair. 'Adoption papers.'

'You want to adopt a baby?'

She sighed at him. 'No, Sol, I already have a baby. Our baby.' She looked him right in the eye. 'And I want you to agree that my new partner can adopt him.'

Chapter 10

6 November 1990

When I come down for breakfast, I see Mrs Moser talking to Hemma and my heart drops. Before she can catch sight of me, I run back to my room. I wish I had better clothes or a nice haircut. Anything to make me not feel like a piece of rubbish in a skip when she tells me she's very sorry but they think it's in everybody's interests if I don't have contact with the little ones for a while.

Tears sting my eyes and my nose is running as I charge to the toilet, but obviously it's locked. I bang on the door.

'Go away.' It's Michaela inside. 'I'm doing a shit.'

'Can I get some bog roll?' I ask. 'Please.'

She groans but the door opens a bit and her hand passes out the roll. I take a wodge and pass it back.

'My dad called last night,' she says. 'He's coming round tonight.'

'That's good,' I tell her.

'Do you want to meet him?'

I'm glad she can't see my face, which must be a right picture. I mean, she's just the latest lass our Jay's shagging and she's not even the only one. We've never had one conversation, Michaela and me. Yet she wants to know if she can introduce me to her dad.

'Okay,' I say, though God knows why. Not that it matters, because there's no way Michaela's dad is coming over.

155

By the time Mrs Moser sees me, I've put on my game face. Hemma leads us into the office, so I know it's really bad news.

'How are you?' Mrs Moser asks, a smile on her lips.

'Look, I know things were bad at the contact centre with our Crystal grizzling and that, but it's hard when there's such big gaps between seeing each other.'

It's a speech I've made before. No one listens or cares.

Mrs Moser's still smiling. 'Relax, Lib.'

'Elizabeth,' Hemma corrects.

'I don't think Lib ever uses her full name,' says Mrs Moser, without looking at Hemma.

Hemma screws up her mouth. You can tell she wants to argue, but Mrs Moser is the sort of woman you don't argue with. Plus she reports back to the court, so Hemma wouldn't want anything bad said about her, would she?

'The contact session was fine, Lib,' Mrs Moser says. 'Crystal soon settled down, once she was over her initial shock at being with you again.'

'Was she all right once she got back to the foster placement?' I ask.

Mrs Moser nods. 'Apparently, she told Mrs Peterson that you smelt exactly the same.' She laughs. 'Anyway, that's not why I'm here. Remember on the way to the centre we talked about you getting back into college?'

'I've been working really hard to make that happen,' says Hemma. 'It didn't help that Elizabeth left her last school without any notice.'

'What do you think of this?' Mrs Moser is talking directly to me, not Hemma. I'm beginning to suspect the guardian isn't too impressed with our resident key worker. She hands me a brochure. 'It's in Wakefield.' I look down at the front cover with a picture of a group of students sitting on a lawn in front of a college. They've all got nice trainers and big smiles. 'I've wangled you an interview if you're interested.'

'Do they know where I live?' I ask.

Mrs Moser leans towards me, and her shirt gapes a bit so I can see a little silver chain around her neck, with a heart locket. 'Your situation means you have priority on school and college places. It's the law. The head of Sandringham College takes his responsibility to looked-after children very seriously.' She leans back. 'Plus he's an old mate and he owes me a favour.'

An hour later, I'm at the college in Mr Whitbred's office, which is full of books. There's a shelf behind his chair crammed with them and there are towers of them on the floor lining the wall. There's one on his desk, open and face down, which you're not meant to do because it breaks the spine.

'How long have you been out of college?' he asks.

'A few weeks,' I tell him. 'But I've been reading and that, trying to keep up.'

'Under normal circumstances I'd suggest restarting the year next September, but I've seen your grades and Gracie, sorry, Mrs Moser, tells me you're exceptionally motivated.'

'I want to go to university,' I tell him.

'Have you thought about where?'

'Oxford,' I say.

He nods. 'Right, then, we'd better get you back into class. Shall we say on Monday?' I don't answer because the truth is too embarrassing. 'Is there a problem?' he asks.

'I'll need a travel warrant to get here,' I say. 'And they always take ages to come through.' He peers at me and I realise he might not know what a travel warrant is. 'It's like a bus pass. I ask one of the key workers and they put in an application but it takes a while. I'm sorry.' My face burns hot. 'I'd walk if it was close enough.'

He runs his finger over his mouth, pulling his bottom lip down so I can see pink skin. 'I don't think you can afford to miss more lessons.' Oh, shit. Why did I say owt? I could try to borrow some cash for the bus fares until the warrant comes through. Then he opens a drawer and takes out a wallet, black leather with the letters CW embossed on it in gold. 'Tell your key worker to get a wiggle on and, in the meantime, here you are.' He pushes a five-pound note across his desk. 'Now go straight to the office to register and I'll see you next Monday, Miss Greenwood.'

Present Day

Liberty ripped off a piece of gaffer tape with her teeth and attached a sheet of brown cardboard over the broken window in her sitting room. She'd arranged for a bloke to come and fix it later, but needed to keep the rain out in the meantime.

She was still mulling over what to do about Angel. Obviously the line the copper was spinning about leaving the Kalkan problem alone if Liberty managed to uncover who had killed Redman was utter nonsense. Liberty and her family would never be safe while Angel had the video clip. But she needed to buy some time as she worked out how to destroy it or get it back, or rid herself of the two people who had seen it and could use it against her. This last course of action would be Jay's first port of call, probably Crystal's too, which was why Liberty still hadn't told them who had broken in. But the death or disappearance of two local police officers would bring an unholy amount of attention, which Liberty couldn't afford right now.

No, she needed enough time to make a plan and the best way to get that time would be to give Angel what she wanted: the name of whoever had killed Joel Redman.

Bunny Hill looked better than she had in years. She'd ditched the Bird's custard hair and pleather clothes that would have made Mel think twice. Yes, she looked older, but twice as attractive. She pressed the button on a coffee machine to heat the water and hummed to herself while she waited.

'You're clearly on good form, Bunny,' said Liberty.

The other woman handed over a cappuccino and a plate of cookies speckled with chocolate chips. 'It's nice to see you, Liberty.'

Liberty bit into the biscuit and tried not to wince at the toothache-sweetness. She hadn't contacted Bunny since her husband had been sent down. It wasn't common knowledge that Liberty had orchestrated that, but no doubt Bunny suspected it. Paul Hill had got a ten stretch at sixty and might even die inside, which wasn't a topic of conversation Liberty had wanted to engage in. 'It's not a social call,' she said.

Bunny slid onto a stool at the kitchen island and smiled. 'Didn't imagine it was.'

Liberty looked around the room. A far cry from her own kitchen, Bunny's was brimming with signs of a well-lived life: a fruit bowl full of apples and grapefruits and mangos, a toaster spilling crumbs, a tube of hand cream at the sink.

'This place was always in my name,' Bunny said, wafting a hand around the room. 'So they couldn't touch it when Paul went away.' She spooned some froth from her coffee and sucked it down. 'Same with the ISAs and what-have-you.'

Liberty laughed. The thought that Bunny Hill had investments in anything more than how deep her tan was seemed unthinkable. 'What about the house in Spain?' she asked. Bunny shrugged. It had clearly gone and she clearly didn't care. 'The club?'

'What can I tell you, Liberty? All the stuff we had to clean money has gone one way or another. But so what? I diverted everything I could into legit businesses so now I don't need them.' She made a hey-presto flick of her hands. 'For years and years I told Paul that was what we should do, but he wouldn't listen.' She tossed her now light brown hair. 'But I make the decisions these days.'

Liberty put down her half-eaten cookie. How had she not realised that Bunny's bimbo act was just that? She'd needed to be something when Paul was in charge, and now she was free to be who she really was.

'Far be it from me to tell you how to crack on,' Bunny said, 'but you'd sleep a lot easier at night if you moved away from the drugs and all the other dodgy stuff.' She eyed Liberty coolly.

'People like us have to start out that way. We don't have families to set us up, do we? But the aim is to get away from that as soon as you can.'

How many times had Liberty told her siblings this? A thousand? A million? Yet when had she last done anything about trying to achieve it?

'Anyway, you're a bright woman, you'll have a plan,' said Bunny. 'And in the meantime why don't you tell me what's up?'

'Joel Redman.'

Bunny reached for a biscuit, broke it in two and nibbled the smaller half. 'He's dead.'

'Know anything about that?' Liberty asked.

'No.' Liberty watched Bunny chase crumbs around the plate with her fingers. 'All that stuff is way behind me,' said Bunny. 'Ancient history.'

'What about Paul?' Liberty asked.

They both knew Paul was ruthless. He'd got Joel Redman in his pocket in the first place by killing some of his family. And he'd kept Redman there with the constant threat of ruining him. Obviously Redman would have done well out of it, but the extra cash wouldn't have been enough on its own.

'Why would he bother?' Bunny asked.

Liberty had given some thought to that. Redman had told the police a few things about Hill that hadn't helped, but ultimately Hill would have gone down anyway. Angel had caught him red-handed with drugs and a weapon in his car. Given his record, there was no way Paul could avoid prison with or without Redman's evidence.

'A warning to anyone else who thinks they can cross Paul?' Liberty suggested.

Bunny laughed. 'A warning to who? We're not in the game any more. You're thinking like a gangster and that's not who we are now.'

160

HARD AS NAILS

★★★

Sol tried to reread the application for adoption for the hundredth time and, like all the previous attempts, the words began to swim before he reached the end. A couple of moments during the night, he'd considered setting the document on fire and he'd even flicked his lighter to do it, but how would that help? He dropped it onto the floor and rubbed his face, the smell of the ink still on his fingers.

Natasha hadn't given him many details, just that she'd had a little girl and wanted her new partner to adopt her.

'Why didn't you tell me you were pregnant?' Sol asked.

'I didn't know,' his wife had explained. 'I was stressed and put it down to that. Then my sister came to visit and she took one look at me at the airport and said I was having a baby.'

'You could have told me then,' Sol muttered.

'*Da.*'

He closed his eyes and tried to think. Maybe Natasha was right and this was for the best. He'd never wanted kids in the first place and he was in no fit state to be a father. He lived in a studio flat on a rolling rental, with a sleeping-bag on the sofa, eating takeaway or nothing at all. But if it was for the best, why did his head feel like it was on fire? He pressed his thumbs against his temples. His mobile rang. Yusef.

'Everything okay?' Sol asked.

'A-fucking-mazing,' Yusef replied.

Sol sighed. There wasn't room in his brain for a row. 'What do you want, Yusef?'

'We need to meet up,' the kid said.

Yusef tapped an old metal toolbox on the floor with his foot and wondered why the people who owned this place before had left so much stuff behind. If this had been back home, the garage would have been picked clean as a bone. In Eritrea, what people couldn't use, they sold.

A few years ago, a teacher at one of the education units Yusef went to, had tried to get him interested in motorbike mechanics, which had seemed random as Yusef had never even been on a motorbike. But then another had said he might like to try a cookery class, so he supposed they were just chatting any old shit to get the kids to listen.

When Sol rolled up, he smelt even worse than normal. Yusef struggled to get a shower every day because there were always too many lads fighting for it, but he sprayed his clothes with Lynx without fail. Sol had worn the same pair of jeans every time Yusef had ever seen him and the stains were just growing. Minging.

'This had better be important,' Sol said.

He was obviously vexed. Well, too bad. Yusef was the one putting his life on the line. Sol just swanned around barking orders.

'I did what Ricky told me and asked around about the youngers who trashed the nail bar up near Gooch,' said Yusef.

'And?'

'No one knows exactly who they are, but they've also done a chicken shop,' said Yusef. 'They took the place apart with hammers and bats. One of the blokes who works there says the place was knee deep in chips where they upturned sacks of them.' Sol turned away. 'Are you even listening?' Yusef shouted.

'How can I not when you're screaming?'

Yusef kicked the toolbox. It was half empty and easily slid across the concrete floor. 'You told me to do what Ricky said and now you don't even give a shit.'

Suddenly Sol was up in Yusef's grille, eyes flashing. Yusef could smell his hot fag-breath, like he hadn't brushed his teeth. 'Then tell Ricky Vine your big news.' He stepped away and spat on the floor.

Yusef felt his skin go hot as he tried not to bang out Sol. 'I'm not wearing a wire,' he said.

'Yeah, you told me that yesterday,' Sol muttered.

Yusef didn't move. Something was up. More than Sol just having the hump. No way would any five-oh let him talk to Vine without listening to every word. He waited for Sol to lose his rag, maybe even throw a punch, but it didn't happen. Instead, Sol just walked away, leaving Yusef alone in the damp garage. This time Yusef picked up the toolbox and chucked it at the old Beemer. It landed on the bonnet with a thump. Then Yusef ran to the box, picked it up and smashed it down. Again and again and again, tears skimming down his cheeks.

All the way over to the gym Yusef constantly checked his phone, expecting Sol to call or text to tell him to get his arse back and taped up, but the only person who did text was Coops to say she needed him at one of the stash houses. Yusef texted back to tell her he was on his way to see Ricky.

Get U Big G she texted back with three laughing emojis. He sent her a bloke shrugging and got off the bus.

The face on security patted Yusef down but not too keenly. Like something had already shifted. Then he showed Yusef into the main exercise area where Ricky was skipping rope, the sound of the whip through the air as it passed over his head going through Yusef's chest. Eventually he stopped and grabbed a towel to wipe his sweaty face, even more pink than usual. The man was like an uncooked sausage.

'Back so soon,' Ricky said.

Yusef nodded. 'I found out a bit about them youngers, like you said.' Ricky yanked off his T-shirt, threw it on the floor. 'No one seems to know exactly who they are, which is well weird.'

'Is it?'

'Yeah. Someone always knows someone round these streets.' Yusef watched Ricky rub his hair with the towel as he walked to a water barrel. Then he drummed on the plastic top with his hands. 'But, anyways, they done over another business, a chicken shop,' he added.

Ricky stopped beating out his tune. 'I know.' Yusef's heart sank. He'd come all the way over here just to tell Ricky something he'd already got wind of. Now he looked stupid. Worse, he'd acted like Ricky was stupid. 'But you've no clue who these muppets are?' Ricky asked. Yusef shook his head. 'Right then, sunshine, I want you to get in among them and find out.'

'What?'

'If you don't know them, then they don't know you,' said Ricky. 'Buy some drugs off them, get talking to them, shag one of the lasses, I don't know and I don't give a toss.' He tapped his head. 'Work it out and tell me who they are.'

Then he was gone, leaving the security to pick up his sweaty T-shirt. 'You heard Ricky, get a shift on.'

Back at the bus stop, Yusef sank to the pavement, not caring that it had been raining. The feds had sent him under cover to spy on Ricky Vine and now Ricky Vine was sending him under cover to spy on some pure-mental youngers. 'How the fuck is this even happening?' he asked himself, knowing there was no answer.

The queue for prison visits was long and slow. Liberty might have had no trouble circumventing the requirement for a visiting order, but Al Capone himself couldn't have avoided security. For a place flooded with drugs, weapons and contraband of every conceivable type, they put on a good show at the door.

The woman behind Liberty told her kids to be quiet as they asked again why they couldn't bring their phones into the jail. 'We're not allowed,' their mum told them.

'But Dad's got one.'

'Shush,' she snapped. 'Anyway, he hasn't.'

'Yes, he has. The number's pinned to the fridge. Oh seven seven four—'

'Sweet Jesus, will you stop right now!' she shouted.

When Liberty had finally been swept by a wand and asked a ton of questions by a guard, she settled at a table in the visiting hall. A few inmates nodded in her direction and she nodded back, despite having no clue who they were.

At last Paul Hill made his way to her. If Bunny had improved since they'd last met, Paul looked infinitely worse. His hair had thinned so pink scalp poked through, like a naughty tongue, shocking against the white strands. He'd always been impeccably dressed, with double-cuff shirts and cashmere scarves, but his prison-issue grey sweatshirt and jogging bottoms hung off him, stained and unironed.

'Liberty,' he said, displaying teeth that were as yellow as his wife's old dye job. 'To what do I owe this pleasure?'

'I spoke to Bunny earlier,' said Liberty.

'She all right?' he asked, tone full of concern. Not long ago he'd treated Bunny like an irritant. Now he'd clearly come to realise that she was all he'd got.

'Fine,' said Liberty. 'Doing well, in fact.'

'I honestly thought she'd fall apart when I landed in here, but it turns out she's as tough as old boots.'

As charming as Paul's new admiration for Bunny was, Liberty didn't have time to listen to it. 'I asked her about Joel Redman.'

'Oh, aye?'

'I want to know who killed him,' said Liberty.

Paul burst out laughing and, in that second, Liberty caught a glimpse of the man he used to be: fearless, remorseless. He pinched the bridge of his nose as if to stop tears of mirth. 'You think it was Bunny?'

'No,' Liberty replied. 'I think it was you.'

Still laughing, Paul shook his head. 'Look around you. Tell me what you see.' Liberty turned her head to take in the room. Rows of tables, like a school exam, except instead of heads bowed over test papers, every face was looking their way. 'You're it now, Liberty.' Paul dropped his voice to a hiss. 'They know who's in charge these days.'

Liberty continued to scan the sea of men. Every single one of them knew the Greenwoods ran the area and that she was head of the family. 'We didn't kill Redman. I know that much.'

'You sure about that?' asked Paul.

Mel was fishing in the mobile-phone box under the bar when Liberty walked into the Cherry. A new girl with legs that seemed to start under her armpits waited nearby, hand outstretched. When she had her phone back, she immediately turned it on.

'Not until you're outside,' Mel snapped. Her anti-surveillance regime was still clearly operating at DEF CON 1. She covered the box with a tea-towel and scowled at Liberty.

'Someone get out of bed on the wrong side?' Liberty asked.

'Could say the same to you.'

Liberty nodded at the office door. 'I need to talk to you.'

Mel reached for a bottle of Jack Daniel's. 'Something tells me I'm going to need this.'

As usual, the back room was piled high with boxes and Mel moved a carton of Princess Leia outfits. The thought of a house-wife in Doncaster wearing a silver bikini complete with Danish pastry side plaits would have made Liberty laugh in any other circumstances.

Mel dragged a couple of glasses from a drawer and poured them both a drink. 'Spit it out, then.'

'I know you love Jay,' Liberty chose her words carefully, 'and you've had his back for a long time now.'

'I've got all your backs,' said Mel.

Liberty nodded. Mel had cleaned up all manner of messes for the family. But there was no denying that if there was a biblical flood it would be Jay who Mel would carry to a boat, held high above her head.

'Thing is, Mel, he's not in the best place right now, what with Becca kicking him out. She kept him on an even keel.' Liberty held out a glass to Mel, took one herself and clinked. 'And I think he's done something.'

'He's always doing something.' Mel knocked back her bourbon in one. 'You know what he's like.'

Liberty took a drink and let the alcohol slide down her throat, causing a mini explosion in her chest. Jay was unpredictable, Crystal too. The only thing you could ever predict about either of them was that they'd do exactly what you weren't expecting. They'd grown up in chaos and could never give up the habit.

'We don't keep stuff from each other, though,' said Liberty. 'We don't lie about what we've done.'

Mel poured herself another slug of JD. 'Why have you come to me instead of asking your brother?'

'Because I just need an answer, not World War Three,' said Liberty. Mel exhaled a long breath. A sign that she was resigned to things. 'Did Jay order Joel Redman's death?'

'Why would he have done that?' Mel asked.

'Like you said, he's always doing something. Let's not pretend it's all part of some finely tuned plan.'

Mel drained her glass and set it down with more force than necessary. 'The trouble is, Lib, that you judge other folk by your own standards.'

'What are you talking about?'

Mel strode to the door, kicking aside a sack of nipple clamps. 'You're the one making decisions without telling Jay or Crystal.' She wagged a finger at Liberty. 'You got Kelly involved in the family business without so much as a word about it. And I know you're not giving the full story about the break-in at your place.' She opened the door and music flooded in from the club. 'There's only one of you tearing this family apart and it's not Jay.'

Chapter 11

On the way home from Sandringham, I can't keep the smile off my face. I'm going back to college. I'm going to get my A levels and I'm going to Oxford University and then I'm going to be a solicitor. I'll earn loads of money and buy a lovely house and our Jay can move in, provided he promises not to bring any lasses home. And the little ones can visit any time they like. They'll be older then, probably at college themselves, so I can help them with their homework.

I touch the bulge made by the crumpled fiver stuffed in my jeans pocket. I'll pay Mr Whitbred back as soon as I can. He might be able to claim it from some sort of expenses, but I'll give it to him anyway and save him the trouble.

'You liked it, then?' Mrs Moser asks, as she pulls up her little red Fiat outside Orchard Grove.

'Yeah,' I say. 'They all seemed really nice.'

And not just Mr Whitbred. When I went down to the office, the ladies helped me fill in lots of forms and not one asked me why I was joining so late in the term.

'Good. That's one thing sorted out at least,' says Mrs Moser.

I thank her for the lift and head inside to find our Jay. I want to tell him the good news. But before I can take my coat off, Hemma barrels down the hallway towards me, face like a wet weekend. 'Can you come to the office, please, Elizabeth?'

What am I meant to have done now? There's no way she's found anything in my room that I'm not allowed. I mean, she's not even supposed to be in there without me but I bet she sneaks in. Tough luck: when I do have a bit of weed, I give it to our Jay to hide. After being in YOI time and again, he's the Lord High Master of finding hiding places. 'Fine,' I say and follow her.

When we get inside the office, she closes the door behind her and I spot a bloke in one of the chairs, looking down at the floor so I can only see the top of his head. But when he lifts his chin, I'm staring straight at Mam and she's staring straight back at me.

'Hello, Lib,' he says.

I swallow cos it's not Mam. He's got the same face but with short brown hair, stubble on his chin and a tattoo of a swallow on his neck.

'This is Ian,' says Hemma. 'Your uncle.'

'Do you remember me?' he asks.

I'm not sure. We never had much to do with Mam's family – well, Dad made sure of that. Sometimes when he was inside, we'd hop on a bus and spend the day with them. There were always uncles that told Mam in hushed tones that if she ever took Steve back they were done with her. Obviously, there's one of Mam's brothers who sticks in my mind for what happened when she died, but it wasn't this bloke Ian.

'No,' I say.

He doesn't seem too worried. 'Well, you were only small, carrying the baby around like a sack of coal.'

'He's called Frankie.'

'How old is he now?' Ian asks.

'Nearly seven.'

Ian stands. 'Look, I'm not here to cause any bother, love. And if you want nothing to do with me, then I'll not call again.'

'It would have helped if you'd got in touch first, Mr Lynch,' says Hemma. 'Then I would have discussed it with my colleagues and we could have decided on an appropriate course of action.'

Ian eyes Hemma as if he's never heard anything so stupid in all his days, then puts a hand on my shoulder. 'You'll soon be shot of all this and *then you can do as you please. In the meantime you can find me in the Turk's Head.' He gives me one heavy pat. 'If you like.'*

Present Day

Liberty's mind reeled as she drove from the club to her house. She spent every second of her days trying to keep her family alive and out of prison, only for Mel to say she was tearing it apart. The unfairness cut through her, so when she saw Angel's car parked up, she was in no mood to play nicely and ignored both coppers when they followed her to her door.

'Why don't you come in through your usual route?' she asked, without looking at them. 'Or maybe break an upstairs window this time.'

'Let's not do this here, Liberty,' said Angel.

Liberty. That spiked her temper. She'd noticed Angel using her first name the last time they met, like they were friends. Liberty turned slowly and stared at them. 'Do what?'

'Wash our dirty laundry in public,' said Angel.

Liberty laughed. 'I think maybe we should do just that.' She pointed at Angel's sidekick. 'What's your name, sunshine?'

'Adam.'

Liberty tapped his chest. 'Well, now, Adam, I'd be interested to know how she got you into this. Because you look like a perfectly normal bloke to me, yet here you are on my doorstep, withholding information about a murder so you can blackmail me to look into your mate's obsession with a bent copper.' She smiled at Adam. 'Have you even wondered why Rose here is so interested in Joel Redman? Why she's willing to go to all this trouble?' The shadow that flew across his face told Liberty that he had indeed considered it. Not as daft as he looked, then. 'Angel put Joel away, which I'm sure plays on her mind, but it's a bit more than that, eh? She feels guilty. Why do you think that is?'

As Liberty tried to step into her house, Angel kicked out her leg, blocking Liberty's passage. 'You can't talk your way out of that video.'

'And you can't talk your way out of how you came to be outside Joel Redman's house when Paul Hill was inside, or where the drugs and the guns came from.' Liberty smiled at Adam. 'Maybe you think she just got lucky that night.'

'I had them under surveillance,' said Angel.

Liberty spoke directly to Adam. 'Ask yourself some questions here, young Adam. Why would Paul Hill, a well-known face round these parts, have a few kilos of gear in the boot of a car registered in his name? And where was his driver?' She stepped over Angel's leg as if it were a fallen tree trunk, dead wood left to rot. 'Here's something I've always believed, Adam. If it's too good to be true, it probably isn't.'

Then she slammed the door in their faces and leaned her back against it, shaking. There was a bang as Angel struck it from outside that made Liberty jump, but then silence.

'What the hell is wrong with you?' Hutch threw the van around a corner in third. 'You've had your phone off all day and now you can't string two words together.'

Actually Sol hadn't turned off his phone, he'd just let it run out of battery while he went to the shop to buy washing powder, shampoo and a new toothbrush. And he hadn't bothered charging it while he stood in the shower for at least half an hour, washing and rewashing his hair, fingers scraping his filthy scalp. When he'd filled the bath, sprinkled in Daz and dunked his jeans into the milky water, he'd finally put his mobile on to charge.

'Maybe I've got fuck-all to say.'

Hutch screeched to a halt, jolting them both forward. 'Kapur gave us a time limit, Sol. You can't spend an entire day in radio silence.'

'What would have been the point of me answering the phone if I had fuck-all to say?' Sol asked.

'You're a seriously difficult man, do you know that?'

'So both my ex-wives told me.'

Hutch flashed the headlights at Yusef who was waiting outside the garage. The kid jogged towards the van and jumped in.

'All right?' Hutch asked him.

'No,' Yusef replied. Sol sniffed and looked out of the side window. He was in no mood for Yusef's tantrums. 'Ricky says I've got to find out what's happening with some youngers stirring up trouble. He told me to buy some drugs off them or chirps one of their girls, get some information.'

'We need you to find out what Ricky's up to, not get yourself a bunk-up,' said Sol.

Yusef kicked the back of Sol's seat. Then he did it again. He was about to have a third go when Sol snaked around his hand and grabbed the lad's foot, twisting it hard. Yusef shouted out, tried to bat his arm away, which just made Sol twist it even harder.

'Stop,' Hutch shouted. 'This is a good thing. An easy way for Yusef to get Ricky to trust him.'

'Except I've got no clue where they're at,' said Yusef.

Half an hour later, Hutch had made some calls and discovered there'd been a report of antisocial behaviour in a flat in Alexandra Park. The woman who had made the report had said she'd also seen a group of kids taking over a children's play area wearing balaclavas and waving hammers.

'I need money,' said Yusef, when Hutch pulled up near the play area.

'For what?' Sol snapped.

'To buy drugs,' said Yusef. 'They ain't gonna give them to me.'

Hutch peeled off two twenties from a roll in the glove compartment. 'You tell us what's happening first, then you tell Ricky. In that order.' They watched Yusef slope away into the night, hands deep in the pockets of his denim jacket. 'This is a massive risk.' Hutch pointed at Yusef's back. 'He could get caught by this lot spying for Vine, or by Vine spying for us.' Sol just shrugged. 'You know there's a reason both your wives are now exes,' said Hutch.

Yusef held both notes tightly in his fist, wondering if it would be enough to get to London. He could probably walk straight through the playground, out the other side and get a bus to Piccadilly, then jump on a train. Did they run this late, though? He knew the trams still ran at all hours, but trains to London? He couldn't get stuck at the station with nowhere to go as that would be the first place the cops and Ricky Vine would look for him.

When he turned the corner and saw three youngers on the swings in the park, he knew he wasn't going anywhere. Between the cops and Ricky, they'd got him trapped. He stuffed the money back into his pocket, lit a fag and wandered over to the first younger. The lad had a graze on his cheek and a bruise at the corner of his eye.

'All right?' said Yusef. The younger spat on the tarmac, between them. 'You serving?'

The one on the middle swing looked over and Yusef saw it was a girl under the hood. 'Depends what you're after,' she said.

'Anything you wanna give me, queen.'

The two lads on either side laughed, but Yusef held eye contact with the girl.

'You do not want to come by with Tia,' said the younger with the battered face.

'Why? She mash you up, did she?' Yusef asked.

He knew he was pushing it, that all three might turn on him and give him a kicking, but this was how he needed to roll. He wasn't some bag head looking for a dig, and they knew that. The younger reached into his coat and Yusef saw the silver blade of a knife. He raised an eyebrow at it to let the lad know he'd seen it and it didn't vex him.

'So, Tia,' said Yusef, using the name he'd picked up, 'you gonna sell a brother a bit of weed or not?'

She jerked her head at the younger with the knife: he gave a big sigh, slid off his swing and held open his hand for the cash. As Yusef gave him one of the notes, he waved goodbye to his ticket to London.

Two minutes later, Yusef rolled a blunt, took a drag and held it out for Tia, who laughed. 'You not got nobody else to share that with?'

'Not as hot as you,' he replied.

'Don't chat shit,' she said, but took the joint from him anyway.

A lot of boys spent half their lives chirpsing girls, sliding into their DMs and all that. Caden had about ten girls he was chatting to on Snapchat. Whenever one of them put up a video or a picture, he'd like it. If he missed one the girls got riled, so he was checking his notifications all day long. Yusef never really bothered. Most of the sex he'd ever had in his life wasn't by choice, just people, men mostly, making him do stuff in exchange for whatever. Endlessly telling girls they looked fit in their selfies wasn't something he could be arsed with for the off-chance of a blow job when their mum was at work. Or, worse, in his sleeping-bag on the floor where he was staying with six other lads tuned in. But he knew how it worked. You said something nice to a girl, they told you to shut up, you said something else nice.

'If it was shit I wouldn't still be here, would I?' he asked Tia.

She blew smoke into the air. 'D'you wanna do something?'

'Depends what it is.'

Tia pulled a bandanna from her pocket, tied it around her mouth. 'A bit of a laugh, bruh.'

***

Liberty stared at the bedroom ceiling, her face hot, her chest tight. Empire Rise was quiet outside, only the odd car passing by, but she still couldn't sleep. When she closed her eyes, she saw bright flashes of light against the purple backdrop of her eyelids. When Sol lived here, he'd always pretended she didn't keep him awake with her tossing and turning.

She put Sol out of her mind and focused on her need to speak to Jay and discuss what was going on. If Jay had killed Redman, Liberty wanted to know, but she was also desperate to ask him why he hadn't told her. Perhaps it was the same reason she hadn't told him about Kelly or Angel. A lack of trust in each other's reaction?

Her mobile was on the bedside table on top of a novel she hadn't opened in months. A bookmark peeped out as if it expected her to pick up where she'd left off, but Liberty couldn't remember what it was about. She racked her brains. There was a murder on a moor and a disgraced copper trying to work it all out. His sidekick was a genius who wore old band T-shirts. It might even be a great novel, but she couldn't concentrate, these days, her mind constantly circling back to the business and the fires she needed to put out.

Liberty grabbed her phone and scrolled through some photos: Jay and his kids, Crystal's ultrasound scan, Frankie in the Cherry, laughing his head off at something, Mel behind him, scowling as usual.

When a call came in, she was disappointed not to see Jay's number. 'Tia?'

'You need to come to Manchester,' said Tia. The kid didn't do panic, but the slight catch in her voice told Liberty it was serious. 'Your man's lost the plot.'

'Kelly?' Liberty's heart hammered. 'What's he done?'

'He's ripped JB's head off.'

Liberty sat up. 'How bad is it?'

'He'd dead, Lib. Kelly's killed JB.'

★★★

The youngers slouched along a wall in the old carpet warehouse. Liberty recognised most of them from her own crew. There were a few new faces, which had been part of the plan. Dead bodies had not been any part of it.

'Tia,' she said, when she saw the girl sitting cross-legged on the floor, head against a lad in a scruffy denim jacket with a sheepskin collar.

Tia pulled herself to her feet and led Liberty away from the others. Then she looked at her boss full on, face tired and pinched.

Liberty's chest tightened. Tia looked her age. Just a kid. 'Are you okay? He didn't hurt you?'

'Not me.'

'Tell me what happened,' Liberty said.

'We went to some kebab shop to make a bit of a mess,' said Tia. 'Like at the other places.' She picked at the skin between her thumb and finger, blew on some dark flakes, which Liberty realised must be dried blood. 'Everything was fine until JB jumps behind the counter and starts to fill up some pitta bread with chips. Then Kelly loses it.' Tia shook her head. 'Like properly goes mental. He's screaming about how a doner kebab is meat and salad, not chips.'

'Are you serious?' Liberty asked.

Tia crossed her heart. 'I mean JB just laughed, cos like it was so random, but I knew then that it was all going to end in shit because you can't look at Kelly twice, you know? You think Frankie was touchy, you've not met Kelly.' Tia puffed out a breath. 'I tried to warn him. I was like "Pack it in, JB," but Kelly was already over the counter and going for him. He picks up one of them massive knives that they use for slicing the meat, you get me? And he cuts him.' She made a slashing motion. 'Blood everywhere, man. JB screaming blue murder. But Kelly just keeps on.' Tia carved the

177

air between them again and again. 'And even when JB was on the floor, making this fucking gurgling sound, Kelly's still going at him.'

'Where is he now?' Liberty asked.

'JB?'

'Kelly.'

Tia pointed to a back door. 'They're both out there.' Liberty nodded and moved across the warehouse. 'Are you packing?' Tia asked, and Liberty nodded again. 'Good. He's not the full ticket, Lib. We gotta be careful here.'

Kelly was in the driver's seat of his van, hands on the steering wheel, staring dead ahead at the wall of the backyard like he might find the answer to a difficult question between the bricks.

As Liberty approached, Tia leaned into her back, hot breath on Liberty's neck, and she whispered, 'If he does anything, I'm taking him out.'

The gun in Liberty's pocket felt solid and she knew Tia's knife would be similarly close to hand as she rapped on the driver's window. At first, Kelly didn't react, eyes still dead ahead, but when Liberty raised her hand a second time, he flicked a glance at her.

'Can I have a word?' Liberty asked.

He blinked once and lowered his window. Even though it was dark outside, Liberty could see from the light seeping from the warehouse that Kelly was covered with blood. There were scarlet smears across his face and on every outstretched finger. His clothes were all black as per usual, but up close they looked wet and shiny.

'Where's my lad?' Liberty asked.

Kelly made a backwards nod to the seat behind him where Liberty could now make out a shape covered with a tarpaulin. 'I told you I was done with lippy youngers,' said Kelly.

Liberty felt Tia bridle behind her and held up a finger in warning. When she was sure Tia wouldn't kill Kelly on the spot, she went to the passenger door and leaned inside the van. The smell unfurled like a ribbon: blood, piss and shit. Holding her breath, Liberty lifted the heavy plastic sheet. Poor dead JB lay on the seat, his chest and face slashed so many times he was more pulp than boy. She dropped the tarp quickly. 'So what now?' she asked Kelly.

He shrugged. 'Get rid of the body.'

'And what about that lot in there?' Liberty stretched her arm in the direction of the warehouse. 'Just pray no one says anything?'

Kelly turned his head to her, owl-like, without moving a muscle of his torso. 'Anyone breathes a word, they'll hear from me.'

Liberty chewed her lip. These were a bunch of kids, and she didn't even know all of them. Suddenly Kelly burst out laughing, his roars echoing around the empty yard. It was more frightening than the silent treatment. At last, he reached behind his seat and grabbed a canvas bag. Then he threw it from his window at Tia, who looked at Liberty with a what-now face but didn't move.

Liberty slammed the passenger door and walked back to Tia. She nudged the bag with her toe. 'What's this?'

'A party,' Kelly replied.

Liberty bent to the bag and unzipped it. There were bags of weed and coke, vials of nox, cans of Red Bull and fliers for pizza delivery.

Kelly started his engine. 'I'll do the necessary with the boy. You get the troops to forget all their troubles.' Then he reversed out of the yard at speed.

Tia took the bag from Liberty and headed back to the warehouse door. 'Can we have garlic bread?'

'Whatever you like,' Liberty replied.

'And some cans of pop? I don't like them energy drinks.'

'Anything else?

'Yeah. When you're done with Kelly, can I get rid of him?' Tia scowled. 'I know JB was a pain in the arse, but still.'

Sol watched Shanie sleep. Was that her name? She'd said something about her dad being called Shane and adding an *i*. Like Nigel Lawson (though that was an A, wasn't it? Nigell-a? Would his own daughter be called Sollie? Solla?). He wanted to get up and have a pee but he didn't want to wake Shanie, so he just lay on his side and stared at her.

After they'd dropped Yusef near the playground, Hutch had virtually chucked Sol out of the van and told him to get a grip. Instead, he'd got a beer at the bar with the fancy gins. The young woman with the black lipstick had been behind the bar again and she'd smiled at him.

'Why so glum?' she'd asked.

He'd toyed with telling her about the baby he'd never met, but instead asked if she wanted a fancy gin. She didn't. But she did take a vodka tonic. And then another. Going back to hers had never been the plan, but he didn't say no.

Shanie gave a noise, a sort of mini-grumble, and turned over, taking most of the duvet with her. Sol almost laughed at the sight of himself, stark bollock naked from the waist down. For some reason he'd left his T-shirt on. He slid his leg off the bed and eased himself up to a sitting position, then picked up his jeans with his big and second toes, dropping them twice before finally grabbing them firmly.

When he was at the bedroom door, Shanie stirred and sat up. 'You're off, then.'

'Work,' he said. 'Sorry.'

'No worries.' She yawned. 'Don't suppose you've got any fags, have you?' He nodded and padded back to her, leaving his packet on his side of the bed. 'Cheers,' she said.

He was going to say something about having had a nice time, when she lay back down, burrowing under her duvet, and went back to sleep. Relief washing over him, Sol escaped.

Outside the block of flats, with no real idea of where he was, Sol hunted for a taxi while he checked his phone. Yusef had called him ten times and left a voicemail. Sol pressed play.

'It's me. Something really bad's happened, yeah? I mean really bad. Can you—' The message cut off.

Chapter 12

7 November 1990

I feel bad for not telling our Jay about Ian turning up, but I need to think it through properly. Jay's got a lot of good qualities, like the way he can make anybody laugh, but thinking stuff over isn't among them. One of the things that's bothering me is why Ian's shown up now. We've been in care for years and he hasn't even written a letter as far as I know.

In the end, I realise there's no point in me trying to guess: I need to just bloody ask him.

The Turk's Head is at the bottom of town, between the chip shop and a zebra crossing. I've passed it a load of times, but never been in. Just inside the door, there's a pay phone and some bloke's feeding ten-pence pieces into it, like a slot machine. He looks me up and down as I pass.

It's almost empty in the bar, which I suppose isn't surprising on a wet Wednesday afternoon in November.

The barmaid stops wiping a glass and smiles at me. 'What can I get you, love?'

'I'm here to see Ian,' I say. 'Ian Lynch.'

She slides the glass onto a shelf above her head. 'And who shall I say is asking after him?'

'Lib Greenwood.' I cough, a bit embarrassed. 'I'm his niece.'

She raises her eyebrow at me. It's so plucked most of it is drawn on with pencil. Then she nips out the back, presumably to find him. I stand there feeling stupid, but at least the bloke leaning against the bar reading the Mirror doesn't look at me.

At last the barmaid reappears with Ian in tow and he smiles when he sees me. 'Fancy a drink, Lib?'

'Hey.' The barmaid flaps her tea-towel at him. 'I doubt she's old enough.'

'Chuffing hell, Janice, I meant a bloody Britvic, not a port and lemon.' He lifts the bar hatch and sits at the nearest table, pats the stool next to him for me to sit down. He takes out a packet of Superkings from a top pocket, and offers it to me. I shake my head. 'Very sensible, love.' He lights up. 'Your mam always said you were the clever one.'

I try not to roll my eyes. I mean, how many times have I heard that?

Janice brings over an orange juice for me and a pint of Guinness for Ian. I smile my thanks at her and take a sip. Ian licks the froth from his top lip. 'So your first question is, why have I got in touch out of the blue? Am I right?' I nod and he sighs. 'There's no easy way of putting it so I'll just spit it out. When your mam died, I was in a bad way, got myself into a lot of bother.' He points the end of his cig at me. 'You lot were the least of my worries.'

I shrug. I never expected any of Mam's family to come for us, certainly not Ian who I can hardly remember.

'Then I met Janice and she straightened me out.' He calls over to her. 'Didn't you, Jan?'

'Didn't I what?'

'Straighten me out?'

She laughs. 'You straight? That'll be the bloody day. You only behave cos you're scared of my brother.'

Ian snorts smoke through his nose. 'One time when we were talking, I told her about your mam and she goes, "Well, what the hell happened to the kiddies?" and I had to admit I didn't know. She called me all sorts of shit and I suppose I agreed with her. So I asked a few questions, found out where you were staying.'

I stare at him. 'But what do you want?'

'Want? World peace and foreign travel at a push.'

'From me,' I say. 'What do you want from me?'

He frowns. 'You're a kid without a pot to piss in, what makes you think I want owt?' His Guinness has left white smears on the inside of his glass that drift slowly down. 'I was thinking maybe I could do something for you.'

'I haven't asked you for anything,' I snap.

Ian laughs. 'Keep your hair on. You've got your mam's gob on you, that's for sure.' He flicks his ash. 'I know it's dead in here right now, but it gets mobbed of a weekend. We could do with an extra pair of hands.'

'Collecting glasses and cleaning up,' Janice shouts. Obviously she's been earwigging. 'You're too young to pull pints.'

'I expect you wouldn't mind earning a few quid,' Ian says.

I finish my juice and stand. 'I'll think about it.'

Present Day

Somebody rigged up a speaker to their phone and when an old Wiley track banged out across the warehouse, everyone jumped up. Tia had only done a couple of lines, but she was bouncing off the ceiling. She threw a slice of pizza at Yusef and it fell off him onto the floor, but a pineapple chunk stuck to his jacket. He peeled it off and lobbed it back at her. She laughed, but it was too much, a bit hysterical as she pumped her fist to the beat.

You wouldn't have guessed that a few hours earlier they'd all watched a lad die. But Yusef had seen it before. There was the shock, then the drained feeling, like every bit of energy poured out of you and you didn't think you'd ever be able to stand up again. Then that passed and all you could think was that you were glad it wasn't you lying in a pile of chips and pitta, your guts spilling out.

He felt his phone vibrate, knew he shouldn't check it in front of anyone.

'I need a piss,' he shouted at Tia.

She mouthed, 'Okay,' and kept on dancing while Yusef went out into the yard. The woman was out there in her Porsche. Yusef had no idea who she was, but Tia had said she worked for her. He must have looked surprised by that because Tia had warned him, 'Don't let her pretty face fool you. She's cold as ice, that one.'

Though Yusef had only just met Tia, he could tell she knew what was what, so he believed her on that score.

He went into a corner and turned to the wall, pulled down his flies and took a leak. With his free hand he checked his phone, keeping it down by his tackle so there was no way Tia's boss could see. Sol had called a ton of times and left a text message – *Where r u?????*

To be fair, Yusef had no idea. Mid-stream, he looked around for any landmarks. It was just an industrial estate. Warehouses and that. Mostly boarded up. Then he noticed a sign above the Porsche 'Carpet Zone'. Tia's boss caught him looking, held up her hands as if to say, 'What?' Yusef shook his head and typed the name of the sign in a text to Sol, then slipped his mobile back into his front pocket.

As he walked back to the party, the woman lowered her window. 'Everything all right?'

'Nice wheels,' he said.

She smiled. 'Wash your hands before you touch Tia.'

The minicab driver had a *bhangra* tune on the radio, dipping his head in time.

'You ever heard of Carpet Zone, mate?' Sol asked him.

The driver thought for a second. 'It might be over on Battle Park.'

'Can you take me there?'

'It's in the other direction.'

'Change of plan,' said Sol. 'I'll see you right, though.' The bloke nodded and, barely slowing, did a U-turn, the beads hanging from his rear-view mirror swinging wildly. 'You should meet my mate at work, you'd have a lot in common. Maybe have a race,' said Sol.

Battle Park turned out to be an old industrial estate with very few businesses still alive. Those that were had metal shutters on doors and windows. The cab driver pulled up outside a disused building, the front entrance long since smashed.

'I really don't think you want me to drop you here, pal,' the driver said. 'It's not safe.'

'Story of my life,' said Sol, and slid some notes into the driver's lap.

As soon as he was out of the car, Sol could hear music and voices from inside. This must be the right place and Yusef must have managed to hook up with the youngers in the swing park. Though God knew how they'd all got over here. It sounded like a decent party was going on inside, but by the sounds of Yusef's text something was very wrong.

Sol sent another text – *R u in the warehouse?*

He waited a couple of minutes for a reply and, when he didn't receive one, set off to investigate. He peered through a window, but all he could see in the darkness inside was even darker figures moving around. A scream echoed across the concrete, but it wasn't a scream of terror, more just a kid messing. Even so, there was no way he was marching in there: youngers were always armed, and if they were off their heads, it could end very badly. Sol had been stabbed twice in his career, both times by cornered kids, frightened of getting caught with a bit of gear up their jaxies.

Instead, he skirted the building towards the back.

The bass from the warehouse was getting on Liberty's nerves as she waited for Kelly to return. He'd been right in thinking the youngers would need to burn off some energy, but there seemed to be no sign of the party abating.

She got out of the car to stretch her legs and yawned. Above her, the lights of a plane coming in to land at Manchester airport twinkled and she imagined passengers looking down on her, their tired tanned faces, desperate to get off and head home, their phones full of pictures of the lovely place they'd visited. It had been a long time since Liberty had been on holiday.

'Lib?'

She turned at the sound of her name, wondering why Kelly hadn't come back in his van, only to find Sol at the entrance to the backyard.

'What the hell are you doing here?' he asked.

She was too shocked to answer as he walked towards her. 'Work,' she muttered at last, their agreed safe-word. Ask me no questions, I'll tell you no lies. 'What about you?'

'Work,' he said.

They stared at one another, still speechless.

'I heard you moved over to Manchester,' Liberty said at last. 'Though that doesn't really explain what you're doing out here at four in the morning.' He patted his pockets and sighed. 'No fags?' she asked.

'As if today couldn't get any worse,' he said.

'That bad?'

'I ended up shagging some barmaid with a pink fringe because Tasha's had a baby without telling me and wants some other bloke to adopt it.'

Liberty laughed. The way he hadn't even tried to dress it up was classic Sol and one of the things she'd always loved about him. She had absolutely no idea what he was doing there, but no way was she going to let Kelly find him and put him in that danger.

'Jump in the car,' she said. 'Let's see if we can find an all-night garage.'

★★★

Sol bought a packet of fags and two take-out coffees while Liberty parked the car by the air pumps and got out. Sol texted Yusef to say he couldn't meet him just yet, then put both cups on the roof of the Porsche with a handful of sugar sachets and watched Liberty shake one, rip it open with her teeth and pour in the granules.

He was glad that he'd had a shower the previous morning and his filthy jeans were still drying on the side of the bath. He didn't look great but hopefully he didn't smell like a compost bin.

Liberty stirred her coffee with the plastic wand, then sucked it clean. 'So Natasha's had a baby?'

'Apparently.'

'I've got to be honest, I never suspected you were cheating on me.' Liberty laughed. 'Although when you started sleeping with me, you were cheating on her so I don't know why I'm shocked.'

She didn't say it by way of accusation. Liberty didn't judge. Morality was a sliding scale for her, with each person doing their best in difficult situations.

'I didn't cheat on you, Lib,' said Sol. 'I haven't seen Tash since I left her. Not until she tracked me down yesterday.'

Liberty blinked, dark eyelashes like a curtain opening and closing. She looked very much like her little brother Frankie tonight.

'What are you going to do?' she asked.

Sol scratched his head. He'd been asking himself the same question. 'I don't think I'd be a very good dad.'

'Why not?'

'I don't know how it works, Lib. Mine was a useless screw-up. When he left I was relieved.'

Three young women, arm in arm, a bit stoned by the look of them, entered the forecourt. The one in the middle wore a woolly hat with pink cat ears knitted onto the top and kept saying,

'Miaow,' which made the other two crease up. Liberty smiled as they entered the garage. 'Kids don't need their parents to be perfect,' she said. 'I mean, look at our Jay.' She shook her head and laughed. 'I don't think his boys would be better off without him.'

'How is he?' Sol asked.

'What can I tell you? Becca's left him and he's banging random women in an arcade for loose change,' she said. 'Look, it's up to you, Sol. If you don't want the hassle of kids, that's fine. But don't pretend it's for their sake.'

If anyone else had said that, Sol would have argued and defended himself, but Liberty didn't say it to hurt or score points. She said it because it was what she believed.

'Why did you never have kids, Lib?' he asked.

The girls emerged from the garage, arms laden with crisps and cans of fizzy drink. The one in the kitten beanie was already demolishing a Cornetto.

Liberty's phone pinged and she read a text, throwing away the dregs of her coffee into the drain. 'You'll get a cab here no bother, I should think.' Then she leaned over and kissed him on the mouth. 'See you, Sol.'

As the Porsche drove away, Sol ran a finger over his lips. So many times he'd wished he'd never set eyes on Liberty Greenwood, yet every time he was with her he felt like he was coming up on MDMA.

His phone rang and Yusef's name flashed.

'You okay?' Sol asked.

Yusef's breath came in ragged little huffs as if he was running. 'I got away on my toes.'

Sol chucked his sleeping-bag at Yusef. 'You're having the floor.'

Yusef sniffed it. 'Fine.' He laid it out under the window with a shrug.

'I'd offer you tea but I'm out of milk,' said Sol. He didn't add that he was also out of teabags. And clean mugs.

'Why do you live in such a shithole,' Yusef asked, 'when you've got a proper job and that?'

'It's temporary.' Sol moved a pair of dirty socks off the sofa and sat down. 'So why don't you tell me what went on tonight?'

'I already have.'

Sol shook his head. 'We need to get this properly straight.'

Yusef got down on his knees, patting the sleeping-bag smooth with a practised hand. Then he kicked off his trainers and zipped himself inside. 'I got talking to the youngers in the park, like Ricky told me to. Like *you* told me to.'

'And?'

'And they asked me if I wanted to roll some kebab shop,' said Yusef. 'I though they meant like rob it, but when we got in, they all went mental, wrecking the place. There was this old bloke going postal and then he stabbed up one of the youngers.'

'You think he died?' asked Sol.

Yusef snapped up his head. 'I don't think he died, man. We all saw it.' Yusef scrunched his face up. 'He was in the van with us on the way back to the warehouse. The smell was disgusting and everybody was like totally silent, even Tia.' Sol felt a tingle at the name. Common enough among teenage girls. Or that was what he'd told himself when Yusef first mentioned her. 'But when we arrived, she called her boss and the next thing is some woman rocks up.'

'Called?'

'No clue. But she wasn't like most people, you know? She was dressed smart and had a banging car.'

Sol hung his head. Whichever way he cut it, Yusef was talking about Liberty. Her crew, including Tia, had been responsible for trashing businesses linked to Ricky Vine. His number two had killed Frankie and now she was taking the war back to him. The fact that a younger had been murdered in the process should come as a shock to no one.

'But Ricky doesn't know who these kids are working for?' Sol asked.

'Not yet.' Yusef flopped onto his back. 'But I'm going to have to go round to the gym later and fill him in, aren't I?'

'Get some sleep,' said Sol. 'Then we'll talk about what to do next.'

Yusef closed his eyes and Sol waited for his breathing to become even. Then he called Hutch. 'There's been a development.'

On the way back to Yorkshire, Liberty went over and over her meeting with Sol. He'd looked even scruffier than usual, but his smile was the same as ever. The way he'd looked at her from under his fringe, she'd wanted to stay and talk to him all night, but once she'd got him safely out of Kelly's way, she'd needed to get back to the warehouse to make sure the youngers didn't do anything stupid.

As she walked through the Cashino, the sound of the machines ringing in her ears, she thought she might be sick at the thought of telling Jay and Crystal what had happened.

In the back room, Jay, Crystal and Mel were waiting for her, faces serious as she closed the door behind her.

'I've screwed up,' she told them. 'Well and truly this time.' She batted away the tears that slid down her cheeks as Jay kicked out a chair for her to sit. 'I don't know what to do to make any of it better.'

'We'll figure it out together,' said Crystal. Liberty flung her arms around her sister's neck and breathed in the smell of her shampoo. Crystal stiffened but didn't push her away. Instead she patted Liberty's back as if she was a dog. 'Can we stop now?' Crystal asked. Liberty laughed and sank into the chair. 'Just tell us what's up, Lib.'

Liberty took a deep breath. 'It was the police who broke into my house.' Jay and Crystal exchanged a glance. 'Rose Angel and her new puppy. They took Kalkan's mobile.'

Jay slammed his fist onto the table, making pound coins dance from their towers. 'I'll kill them both.'

'There's got to be another way, surely,' said Liberty.

Crystal popped a stick of Juicy Fruit into her mouth. 'What do they want?'

'Angel's saying she wants to know who got rid of Joel Redman. When I give her that information, she'll give me back the mobile.'

'Of course she won't,' said Crystal. 'You're not that naïve, Lib.'

Liberty shook her head. 'I know she won't but I thought I could buy some time by finding out.' She smiled weakly at Jay. 'But now I know who it was and I can't tell her, can I?'

Crystal stopped mid-chew and stared at Jay. 'You killed the copper? Why in the name of all things holy did you do that?'

'I didn't,' said Jay. 'At least, not on purpose.' Mel groaned in the background and banged her head gently against the wall. Jay shrugged. 'I just wanted to make a point to some of the other police we've got on payroll who've been asking for too much money. He wasn't meant to die.'

'So now we've got Angel digging around about that and the Kalkans?' said Crystal. 'Great job, well done, Jay. Next time you want to send a message, try a horse's head in the bed.'

'To be fair, apart from Angel, no one cares about Redman. The police are glad he's dead,' said Liberty. 'Same with Kalkan, really. His wife hasn't even reported him missing. Without that video there's nothing to say he didn't just bugger off back to Turkey.'

'Then we get rid of Angel and the muppet she's convinced to help her,' said Jay. 'Problem solved.'

'If we do that, the police will have to investigate us,' said Liberty.

Mel snorted. 'When were the police ever not investigating the Greenwoods?'

Crystal and Jay laughed. The police had been knocking on their door since they were toddlers. But this was worse. Liberty swallowed, knowing that she was going to have to tell them.

'Thing is, this is a particularly bad time for police interest in us,' said Liberty.

Crystal frowned. 'Because?'

'You were right about Kelly,' Liberty said. 'I couldn't control him.' All six eyes bored into her. God, Liberty needed a drink. 'And he killed one of our youngers last night.'

'What?' Jay's voice was deep and low, the word more a growl.

'They went to cause a few problems in one of Vine's places and Kelly lost the plot,' said Liberty. 'He stabbed one of Tia's boys.'

No one said a word for a long moment.

'So let's get this straight,' said Mel. 'The police know we killed Kalkan and it's only a matter of time until they know we killed Redman? And Ricky Vine can't be far off guessing that we've decided to pay him back for fire-bombing the car? Oh, and while we're at it, we've roped in some nutter to help us with Vine but he's ended up killing one of our own?'

Jay's shoulders began to quiver and Liberty braced herself for the table going over, but actually he just gave a bark of laughter. 'Honestly, Lib, our Frankie would be like a pig in shit with this mess.'

'It's not funny,' said Mel, but even she cracked a smile.

'There is one other thing,' said Liberty.

'Don't tell us,' said Crystal. 'Tia's an informer, working with MI5.'

Everyone laughed.

'It's Sol,' said Liberty. 'I think he must know what's going on in Manchester.' Everyone stopped laughing. 'He turned up out of the blue at the warehouse. I managed to keep him away from

Kelly, but it was just too much of a coincidence that he was there at all.'

'He followed you?' asked Crystal.

Liberty paused and replayed his face when he saw her in the yard. He'd seemed as shocked to bump into Liberty as she had been to find him there, but it made no sense that he'd arrived at that exact moment.

'You need to find out what he knows,' said Crystal.

'He's not going to tell me that.'

Crystal cocked her head to one side. 'The man's tongue hangs out of his head at the sight of you.'

'That was a long time ago,' said Liberty. 'Things change.'

Crystal shrugged. 'Then you'd better put on some make-up and buy a pair of lacy knickers.'

Chapter 13

9 November 1990

It's not even half seven but it's already mobbed in the Turk's Head with every seat taken and loads of folk standing. I grab as many empty glasses as I can stack and ferry them to the potman, so he can get them washed and back to Janice and Ian. They've got a couple of lasses working the bar who do Friday and Saturday nights. One's called Jo and she wears her hair in a bit of a rockabilly quiff that I like. The other one's Anya and she rubs cream between her fingers all the time. I don't blame her: the skin looks really sore.

Janice never stops smiling, chatting, pulling pints. When some bloke gets arsy with Anya about the price of an orange and lemonade, Janice makes him laugh so that in the end he pops some change in the tips jar.

There's only one bloke she can't seem to win round, so she shouts over to the bouncer to chuck him out. 'Give him a hiding,' she mutters in his ear, which I think is a bit over the top considering, but maybe he causes trouble every week.

When Ian calls time and Janice shoves the last straggler out of the door, I'm absolutely knackered. I hope I did all right. There didn't seem to be a shortage of glasses from what I could tell and I only broke one, which wasn't even my fault.

Ian locks the door and gives everyone a drink. I ask for a Coke but he gives me half a lager. 'Come on, Janice, she's bloody earned this.'

Jo fetches her and Anya's coats ready for off, while Janice shares out the tips. I'm shocked when she pushes some at me.

'What?' says Anya. 'You worked the same as the rest of us.'

I want to count them up but that would look too desperate so I thank everybody and push the coins into my pocket.

Ian walks the barmaids to the main road, where Jo's husband is picking them up after his shift on the door of another pub in town. Janice bobs to look in the mirror behind the bar.

'Ian will drop you home, Lib.' She licks her finger and wipes under her eye where the mascara has run. 'I mean, I know it's not your house, but you get my drift.' She turns and smiles at me. 'So do you all live there, together?'

'No. Just me and our Jay,' I tell her. 'The little ones are in foster care.'

'What a shame they've split you up,' she says.

I shrug. 'They're going to put the other three together soon, so that will be good.'

'And what about you?' she asks. 'They can't leave you on your own, surely?'

'I won't be in care much longer so it doesn't matter.' I nod at her that it's going to be all right. 'Honest, Janice, I just want them all settled.'

'Well, there's always a bed here for you.' The door opens and Ian comes back, blowing on his hands. 'The girls go off all right, then?' Janice asks.

'Yeah. Though Barry said there was a lot of trouble in town tonight.'

'Not too bad here,' says Janice.

'That's cos everyone knows not to cross you,' says Ian. He grabs a set of car keys. 'Ready, Lib?'

When I get back to Orchard Grove with my wages and my tips, I'm in no mood to find Hemma standing guard outside my bedroom door.

'Where have you been, Elizabeth?' she asks.

Obviously I'm not going to tell her. 'Out.'

'You know the rules about returning by curfew.'

I bet if I open each bedroom door, half the kids would be missing. I bet if I open Michaela's door, our Jay will be in there. I bet if I open the door at the end of the corridor, the new lad will be banging up a bag of brown. But here's Hemma hassling me, the best behaved in the whole place.

'What are you gonna do?' I say. 'Handcuff me to the radiator?'

She crosses her arms. 'We can stop your allowance for a start.' I laugh. I haven't had a penny since we got back from Manchester. My application is 'being processed'. And, anyway, I've just earned myself more than a few quid without having to fill in stupid paperwork or have anyone make me feel like I need to beg for it. 'And we can look again at contact sessions with your brother and sister,' she says.

'You can't threaten me with that.' I point my finger at her. 'It's not up to you and you know it.'

'I can make recommendations,' says Hemma.

'And no one will listen to you. No one even cares what you think.' I push past her and unlock my door. 'Mrs Moser wants me to have contact with them and she's going to tell the judge that.'

I slam the door and smile. I'm sick and tired of playing nicely.

Present Day

While Yusef had a shower, Sol popped to the corner shop. He threw a ton of food into a basket; bread, butter, some giant crumpets, a malt loaf, milk and orange juice without bits. He was weighing up what sort of jam to buy when his mobile rang and his heart gave a bang.

'Lib?'

She sounded raspy, like she hadn't slept. 'Can you talk?'

He chucked in two jars of jam, one apricot, one strawberry, and went to the till. 'Sure.'

'It was so weird seeing you last night,' she said. 'And don't worry, I'm not going to ask you what you were doing there. Not my business.' He waited for the assistant to fill two plastic bags with his stuff and tapped his card with a smile at her. 'But it felt good anyway, you know?'

Sol let someone into the shop first, then stepped outside. 'Yeah. Weird but good.'

'I wish things had worked out differently between us,' she said.

The bags weighed heavy in Sol's hand and his chest weighed heavier still. 'Me too.'

'I was thinking maybe we could meet up properly? Get some dinner?' she said.

'Like a date?'

She gave a deep laugh. Sol and Liberty had never had a date. They'd met when he'd been investigating Jay for GBH. They'd had sex. And when Natasha had kicked him out, Sol had moved into Liberty's place because he'd had nowhere else to go. Never once had they booked a table in a restaurant and eaten out together or gone to the cinema or even had a drink in the pub as a couple.

'I just . . . I don't know . . . Maybe it's a bad idea,' she said.

It was definitely a bad idea. 'Lib, I think about you all the time, but there's no easy way to put this. I'm a copper – well, sort of – and you're a . . .' He stopped himself saying 'gangster'. 'You do what you do.'

'I didn't plan to live like this,' she said.

'I know,' he said. 'But it *is* how you live now.'

'Okay,' she said, and hung up.

As Sol walked back to his flat, he passed a couple of old women on a bench outside the fire station. One had a scruffy Yorkshire terrier tucked inside her fleece, its head poking out, giving little warning barks at anyone who passed. The woman tapped its nose. 'Who do you think you are?' she asked the dog. 'You need to look in a mirror.'

The other woman chuckled and patted the dog's head. 'In his mind, he's a wolfhound. Isn't that right, Archie?'

Sol listened to the high-pitched yelps as he searched for his key. Upstairs was a kid Sol was blackmailing to snitch for him. A boy who was more terrified of being sent home than of being sent to jail. As he carried his shopping inside, Sol looked in the mirror in the communal hallway. Christ, he needed a haircut.

In his kitchen, Sol buttered a couple of crumpets as Yusef complained that Sol had only one towel. 'Drying myself with this when it's already wet from rubbing your arse.' Yusef flapped it at Sol. 'And there was a pair of jeans in the bath.'

Sol handed the plate to Yusef. 'Tell me you took them out before you had a shower.'

'Chucked them on the floor, didn't I?' Yusef replied. 'Is that jam?'

Sol had both jars lined up on the counter and Yusef's fingers dangled above them as he decided which flavour to go for.

'Listen,' said Sol. 'You need to head over to the gym or Ricky will get suspicious.'

'Do you think I don't know that?'

'But you have to be careful about what you tell him,' said Sol.

Yusef plunged an already buttery knife into the apricot jam and slathered some across a crumpet. 'Nah, man, he's getting the whole story.'

'It's not that simple,' said Sol.

'Yeah, it is.' Yusef took a bite, the melted butter running down his chin. 'I need Ricky to trust me.' He waved the crumpet at Sol. 'You said that. If I don't tell him exactly what went down he won't. And he'll kill me when he does find out.'

'I'm not saying to make up a load of rubbish, just leave out the bit about the woman who turned up,' said Sol.

'Why?'

'If Vine knows she's involved, he'll ignore everything except sorting her out and a war will kick off, believe me. Right now, I just want him to go about his business so that I can nick him.' A third crumpet popped out of the toaster and Sol plonked it on Yusef's plate. 'Then you'll be free to do whatever you want to do.'

'So what do I say?' Yusef asked.

'That Kelly has a load of youngers causing trouble. That last night he killed one of them.'

Yusef grabbed the butter and shoved in his knife, leaving smears of jam over the surface. 'But won't Ricky just kick off with Kelly? Won't that be a war?'

'Vine can deal with him in a few seconds. Job done,' Sol answered. 'If Ricky and the woman you saw go toe to toe, it'll be a different story and a lot of people are going to get hurt.'

Pah, pah, pah. The sound of fist against punch bag rang across the gym. Pah, pah, pah. Yusef tried not to think about those knuckles smacking against his jaw.

'Shall I come back later?' he asked Moody.

'You got somewhere better to be?' Moody replied.

'Nah. I'm just thinking Ricky would probably want me to be out grafting rather than hanging around here.'

Moody beat the bag with another volley of punches. 'He wants you to wait here for him, so that's what you'll do. Right?'

Yusef nodded.

Pah, pah, pah. Yusef put down his head and covered his ears with his hands.

Liberty cursed herself for listening to Crystal. Of course Sol wasn't going to come running just because she called him. Things had been over between them for a long time, if they could ever be said to have properly begun. He'd always made it clear how much he detested the Greenwoods' business, and now, with a baby thrown into the mix, how the hell did she expect him to react? The trouble was, when you spent too much time in a strip club, you got a skewed idea of what men were like. And Jay was living proof that even the smallest encouragement from any woman was like an irresistible drug.

The doorbell rang and Liberty groaned. If it was Angel and her lapdog, she might just put a bullet in both their brains right here and now.

She threw open the front door. 'What?'

'I knew I should have brought flowers.'

Liberty stared at Sol on her doorstep. 'What the hell are you doing here?'

He laughed. 'Shall we say I'm predictable if nothing else?' He leaned across and kissed her hard.

'Have you got enough energy for this after your night of passion with a pink fringe?' Liberty asked.

He pushed her inside and closed the door behind him with his heel. 'Well, I'm not sixteen any more, but I'll do my best.'

Later, Liberty watched the slow rise and fall of Sol's chest as he slept and smiled to herself. She hadn't been lying when she'd said it had been good to bump into him and that she wanted to see him again. Clearly he felt the same. She was almost certain he hadn't been expecting to find her outside the warehouse so what had he been doing there?

She gave him a nudge and when she was sure he was in a deep sleep, she rifled his pockets for his mobile.

Quickly, she unlocked his phone. His pin was the same as it had been on all his phones – his mum's birthday. Just like his password was always the same – his nan's first name, Michaela. A lifetime ago, Liberty had known a girl called that. She'd been an angry, serious kid, who had been one of Jay's girlfriends for ten minutes, always waiting for her dad to ring. Probably still waiting now.

Sol's emails were the usual mix of endless unread messages from Netflix to Sports Direct and a smattering of work emails. The latter were nearly all from his mate Hutch and, although they weren't explicit, they told the story of a drugs operation.

Texts were more interesting. Lots from someone called only Y who had obviously been at the warehouse the previous night. Liberty slid a glance at Sol, still fast on, and shook her head. The man hadn't learned his lesson after what had happened with Mads. He'd tried to get that poor kid informing on drug dealers, sending her deep under cover, and now he'd obviously got another kid working for him. But for what? Why bother sending in a kid to inform on Kelly? He was no one in Manchester, these days. It made no sense. Then it dawned on her, and she couldn't believe how stupid she'd been. Sol must have got wind that Kelly was working with her. And he'd sent in Y not to spy on Kelly, but on Liberty. She swallowed hard at the realisation that Sol was building a case against her and that he intended to send her down.

Had he come to see her today as part of some operation? What was it called? A honey trap? Was he just using her and she'd been too desperate to notice?

Sol murmured and turned over in bed, so Liberty memorised the number for Y, relocked Sol's phone and slid it back into the pocket of his discarded jeans. Then she pulled on a T-shirt and padded out of the bedroom and downstairs.

In the kitchen, she shut the door and called Tia, who answered after one ring.

'Hey.'

'Is there a younger who's name begins with Y?' Liberty asked.

'Why?'

'Very funny,' said Liberty. 'He won't be part of the old crew from these parts, he'll be from that end. Maybe a new face.'

'Don't think so,' said Tia. 'No, wait. There was this lad called Yusef but he's not with us, you know. He came along last night just because—'

'That'll be him,' Liberty snapped.

'What's he done?' Tia asked.

'Hopefully nothing yet. But I need to talk to him, okay?'

Tia exhaled a long breath. 'I'll try to find him, but I literally just met him last night.'

'I'll text you his number,' said Liberty. 'Offer him whatever you need to get him to come to you. I want to speak to that boy.'

Yusef tried to block out the pah, pah, pah and concentrate on building a swimming pool on Minecraft. His library was sick, if he did say so himself, but he was struggling with the pool, what with the noise of Moody smashing the punch bag.

'All right, kid.'

Yusef looked up to find Ricky Vine standing above him. His heart slowed right down, then went into overdrive as he tried to decide if he was shit scared or relieved.

'What you playing?' Ricky asked, nodding at Yusef's phone.

'Minecraft.'

'My eldest loves that,' said Ricky. 'His mam goes pure mental at the time he spends on it, but I can't see the harm. Better than hanging about the streets, eh?' Ricky laughed hard as if he'd just told the sweetest joke and Yusef tried to join in. 'So did you find them youngers?' Ricky asked.

Yusef nodded. 'They were dealing up the Ally Park estate.'

Ricky raised an eyebrow. 'Were they now? And who are they working for?'

'Some bloke called Kelly.'

Ricky laughed. Yusef tried again to join in, but Ricky grabbed his face, squashing his cheeks with fingers and thumb. 'Take the piss like that again and I'll carve you up. Understand?' Yusef nodded, as Ricky dug in his nails. 'So I'll ask again, who do these kids work for?'

At last Ricky let go and Yusef's hand flew to his stinging cheeks. A wet feeling on his fingers, told him he was bleeding. He tried to breathe.

'Maybe I got the name wrong,' Yusef mumbled, though he was sure the name was Kelly.

Moody wandered over, bringing the stink of sweat with him.

'This joker says that Kelly's the one been causing all the bother up Ally Park,' said Ricky. Moody ran his forearm across his eyes with a laugh. 'But he might have the name wrong.' Ricky did an impersonation of Yusef.

Moody kicked out a foot and knocked Yusef off the chair. He fell backwards, banging his head on the concrete floor. When he looked up, Ricky and Moody both loomed over him, sweat dripping onto Yusef's chest from Moody's face. He was going to get a kicking.

'Kelly is such old news that I bet you've never even heard of him, lad,' said Ricky.

'Not till last night I hadn't,' said Yusef.

Bang. He felt the wind fly from his belly, before the pain of Moody's foot in it. Then he rolled onto his side with a groan, clutching himself. While Yusef tried to steady himself, Moody lit a fag. When he thought he'd be able to speak without throwing up, Yusef said, 'I don't know what to tell you. Someone told me that was his name.'

Bang. Another kick, this time in his thigh. Yusef bit down hard on his lip until he could taste blood, so as not to scream. He screwed up his eyes against tears.

Moody crouched next to Yusef's head, grabbed a fistful of hair and pulled it off the floor. Then he held the lit cigarette inches from Yusef's eye.

From above, Ricky spoke, but Yusef couldn't stop looking at the orange end of the fag. He'd been beaten, kicked and stamped on more times than he could remember. He'd been stabbed and cut and one time whipped with a hosepipe. He'd never been burned. But he'd heard the noises people made when it happened.

'No chance has Lee Kelly taken me on,' said Ricky. 'He's thick, but not that thick.'

Yusef blinked against the smoke and the heat of the hot fag end. There'd been a lad with a milky eye in the Jungle. Yusef didn't know how it had got like that, but just the sight of it used to freak him out.

'He's not working on his own,' Yusef babbled. 'There's someone else and they brought their youngers from their own ends.'

Moody looked up at Ricky.

'Who?' Ricky asked at last.

'I haven't got a name,' said Yusef.

The fag end pressed into his temple with a sizzle and this time Yusef couldn't help but scream. 'A woman,' he yelped. 'Not from round here. Long dark hair. Posh.' Sol had told Yusef not to pass on this information, but Yusef didn't care. Let's see if Sol would keep his mouth closed with someone using his face as an ashtray. 'Nice car, you know?'

Ricky reached down, grabbed Yusef's jacket and pulled him to his feet. Yusef's face was covered with blood, tears and snot, but he tried to look Ricky in the eye.

'Are you a hundred per cent sure about this, lad?' Ricky asked.

Yusef nodded so hard his head felt like it would fall off. 'Met her myself after we'd done the kebab shop.'

At last Ricky let go. Yusef staggered backwards, the leg Moody had kicked unable to take his weight.

Chapter 14

12 November 1990

As soon as I arrive at college, I go straight to Mr Whitbred's room.

'Well, good morning, young lady,' he says. 'Bright and early, I see.'

I pop the money he gave me onto his desk. 'I wanted to pay this back.'

'Aha. Your bus pass arrived quicker than you thought?' he says.

'Yeah,' I lie. I'm not going to tell him about my shift in the Turk's Head because he won't understand. Even nice people who mean well don't really understand.

He slips the cash back into his wallet and smiles. 'Have you been to see Brenda in the office?'

'I came here first,' I say.

'Well, Brenda is your next port of call,' he says. 'She'll have your timetable and anything else you might need.' I'm about to leave when he puts up a finger. 'At lunchtime there's the weekly meeting in the library for the Oxbridge candidates. You'll want to go to that.'

The morning's lessons go well, and in English I end up sitting next to a lad called Paul. He's got one of them pink faces that always looks like he's just got out of a hot bath. But he doesn't ask me a load of questions about why I'm joining late in the term, which I like. A lot. At lunchtime he just tells me he's going to a sandwich shop with some mates and I can come if I want.

'I've got to go to a meeting in the library,' I say.

He whistles. 'Brainbox, eh?'

'I wish,' I say, because although I know I'm clever, it doesn't do you any favours to brag about it.

When I get to the library, three boys and a girl are sitting around some boxes of pizza and laughing. The lass picks up a slice and flicks off the black olives to land with all the others that have already been flicked off.

'Is there another library?' I ask them.

'Don't think so,' says the girl, and frowns at the lads. 'Is there?'

I look around for any signs of the meeting, but they're the only people in here.

At last a teacher walks in, rubbing his hands, and grabs himself a slice of pizza. He looks at me, mouth full of cheese. 'Are you Lib?' I nod. 'Excellent,' he says, and offers me one of the boxes. 'Margherita or pepperoni?'

'It's not a Margherita if it's covered with olives,' says the girl.

'Ignore Sinead,' the teacher says. 'She'd prefer it if we brought in jam sarnies.'

So it turns out that this is the meeting for Oxford and Cambridge and the teacher, Mr Stark, is here to help us with our applications. There's Sinead going for history, Pete and Dom both going for maths, and Pritpal going for law, though he says he doesn't stand a chance.

'Obviously you're late getting started,' Mr Stark tells me. 'The entrance exams are in a couple of weeks. But the good thing about English is that there's no real prep you can do. Basically they stick a piece of unseen text under your nose and you attack it as best you can.' He hands me a brown file. 'Here are the papers for the last couple of years. Have a go and I'll mark them.'

He offers me the last slice of pizza and I wolf it down, olives and all.

Back at Orchard Grove, our Jay can't believe his ears about my free lunch. But I point out that he's going to have an overnight stay at the Petersons' soon and they're bound to take him to McDonald's again.

'This time I'm not having a Happy Meal neither,' he says.

I slap the top of his arm. 'You'll have whatever they offer. And say thank you for it.' He's about to argue, when Hemma opens my door without knocking. 'Come in,' I tell her.

'Phone,' she says, and marches away because she's still got the hump about me breaking last Friday night's curfew.

Downstairs, I grab the receiver expecting Tiny or maybe Ian offering me another shift. But it's Connor.

'Hello, gorgeous,' he says.

There's noise in the background: shouting, laughing, a voice over a tannoy.

'Hiya,' I say.

'Look, I haven't got much time left on my card,' he says. 'Mam spent ten minutes yapping about her new hearing aid.' There's a crackling sound as Connor covers the receiver and a muffled exchange between him and someone else. 'Sorry about that,' he says. 'There was a mad one at last weekend's football and a load of the lads ended up in here. Honestly, it's like doing time with a pack of dogs on acid.' He laughs. 'So how are you?'

I lean against the wall, covered with a thousand numbers people have scribbled on the paintwork. 'I'm all right,' I tell him. 'I'm going to do my exams for uni soon.'

'You'll smash 'em,' he says. 'No bother.'

'I don't know about that. You have to be really clever to get in.'

Connor laughs again. 'You are really clever, Lib.'

'Thanks.'

'Listen,' he says, as some blokes crank up a chant behind him. 'I've got another home stay coming soon so I was wondering if we could go out. Pictures, maybe. A Chinese?' He knows I love a Chinese. 'Even if you don't want to be my girlfriend any more, I still want you to be my friend. If that's okay?'

'Yeah,' I say. 'But only if we get extra prawn crackers.'

'Of cour—'

The phone cuts off so I hang up and realise I'm smiling. Then Michaela sticks her head around the kitchen door and goes, 'Was that my dad?'

HARD AS NAILS

Present Day

When Sol woke up, Liberty wasn't in bed, but he could hear her voice downstairs so he got dressed.

She was in the kitchen in a T-shirt and some fancy red knickers he'd never seen before, barking an order into her phone. She hung up when she saw him in the doorway.

'Do you want something to drink?' she asked.

His mobile vibrated and he unlocked the screen to see that Yusef had sent him a whole load of texts. Shit. Sol needed to find out how it had gone with Vine.

Liberty stared hard at his phone. 'Everything okay?' Her voice sounded harder still.

'Work,' said Sol, with a shrug.

Liberty scratched her thigh, the skin very white. He couldn't imagine her with a tan, or sunning herself on a beach. To be honest, he couldn't imagine her on holiday. The last one he'd been on had been his honeymoon with Natasha. Golden sands and blue sea. Had he enjoyed it? He couldn't remember. There'd been pictures of him smiling, so maybe he'd loved it.

His phone vibrated again.

'You'd better get that,' said Liberty. 'Could be important.'

He wanted to tell her that he knew she was working with Kelly. That she should stop right now. That she didn't need to go after Ricky Vine because he was going to put the man away himself. That for someone like Vine, it would be far worse to do twenty years in jail, his family stripped of all their assets, than to feel a second's fear when she put a bullet into him. That killing Vine would hurt her far more than him.

'Lib,' he said. 'I don't want you to get hurt anymore.'

She pressed her lips together, eyes locked with his, and said, 'I think I stopped feeling pain a long time ago.'

***

Crystal pushed a glass against the ice dispenser and watched the cubes rattle down the shaft and splash into the apple juice. Then she took a sip as Liberty paced her kitchen.

'So the fancy knickers worked, then?' she asked.

'Yep,' Liberty replied.

'And you found out what Sol's up to?'

'Yep,' Liberty replied.

'And the fact you're here wearing out my tiles, rather than talking to Jay, means it wasn't good,' said Crystal. Liberty pressed all ten fingers against the floor-to-ceiling window and stared out. 'What does Sol know, Lib?' Crystal asked.

Liberty sighed, her breath frosting the glass. 'Possibly a lot.'

'How?'

From behind, Liberty could hear the tinkle as Crystal swirled the ice in her drink.

'He's had a kid, a younger, join the crew in Moss Side,' she said.

'What?'

Liberty turned to find Crystal, glass hovering at her lips, frozen mid-gulp. 'He's sent in an informer.'

'So he knows about Kelly?' Crystal asked. 'And the dead kid in the kebab shop?'

'I reckon so,' said Liberty.

Crystal put down her apple juice carefully, as if every drop was precious. 'And you haven't told Jay because he'll kill Sol.'

Liberty nodded. That was the size of it. Even though Sol had crossed an unforgivable line, Liberty couldn't bear the thought of him dead.

'Leave it to me,' said Crystal.

'What are you going to do?'

'I'm going to keep Sol in line, so our Jay won't need to break his skull. Though I never in a million years thought he'd do something like this to you.'

'It's his job,' said Liberty.

'He's not even a cop any more,' said Crystal.

'He still works for them.'

Crystal rubbed her face. 'Why?'

'Because he thinks criminals shouldn't be allowed to get away with it.'

'But you're a criminal,' said Crystal.

'I know! Look, promise me you'll just leave Sol to me.'

Sol helped Yusef up the stairs to his flat, arm around the kid's waist, then lowered him onto the sofa. There were scratches on his face and a nasty fag burn on his temple, but Yusef's leg seemed to be giving him the most pain.

'Can I look?' Sol asked. Yusef nodded, so Sol unzipped his jeans and pulled them down. 'Don't want you calling me a pervert again.' He stopped speaking when he saw the black bruise that covered the entirety of Yusef's thigh. 'Wait here.' He went to the kitchen and pulled out of the freezer a bag of frozen peas that had been in there when he moved in. He lowered it gently onto Yusef's thigh. Yusef rolled his head back and forth against the ratty cushions of the sofa.

'So why did Ricky do this?' Sol asked at last.

Yusef's eyes opened wide. 'Because he didn't believe that Kelly had done over the kebab shop and all that. I told you that would happen, didn't I?'

'But you stuck to the story, right?' Sol asked. Yusef nodded, then screwed his eyes shut tight. 'Yusef, tell me what you actually said.'

Yusef put his forearm over his face with a grimace. 'What does it matter?'

'I told you, I don't want Ricky Vine getting sidetracked with a war.'

Yusef laughed. 'As long as you get what you want, then we're all good.' The kid kissed his teeth. 'Doesn't matter that he mashed me up. That my leg's broke.'

'It's not broken,' said Sol.

Yusef tore the bag of peas off his leg and threw it at Sol. 'He was going to send me blind, man. Don't you get it? If I hadn't told him the truth I'd only have one eye right now, maybe none.'

'So you told him about Liberty?' asked Sol.

'I didn't know her name or nothing. Just said some woman with a posh voice,' replied Yusef. Sol sighed. Ricky Vine would know in an instant who Yusef was talking about. 'What does it matter, anyway? So what if Ricky goes after her? Why do you care so much, Sol?'

Sol pressed the peas back onto Yusef's swollen leg and rubbed the kid's arm when he cried out in pain, asking himself the same question: why did he care so much?

When Yusef had calmed down, Sol draped his sleeping-bag over the kid and told him to get some sleep. Then he nipped out to the shops to buy some painkillers, a tube of cream for the burn on Yusef's face and some fags for them both. As an afterthought, he also stuck in a six-pack of beer.

He couldn't blame the kid for cracking, could he? Faced with Ricky Vine and one of his goons, anyone would have told the truth. Even spies usually broke under torture. Isn't that why they used to give them a cyanide capsule? Or was that bullshit?

On his way back to the flat, he lit up a smoke. By now, Vine would have decided how to deal with Liberty. And he'd have the element of surprise. But if Sol warned her, he could kiss goodbye to the operation as Ricky would definitely work out who had raised the alarm.

He pulled out his phone and called her, not sure what he was going to say until she replied.

'Sol?'

'I need to tell you something, Lib,' he said.

'Go on.'

'The reason why we bumped into each other the other night,' he said.

'Is because you've got me under surveillance,' she said. Sol stopped in his tracks. 'You've sent in someone to report back on me so you can get me put away. Right?' she asked.

'What?'

'I *know*, Sol,' Liberty said. 'A kid called Yusef. He's one of your snitches.' Sol shook his head. 'You like kids doing your dirty work, eh?' she said.

'And you don't?'

'Is this what it's come to? You hate me so much you want to send me to jail?' she asked. 'Well, get in the queue, mate.'

'I don't hate you, Lib.' There was a moment of silence. 'None of this is about you.'

She laughed loudly and Sol sank onto the bench outside the fire station. The wood was hard and cold. He dropped the shopping bag onto the ground.

'Then who?' Liberty asked. 'Jay? Crystal? She's pregnant, for God's sake.'

'Ricky Vine,' Sol said, head bowed over his knees. 'I'm trying to put Vine away. Yusef's been taping him for me.'

'So why was he with Kelly in the kebab shop?'

'Vine told Yusef to find out who'd been causing ructions in his yard,' said Sol. 'The kid was just doing what he was told.'

'So Ricky knows about Kelly then?' Liberty asked.

'And you.' Sol felt his heart slide down in his chest. 'He knows what you've been doing so you need to be careful, Lib.'

'I need to . . .' She let the words trail away. They both knew what she was going to do now. 'You've taken a massive risk to tell me this, Sol.'

He flicked away his fag. 'Yeah, well, you know how it is when you really hate someone.'

★★★

As soon as she hung up, Liberty called Crystal. 'Do not do anything to Sol.'

'Lib—'

'He's not after me, he's after Vine.' The silence was deafening. 'Crystal, what have you done?'

Still on the bench, Sol pulled the ring on one of the beers, took a long gulp and realised it was raining. He looked up to the sky and didn't mind that his face was getting wet.

Hutch would be furious when he heard what Sol had done, probably wouldn't speak to him ever again. The operation was over. Yusef was compromised.

He took another swallow of beer. Once again, he'd given up everything for Liberty Greenwood.

His phone vibrated and an unknown number flashed up. A text with an attachment. He opened it and found a video. When he played it, he dropped his can of beer. There was Tash with a baby, presumably his baby, and there was Crystal. He couldn't see her face, but he'd know her anywhere. And there was a gun.

He'd just laid his life on the line for Liberty and, in return, she'd threatened to kill his baby.

Chapter 15

16 November 1990

I settle down on my bed to reread the Oxford papers Mr Stark's marked for me. He hasn't given me a grade, just comments in the margin in red biro. At the bottom of one he's written 'I've never read anything like this.'

That made me panic at first, but then he told me it was a good thing. 'They love reading original stuff,' he said. 'And this is really original.' I must have looked a bit worried, because he put a hand on my shoulder and gave it a squeeze. 'Your mind works differently from other people's.'

I don't think that's true, but if he says it's a good thing for this entrance exam, I'll take it.

Our Jay waltzes in and I laugh cos he's wearing a school shirt that's obviously come straight out of the packet, with big square creases where it's been folded up.

'Shut up.' He smooths the shirt. 'I nicked it fresh this morning.'

'You'd better bloody not have,' I say.

'Yesterday morning,' he says, with a laugh.

He doesn't even have to wear a uniform for his PRU and he doesn't go there most of the time, but he's got an overnight stay at the Petersons', so he's trying to make a good impression. I check his neck for a tidemark, his ears for wax, and when I'm satisfied I kiss him on the cheek. 'Be good.'

'I'll give the kids them sweets you got them,' he says.

I kiss him again and he's off. I'm really sad I won't be seeing Crystal or Frankie, like he is, but I know these overnights have to prove to the Petersons that they can all live together okay. I decide there's no point moping so I call the Turk's Head and speak to Janice. 'I'm just wondering if I can have another shift tonight?' I ask her.

'We were expecting you, love,' she says.

A couple of hours later, I'm collecting all the empties and chatting to Jo about her sister, who's failed her driving test four times. Apparently, she hit the kerb so hard on her last try that the examiner had to get one of them collars for whiplash.

I notice that the bloke who got chucked out last week hasn't come back.

When the shift's over, I get even more tips than last time and Ian gives me a lift back to Orchard Lodge. But I'm just about to wave him goodbye when Hemma comes marching out, face like thunder. 'This is absolutely your last chance, Elizabeth,' she shouts at me. 'If you cannot keep to the rules of the unit, you'll have to move on.'

'Mrs Moser won't let you chuck me out,' I shout.

Hemma gets up in my face. 'Mrs Moser has no authority here. I don't need her permission or anyone else's to move a resident.'

Heat flares across my face. It's not that I love this place, and pretty soon our Jay won't even be here, but I don't think I can face starting somewhere else. Somewhere not close enough to college. Somewhere miles away from the Petersons'.

I haven't noticed Ian's got out of his car, until I feel his arm around my shoulders, the roughness of his jacket against my cheek.

'What the bloody hell's the problem?' he asks Hemma. 'It's not even midnight.'

'Elizabeth, like every resident here, needs to be in by ten,' Hemma replies. 'She's not a special case.'

'She was with me,' says Ian. 'Family.'

Hemma's eyes flash. 'And she's not allowed to do that without permission. My permission.'

Ian shakes his head and laughs. It reminds me of Mam. She didn't laugh a lot, but when she did you could hear her across the estate. 'Get back in the car, Lib.'

'No.' Hemma puts up a finger, like she's testing the wind. 'That can't happen.'

'Call the police, then, love,' Ian says to Hemma. 'Tell them that a seventeen-year-old lass has gone to stay with her uncle. See how far you get.'

And then we drive back to the Turk's Head, with Ian still laughing all the way.

Present Day

There were tons of cars parked outside the Cashino, forcing Liberty to leave hers a few streets away. By the time she fell through the arcade's entrance, she was wet from the rain, hair sticking to the nape of her neck.

In the back room, Jay was waiting with Crystal, who had pulled off her shoes and socks and was rubbing the soles of her bare feet against the carpet. 'Itchy,' she said.

'Is that a pregnancy thing?' Jay asked.

'I dunno,' Crystal replied.

'What did you do?' Liberty demanded of Crystal.

'We just needed a bit of insurance.'

'No, we didn't,' Liberty shouted.

'Well, we got it anyway,' Crystal replied.

Liberty stared hard at her sister until she sighed and pulled out her phone. She went into her photos, found a video and pressed play. Liberty's head felt hot as she waited to see what would happen. There on the screen was a small house in what looked like a student area, from the recycling boxes full of Aldi vodka bottles. But one house had clean windows, the curtains open as the camera zoomed in. The front door opened and a woman appeared with a baby on her hip. Liberty gasped as she recognised

Natasha, Sol's wife. They'd never met but she'd seen pictures and, frankly, the woman was unforgettably beautiful.

'I've gotta say our Sol's got good taste in women,' said Jay.

Liberty resisted the urge to punch him as she watched Natasha speak to someone from her doorstep. She could only see the back of the person, but it was obviously Crystal. Liberty pressed pause.

'You went to see Sol's wife?' Liberty asked.

Crystal shrugged and went back to pushing her itchy feet into the carpet. With dread passing through every nerve ending, Liberty pressed play and watched as Crystal chatted to Natasha, even rubbing the baby's cheek. Then, at the last second, she put her hands in the small of her back. An innocent gesture from a heavily pregnant woman, but as she did so, her silk shirt lifted to reveal a gun.

Liberty tried to keep her voice calm. 'You sent this to Sol?'

'He needed to know we're not messing around,' said Crystal. 'Like we discussed, so that Jay wouldn't kill him.'

'Charming that you both think I'm a nutter,' said Jay.

'You are a nutter,' said Crystal.

Liberty's head bounced. Sol now thought she would stoop to threatening his baby. Sol, who had given up everything to be with her and had just risked everything he believed in to warn her to be careful. She felt the bile rise in her throat and threw up in Jay's bin.

Ten minutes and two bottles of water later, Jay pressed a third into Liberty's hands. 'I know you're pissed off about the Sol thing, but we need to sort out Vine.'

Crystal nodded and Jay got up with a set of keys, opened the back of the broken slot machine still in the corner. Inside were several guns. He slid them all into a rucksack. Then he went into the drawer of the desk and pulled out a family bag of Revels. 'For the journey,' he said. 'I'll take all the orange ones, if it'll make you feel better.'

'What about the coffee creams?' Liberty asked.
'Now you're just taking the piss.'

Rose and Adam dived into Scottish Tony's to shelter from the rain
and took a table in the window. Rivulets of water ran off Rose's
nylon hi-vis jacket onto the floor. Without a word, Adam went to
the counter to fetch tea, hands pushed deep into his pockets, as if
he was trying to find something right at the bottom.

He came back with two mugs, one with a tea plate balanced
on top, a jam doughnut in the middle. Rose watched him take a
bite, lips coated with sugar as he chewed. It had been days now
since she had done a deal with Greenwood, and she hadn't sent
even one message to keep them up to date with how the search
for Joel's killer was going. Adam hadn't mentioned it, but it hung
in the air between them, like steam from their tea.

'I think we need to apply some pressure,' she said.

He peered at the bitten end of his doughnut, the jam centre like
a wound in the white dough. He stuck in his tongue and licked it
out. 'Pressure on what?'

Rose shook her head. He knew exactly what she was talking
about.

Adam licked his lips. 'Here's what I think, Rose. I think
we had the chance to report a murder and hand in some evidence, but instead we let the murderer off when she said she'd
get some information for us. And it's no great surprise that the
murderer in question couldn't be trusted to do what she said she
would.'

'We didn't let her off,' said Rose. 'We have the phone. Well,
you do.' The tips of Adam's ears went pink. 'So, like I say, now
we apply a bit of pressure, so she knows she can't put us off any
longer.'

She pulled out her own mobile and sent a text to Greenwood:

If you don't let me know who killed Joel R by tonight, Mr K's mobile will be sent to my boss.

Bunny listened to Liberty as she explained the situation, saying nothing, tapping her toe against the footrest of her stool at the island.

At last when Liberty had finished, the timer on the oven went off and Bunny donned oven gloves to remove a tray of biscuits. 'They're still a bit too hot to eat,' she said.

'No worries,' Liberty replied, as she recalled how sweet the last batch had been. 'So can you help? Obviously we'll make it worth your while.'

Bunny used a fish slice to scoop each cookie onto a wire tray, with a small smile that said she was happy with how they'd turned out. 'I told you last time, we're not in the game anymore.'

'You still know a lot of people,' said Liberty.

'Oh, they're all too old now.' Bunny rinsed the fish slice under the tap. 'Like me and Paul.'

'I'm not asking them to run the streets for me,' said Liberty, 'just keep things ticking for a few days while I take my crew to Moss Side.' She pressed her fingers into the granite of the island. 'I'll make sure everyone's sorted out properly.'

Bunny wiped her hands on a tea-towel and gestured for Liberty to follow her out of the kitchen. Once in the living room, Liberty was surprised to find a model of a building on a table in the middle of the room.

'This is the Hôtel Lapin,' said Bunny, in a reasonable French accent. 'Two hundred rooms including honeymoon suite.' She pointed at the lower tier of the model. 'Wellness centre – that's a spa to you and me – restaurant, two bars.' She tapped the top. 'Rooftop casino.'

'Nice,' said Liberty.

'I need investors,' said Bunny. 'Not small change either. I do you this favour, you come in with me as a business partner.'

Liberty looked at the model. 'Where's it going to be?'

'Mallorca. Nice side of the island.' Bunny smiled. 'Nowhere near Shagaluff or the bucket-and-spade brigade.'

'And it's going to be legit?' Liberty asked.

Bunny licked her finger and crossed her heart. 'A hundred per cent. Even gonna pay all the taxes. Well, the ones I can't not pay, anyway.'

Bunny held out her hand. Was it possible that the answer to Liberty's prayers had arrived in the shape of Bunny Hill? Liberty spat in her palm and shook.

'Jesus Christ, Lib.' Bunny wiped her hand down her trousers. 'You've gone feral.'

Liberty and Jay ordered pie and chips from Amy in the Halfway House.

'You two are brother and sister, I hear,' Amy said, as she put cutlery and sachets of sauce on their table. 'I can see the likeness now I know.'

'I'm a lot better-looking, though, don't you think?' asked Jay.

Amy laughed. 'You've certainly got a lot to say for yourself, that's for sure.'

'Ain't that the truth,' muttered Liberty.

When Amy returned to the bar, Jay watched her pert arse wiggle with a hungry look on his face. Liberty banged down her Peroni to attract his attention. 'Can we at least try to concentrate?' Jay put both elbows on the table, his chin in his hands, and stared up at her with huge brown eyes. He blinked like Bambi, lashes fluttering. 'Why are you doing that?' Liberty asked.

'I'm paying attention,' he said.

She picked up a chip from her plate and stuffed it into her

brother's mouth. He chewed with a grin. Then he took another chip from Liberty's plate and ate it. When he went for a third, she slapped his hand.

No one at the bar looked up when Kelly walked in with Tia, both of them soaked. But Liberty saw Amy nod in her direction and Kelly made his way over.

Tia tore off her hood and shook her baseball cap. 'It's chucking it down,' she said, as if Liberty and Jay might not know. 'Like bucketing it.'

Her eyes lit up at the sight of food and Liberty pushed a tenner into her hand. 'Get yourself whatever you want.'

Tia held it up to the light. 'Just checking it's kosher.'

Liberty smiled. After today was over and she'd done what needed to be done, she was taking Tia back to her house on Empire Rise. The kid would argue, but Liberty didn't care. She'd ply her with takeaways and Netflix until Tia capitulated.

With Tia at the bar, making a song and dance about her order, Kelly sat on a stool opposite Liberty. Jay stabbed a fork into his pie, breaking the crust, and looked at Kelly as if he hated him just for being alive.

'Have you got more people arriving?' Kelly asked.

Jay laughed. Not his usual gift-wrapped present, but a scoffing sound.

'On their way,' said Liberty.

'I want to be the one to kill Ricky,' said Kelly.

Jay pointed his fork at the other man. 'Haven't you killed enough people?'

It was a fair point. Kelly had killed JB, one of *their* youngers, and hadn't even attempted an explanation, but right now, Liberty could do without Jay kicking off.

'We've got groups going to the gym, his flat, his girlfriend's flat, and five or six other places,' said Liberty. 'We hit them all at exactly the same time.'

'When?' Kelly asked.

'Soon,' Liberty replied. 'He knows what we've done and he'll be coming for both of us, so we need to act first.'

Kelly glanced over his shoulder at the door.

'Feeling worried?' Jay asked.

Kelly leaned towards Jay, hands on the edge of the table, knuckles white. 'I've been waiting for this day for a very long time.'

Yusef limped through the rain, his leg killing him. He'd had four paracetamol and two beers but they'd just made him feel tired. He raked a hand across his head and felt how tight his curls were getting. Usually, he'd wear a hat in this weather, but today he didn't care. He was glad of the rain running down his face so he couldn't feel his tears.

When Sol had got back from the shop, Yusef had tried to talk to him, but Sol just kept staring at some video on his phone of a woman and a baby. Yusef had helped himself to the pills and the cans of lager, because it didn't look like Sol would be offering any time soon.

He'd admitted to Sol that he'd told Ricky about the posh woman, and he'd wanted to admit the rest, but Sol couldn't take his eyes off the phone. In the end, Yusef just left without saying goodbye.

When he was outside the stash house he called Coops and she let him in.

In the kitchen, she threw him the once-up-and-down. 'You look like shit.' Yusef shrugged. What could he say? He felt every bit as raw as he looked. 'Can't be riling up Ricky, you know,' Coops said.

No point answering that one either. He hadn't riled up Ricky. Ricky had riled himself up. People like that always did. Same as Kelly when he'd killed the kid in the kebab shop. Same as Coops whenever someone gave her the side-eye or spoke out of line. Yusef himself was no angel: when he got vexed he went off on one, which was why he had the rep he did.

There was a ping-pong bat and ball on the draining-board next to the sink. Coops picked them up, one in each hand. She dropped the ball, let it bounce up, then hit it against the wall, again and again and again. Bat, wall, bounce. Bat, wall, bounce. Yusef leaned against a chair to take the weight off his leg.

'Ricky likes you, though,' said Coops. 'Or you wouldn't be standing here.' At last she snatched the ball in her hand and reached into her pocket. 'That girl called you?'

'Like a million times,' said Yusef.

Coops pulled out a gun and handed it to him. 'You know what to do, then.'

Tia ripped open another sachet of tartare sauce with her teeth and squeezed it over the last bit of her fish with one hand and typed out a text with the other. 'It's Yusef,' she told Liberty. 'Finally woken up by the sound of it. Been trying to get him to meet me, like you said.'

'I think we can safely say events have overtaken us,' said Liberty.

When Tia's sachet was empty, she rifled through the rest. 'Why do they give you so much mustard? And only three or four tartare sauce?'

'Because they assume people actually want to taste the fish,' said Liberty.

Tia huffed and went back to the bar to harass Amy for more sachets of tartare sauce, leaving Liberty with Jay and Kelly, who were ignoring each other.

The pub door opened again, and a boy stood on the threshold, smoking the last drags of a blunt. Liberty recognised him as the younger who had had a pee outside the warehouse.

HARD AS NAILS

★★★

Yusef threw the dog end into the overflowing gutter full of take-away food boxes and plastic bottles. The wind had got up and a Tesco carrier bag blew past. People always talked about Africa as if it was some kind of shithole but, man, the people who lived round here were dirty. There were bins on every corner, but they still lobbed their crap out of their car windows.

He was wet right through to his skin now and couldn't tell what was rain and what was sweat as he checked his phone to make sure this was the place Tia had told him she was at. When he stepped into the pub, he clocked the woman straight away, sitting with Kelly and another bloke. Then she clocked him and he almost pissed himself. He was going to have to do this quick.

Holding his breath, he marched towards her, his hand already on the handle of the gun. Her eyes opened wide and she reached behind her.

Kelly must have caught the look on her face because he turned and reacted quicker than the woman, producing his own piece.

Yusef knew Kelly would kill him so he pulled the trigger first.

Kelly's body jerked, like a wave of electricity had passed through him from his belly up his chest and out through his mouth, with a scream. His knees buckled and he went down clutching himself, blood pouring through his fingers.

Then Yusef heard another scream and, out of the corner of his eye, saw Tia at the bar, a glass raised above her head. He felt the crack against his skull as it hit him and he staggered backwards.

Tia charged towards him, and there was a third scream, this time from the woman. Then Tia jumped at Yusef, crashing into him so that they both fell against a table, glasses and bottles dancing in the air. Tia clawed at his hair, then banged his head against the floor. Little lights danced across his eyes and he tried to breathe as she smashed his head again.

225

Then he pulled the trigger. And she stopped. Her eyes and mouth both made the same shape. Her hands went limp in his hair. Her face hit Yusef's, their lips colliding so hard his teeth made a clang.

Then black.

Chapter 16

17 November 1990

*I chuck a stone at Michaela's window and she opens it. 'Is our Jay there?'
I shout up.*

'No,' she says, far too quickly.

'I don't care if he is,' I say.

*She shakes her head. 'Yes, you do. You're always going on at him for
being in here.'*

*'That's only because I don't want to hear the pair of you going at it.' I
roll my eyes. 'Right now I just need to talk to him.'*

*She looks behind her and says something I can't catch. Then Jay
appears. 'I'm just helping Kayla with something,' he says. 'We're not . . .
you know.'*

*'I don't care,' I yell. His face says this is news to him. 'Look, can you
come down here?' I hold up a tray of chips. 'We can share these.'*

*We sit on the low wall outside and eat the chips. I've brought two little
wooden forks, but Jay just uses his fingers.*

'How did it go with the Petersons?' I ask him.

*'All right,' he says. 'But they wouldn't let the kids have them sweets
you sent.'*

'Why not?'

'E numbers and all that,' he says.

*'I hope you didn't kick up a fuss,' I say. 'You can't be making any
trouble.'*

'Whereas you can?'

I let him have the rest of the chips with a sigh. 'It weren't my fault. Hemma was threatening to send me off somewhere.'

'Hemma's a fucking bitch,' says Jay.

I nod, because Hemma is indeed a fucking bitch. 'Anyway, I'm fine to stay where I am.' Janice and Ian have said I can have the spare room as long as I like. It's only a little box room, with a camp bed, but I don't mind at all. There's a wardrobe in the corner full of Janice's clothes.

'It's just old stuff I should sling out,' she'd said. 'I'll make room for all yours. Take some of this lot to the charity shop.'

I told her I've hardly got anything and she laughed and said we'd have to go shopping.

'Can't I come and stay with you?' Jay asks, licking up the last few scraps.

'No,' I say. 'You can't do anything that'll make the Petersons think you'll be hard work.' He nods, but I can tell he's not happy. 'I'll come by every couple of days to see you.'

'Bet you don't.'

I grab his chin and force him to look me in the eye. 'Yes, I will, Jay.'

'And what about when you go to Oxford?'

Even our Jay's not daft enough to think I can keep coming home every pair of plates. 'I'll get the bus back as often as I can,' I say.

'That'll cost a bomb,' he says.

'I'll get a grant every term,' I say. 'It'll easily cover bus fares and that.'

His face registers shock. 'They'll pay you to go?' I nod. 'Maybe I should apply,' he says.

'You'll have to start going to school first,' I tell him.

Half an hour later, he's pushed all my clothes and books into three carriers and I give him a hug. He smells of the Matey bubble bath I gave him. When I pull away, he looks sadder than I've ever seen him.

'At least without me there, you can shag Michaela as much as you like,' I say.

He tries to smile. 'Promise you'll be back soon, Lib.'

I kiss my fingers and press them to his mouth. 'Promise.'

HARD AS NAILS

Present Day

'Tia.' Liberty could hear someone screaming Tia's name, long before she realised she was the one doing the screaming. She shook Tia's shoulders, but knew it was useless. The girl was dead. Then Liberty felt herself dragged away, her hands still outstretched to Tia, through the pub, out into the street, into the rain.

Jay threw Liberty into the car and drove away, the tyres squealing.

Tia was gone. Tia who could break eardrums with her endless rattle, topics of conversation swerving wildly from one to another. Tia, who got cross when Liberty risked getting arrested. Tia, who called her 'Mum' when she was taking the mick.

'I didn't talk until I was two and a half,' she once told Liberty. 'My mam thought I might be backward, but then one day she told me off for climbing into my doll's pushchair and I turned round to her and said my first words, "Why? Is it dangerous?"'

The windscreen wipers beat fast as Jay sped through the streets of Moss Side.

'That younger had come for you,' he said.

Liberty nodded. Tia had saved her life. Someone had pointed a gun at Liberty and Tia had thrown herself at him. 'Idiot,' Liberty murmured, under her breath. 'Tia, you bloody idiot.'

Jay shot across town until they reached the industrial estate and he pulled into the yard behind the carpet warehouse. There were already several cars and vans parked up, crew of all ages and sizes inside, a few having a smoke in the shelter of the warehouse entrance.

Jay put a hand on her knee. 'You all right?'

Liberty felt as if she had splintered into tiny pieces, but she knew she had to put on her poker face for her people. She pushed her hair from her face, tied it at the base of her neck and took a massive breath.

'Ricky Vine is about to get what's coming to him,' said Jay.

229

Liberty nodded and sent a quick text to Crystal, then stepped out of the car into the torrential rain. 'A lot of people are.'

Rose and Adam trudged through the estate to Salty's garage and banged on the metal door. He'd left a message for Rose at the nick, saying he had some information she'd want to hear about the Greenwoods, so they'd dropped a charge of indecent exposure and made their way straight over. The custody sergeant had been only too happy to see the back of a flasher from his cell area.

'This had better be good, Salty,' Rose shouted.

Adam scowled at the sky as if he could scare away the storm clouds. 'I need to get a job in an office.'

'You? In an office?' said Rose, with a laugh. 'Doing what?'

'Filing?'

'I don't think that's a full-time job, Adam,' said Rose. 'I doubt it's even a part-time job, these days, with everyone sending emails.'

'Photocopying?'

'Did I just mention emails?' Rose asked, and hammered on the door again. 'I will nick you, Salty, if you don't get your arse out here in ten seconds.'

The door creaked and opened a few inches. Salty's voice leaked out: 'Give me a minute.'

'No, Salty, I will not give you a minute,' said Rose, and kicked out at the door.

When it opened further, Rose froze solid. Salty pointed a gun at her head with a shaking hand. At her side, Adam went for his baton, then he, too, froze when he heard the click of a trigger safety from behind.

'Let's not do anything daft,' said a woman.

When the woman moved into view, Rose took in the hugely pregnant belly before the face.

Crystal Greenwood looked Adam up and down, weapon

pointed. 'My sister said you were a bit of eye candy.' She laughed, then turned to Salty. 'Put the gun down, mate, before you take someone's head off.'

Sol finished the last can of lager, crunched it in his fist and threw it across the room. He didn't know what was worse, that Liberty would threaten his child to get what she wanted or that he was so terrified for a child he hadn't even known was his until days ago. Recently, he'd worried that his grasp on reality was fraying at the edges, but right now it felt ripped clean.

Somewhere in the flat, his mobile rang. He'd put it away to stop himself watching that video, but where? He listened to the ring tone and tried to follow the sound. When it stopped he sank back into the sofa. Whoever it was, he didn't want to speak to them anyway.

It rang again, and this time he could tell it was coming from the kitchen so he dragged himself towards it and spotted it peeking out from under an almost empty packet of crumpets.

'Yeah?'

'Sol? Where the hell have you been?' It was Hutch, armed and ready to give him another bollocking.

'Here,' said Sol, because it was true.

There was a moment of silence. Well, not silence: Hutch didn't speak but there were other voices in the background. Urgent voices.

'Yusef's in hospital,' said Hutch.

Sol could hear the rapid pounding of his heart in his ears. 'What happened?'

'There's been a shooting,' said Hutch.

The sound of Sol's lungs contracting joined his heartbeat. 'Is he okay?' Hutch didn't speak. 'Hutch? Is Yusef okay?' Sol shouted.

'Yeah. He's taken a blow to the head, but they say he'll be fine,' Hutch replied.

Sol breathed a sigh of relief. 'So what happened?'

'Yusef went into a pub in Moss Side and he shot two people.' Hutch paused and Sol could hear the rustle of paper. 'A bloke called Lee Kelly and a kid called Tia something. Sorry can't read my writing.'

Sol's mouth went dry. He worked his tongue back and forth until he had enough saliva to speak. 'Is anyone dead?'

'Kelly's alive just about,' said Hutch. 'But Tia died instantly.'

Sol let the phone fall from his hands, bent forward from his waist and vomited onto the kitchen floor.

A group of kids in school uniform, all fancy green felt blazers, jumped out of the way at the sight of Sol crashing through the hospital reception, breathless and sweating. He raced past them and dashed up the stairs, almost careering into Hutch at the door to the ward.

'This is not good, mate,' said Hutch. Even in an emergency like this and even in a storm with rain driving like rods, Hutch managed to look great. Sol peered down at the T-shirt he'd thrown on, stained from yesterday, now sopping. 'The boss has called me three times already,' Hutch added.

'What did you tell her?' Sol asked.

Hutch slapped his sides with his palms. 'That we don't know what's happened.'

'I'll talk to Yusef,' said Sol.

As he moved to enter the ward, Hutch pushed his hand into Sol's chest to stop him. 'He needs to say that none of this has anything to do with the operation.' Sol snorted. 'I mean it,' said Hutch. 'If Kapur thinks this is linked, we'll be handed our arses on a plate.'

The hand in Sol's chest pushed just a little harder, making Hutch's meaning clear. Coldly, Sol nudged it away and went onto the ward.

HARD AS NAILS

***

A small bar of light, no thicker than a pencil, shone under the garage door. It sputtered as someone walked past. Rose fought the urge to scream for attention because her mouth was stuffed with a huge wad of filthy cotton held in place by gaffer tape. If she tried to do anything except breathe through her nose, she'd choke.

She glanced at Adam. On the garage floor, hands cuffed behind his back, ankles secured with more gaffer tape, he, too, looked up at the noise of the footsteps outside.

A scrabbling sound in the corner made them both twist their necks in the opposite direction. A scratchy rustle in one of the disintegrating cardboard boxes that lined the concrete wall. Rose shuddered at the thought that there were rats in here.

More scratching, like little claws, trying to climb out of the box.

Adam kicked at something, probably one of the used syringes that littered the place. He tried to scoop it up and send it at the box, but it missed by three or four yards and hit what looked like an old toolkit. He bowed his head again in defeat and his shoulders shook. Was he crying?

Rose stamped a foot to gain his attention and when they locked eyes, she shook her head – don't cry. Tears would block his nose and then he wouldn't be able to breathe at all.

When Crystal Greenwood had tied them up at gunpoint, Rose had never been more terrified in her life. Liberty was tough, hard to read, but Crystal was on another level. Almost comically pregnant, she lumbered around, her lips smacking away on chewing gum, yet when Adam had asked her what she wanted, she'd smacked him in the mouth with the handle of her gun without a word in response.

At that point, Rose had been tempted to order Adam to tell Crystal where he'd hidden Kalkan's phone, but once the

Greenwoods had that, what reason was there not to kill them both? Rose assumed that was why Crystal had left them in here: to stew. Locked in a dark garage, stinking of puke and crack, with rats in the corner, concentrating on their breathing so that they didn't suffocate, Crystal would expect them to tell her what she needed in short order. Rose just prayed that when Crystal got back Adam wouldn't instantly spill the beans or they'd lose the only leverage they had to stay alive.

Another noise outside. Low voices and shuffling feet. Rose threw Adam a plea. He was not what she'd call bright or brave, but surely he understood he couldn't tell Crystal where the phone was.

Sol dragged a chair next to Yusef's bed and sat down.

The kid looked terrible. The medics had shaved off half of his hair and swathed his head in pearly white bandages. But it was his expression that got Sol. Yusef seemed hollowed out. Like any spark he'd once had was gone, leaving just a dry shell.

'Talk to me, Yusef,' said Sol. The boy's bloodshot eyes blinked. 'Explain to me what's just happened.' Yusef stared at Sol and there was a strange moment when Sol thought he might let himself cry. This lad had been through more in his few years than Sol would ever have to, and instead of trying to protect him or help him make a better life, Sol had used him and placed him in more danger. 'Why did you kill Tia?'

A single tear slid out of Yusef's left eye, down his cheek and onto the pillow.

'Did Ricky tell you to kill her?' Sol asked. Yusef moved his head a fraction. 'Then why?' Yusef closed his eyes. 'I'm trying to help you here,' said Sol.

Was that even true? Wasn't Sol trying to protect himself and Hutch?

'Didn't mean to.' Yusef spoke so quietly Sol had to strain to hear him. He leaned in, head cocked. 'She hit me with a pint pot and I couldn't see straight. Then she jumped me, dashed me to the ground. And then it just . . . I liked her, you know? She was a laugh.'

'So you went to kill Kelly?' Sol asked.

'Nah,' said Yusef. 'I didn't even know he'd be there. Tia told me she was there with her boss and that she wanted to talk to me. But Ricky told me to pop the woman as soon as I got the chance.'

Sol snapped to attention as if he'd just been rewired. 'The dark-haired woman?'

'Yeah. Kelly tried to stop me so I had to do what I did.'

Sol jumped up, knocking his chair backwards. Liberty was back in Manchester. Ricky Vine had ordered a hit on her and he must know by now that it hadn't been successful.

Sol ran from the ward, down the stairs, his phone to his ear. Outside on the greasy pavement, he tried Liberty again.

'Sol?'

'Liberty, listen. I know Ricky Vine just tried to kill you,' he said. 'And I know what you'll do about that, but just for one second stop and think.'

'I didn't know Crystal sent that video to you,' she said.

'What?' Sol spun around on the spot. 'I don't care about that.'

'I didn't know anything about it. I'd never, ever hurt your child,' she said. 'And I'd never let Crystal or Jay hurt her either. You must know that.'

'Lib, please don't do this. If you go after Ricky, he might get you first.'

'I know.'

The tears that Sol had thought might spill on the ward came now. 'We could leave. We could go anywhere we wanted, Lib. And we could take Jay and Crystal with us, if that's what you want.'

'No, Sol. You need to stick around for your little girl.'

Sol let out a sob. 'I love you.' There was a pause. 'Lib?'

'I wish I'd met you when I was young,' she said. 'I wasn't always like this.'

'Lib, please, don't do this.'

'Kiss your baby as often as you can, Sol.'

Then she hung up.

Chapter 17

24 November 1990

When Connor comes to the Turk's Head to pick me up, all his clothes smell of Lenor and he's had a trim since I last saw him. When I go to ruffle his hair, he doesn't even try to dodge out of the way. 'You've changed,' I say. 'You used to go crackers if anyone even got within touching distance of the precious locks.'

He gives me a massive smile. 'You can touch any part of me you like, Lib.'

As soon as we're sitting down in the Oriental, he asks the waitress for two portions of prawn crackers while we look at the menu.

'So how did it go?' he asks.

He's talking about my entrance exam to Oxford.

'All right,' I say. He crunches a cracker, waiting for more details. 'Look, I don't know,' I say and grab one myself. 'Like a million people try to get in.'

'I'll order some champagne now, then,' he says.

I slap him with my menu. 'We are not tempting Fate.'

Later, as he walks me back to Ian's, he touches my hand with his finger. 'Do you think you'll ever forgive me, Lib?'

'Well, I'd not be here if I was holding a grudge,' I say.

The town centre's busy, people walking between pubs. There's a woman crying outside Woolworth's, one of her mates rubbing her back in sympathy, although she keeps looking at her wrist, checking the time.

As we pass the old record shop, Connor nudges me with his elbow. 'We met in there.'

'I haven't got amnesia,' I tell him.

'I remember how you stamped up to the counter, trying to sell that record to Rob.'

'And he accused me of nicking it,' I say. 'Cheeky beggar.'

'Hadn't Vicky nicked it?'

'Well, yeah, but that's not the point,' I say.

He smiles at the shop window, now covered with posters for holidays in Spain. 'I thought you were the most beautiful thing I'd ever seen.'

I stare at the turquoise waves, lapping golden sands, and slide my hand into his. When I look up at him, he turns away and I think he might be crying because he wipes his face with his other hand.

'Are you not going to kiss me, then?' I ask.

He faces me now, and I can see that he is crying, but he's laughing as well. Then he puts a hand on either side of my head and kisses me. He tastes of soy sauce and snot, and I laugh as well.

Back at the door to the Turk's Head, I tell him I can't ask him to stay because I don't know what Ian and Janice would think of that.

'I do not want to get on the wrong side of Ian Lynch, that's for certain,' he says.

'Do you know him, then?'

'I know of him. And his missus,' Connor says, and taps my chin with his knuckle. 'Watch yourself, Lib.'

Present Day

The plan was to hit various places linked to Vine at the same time, so when Liberty pulled up at the gym, she knew she'd have to wait.

A van followed close by with five or six youngers in the back, the driver an ex-bouncer Jay knew from way back. Jay was on his way to Vine's house and had just called to say he was going to arrive in minutes.

It was late afternoon, that time in winter when darkness came even before the day was over. One of the youngers got out of the van and walked around the block. When he returned, he put up a thumb to Liberty: Vine's car was in the car park. She felt something prickle in her scalp in anticipation.

When her phone told her it was exactly five thirty, Liberty got out of her car and moved to the back of the building. There was a thick metal door that would be reinforced inside, but next to it was a window, covered with bars. She put up her hand to her men and gave them the silent count down. Five, four, three, two, one.

The crew produced two police-issue battering rams, hauled them above their heads and crashed them into the steel bars. The noise rang through Liberty's body and she shivered. When the second ram hit, she felt her teeth move. On the third stroke, the bars gave way and the glass behind danced into a thousand splinters.

It took less than a couple of seconds to clear away the rest of the glass with hammers. Then, one by one, they leaped inside, Liberty second to last, with Jay's ex-bouncer to protect her back.

They split into two groups, the first charging down the corridor to the training gym, Liberty and her men streaking up the stairs to the treatment room.

Liberty kicked open the door and they found Moody, alone and wiping down the massage table with a sponge. He laughed when he saw them, but Liberty could see he was scared. She knew all about fear and she could smell it coming off him like cheap scent.

'Where is he?' Liberty shouted, gun raised to Moody's head. 'Don't make me ask twice.'

Moody screwed his eyes shut. Didn't even open them when she pressed the barrel of her gun into his mouth, just gave a long, low moan.

But Liberty knew that one thing would make people talk faster than fear and that was pain. She lowered her gun and shot his kneecap.

Moody crumpled to the ground, clutching the shattered mess of his leg, screaming in agony.

'Tell me where he is, or you lose the other knee,' said Liberty.

When he didn't speak, she took aim.

'He went to teach you a lesson.' Moody groaned.

'What does that mean?' Liberty demanded.

She jabbed Moody's injured knee with her foot. It felt weirdly soft. Moody screamed. She lifted her foot for another kick.

'Yorkshire.' Moody panted between each word. 'He went across to your area.' He gave a gurgle, an almost-laugh. 'He's gone to destroy everything you care about while you're running about over here.'

Liberty stared at him for a second, then put a bullet in his throat.

Angel was relieved to see Salty had returned on his own. Once inside the garage, he flicked a lighter to the end of a roll-up, then lit a few candle stubs dotted around the place. He picked up a litre bottle of Tesco's lemonade from the floor and undid the top. He had a swig and turned to Adam.

'Want a drink, pretty boy?' Salty asked. Adam nodded and Salty produced a razor blade from his back pocket. As he approached the tape on Adam's face, Adam flinched. 'Don't worry, I'm not going to spoil your good looks.'

Salty sliced through the tape, yanked the cotton wad from Adam's mouth and dropped it onto the floor. 'Before you think about screaming,' said Salty, 'remember I'm the one with the gun and the razor blade.' He held the bottle to Adam's lips and Adam gratefully gulped it down.

Rose felt her own mouth fill with saliva at just the thought of a drink and she tried not to gag.

'Let's not tell Crystal about this, shall we?' said Salty. 'She isn't what you'd call the caring type. God help that kid of hers when it arrives. Though she'll probably have it trained to kill by the time it can walk.'

'Why do you work for her?' Adam asked.

Salty raised an eyebrow. They all knew the answer. A bit of gear. A bit of cash. The chance not to wake up in a ditch.

'People like that,' said Adam, 'they think they're untouchable.'

The fag between Salty's cracked lips had gone out and he brought a new flame to it. 'They *are* untouchable, you muppet.'

Adam shook his head. 'They ruin too many lives. I mean, how old were you when you started buying gear from them?'

'Thirteen,' Salty replied, with a shrug. 'Maybe a bit less than that.'

Rose watched Adam's face register shock. Was that real? Or was he just trying to make a connection with Salty? She'd seen him do it before, and while his way with people seemed genuine, she'd also noticed that he used it to his advantage.

'Imagine if you'd never met the Greenwoods,' said Adam. Salty didn't answer but held up the bottle of pop to Adam in a 'Cheers'. Rose would literally lick the soles of Salty's feet for a drink right now. She let out a tiny squeak of despair. Adam sighed sadly. 'You don't owe them anything, mate.'

Salty held the bottle once more to Adam's mouth and the sound of his gulps filled the garage. Then Salty dropped his fag into the bottle and it went out with a sizzle. He sniffed at Adam. 'Don't get it into your head that your mate here's any better than the Greenwoods, pretty boy. She uses me every bit as much as Crystal.' He picked up the roll of gaffer tape and waved it in Rose's direction. 'I wouldn't trust her if I were you.'

'Can I have a pee before you do that?' Adam asked.

Salty shook his head with a giggle. 'Are you serious?'

'It's the pop.'

'Fine.' Salty helped Adam to his feet and dragged over an

already full bucket that sloshed dangerously. He went to undo Adam's zip.

'Oh, come on,' said Adam. 'You're not actually going to pull out my dick?'

'Well, what's your plan?' Salty asked.

'Clip off my cuffs and I'll do the work.'

'As if.'

'I'm serious,' said Adam. 'You might be a bag head but I know you're not a nonce.' Salty chewed his lip. 'You can tape my hands straight back up,' Adam said.

Salty grabbed a pair of pliers from the rusty toolkit and also pulled out his gun. 'If you do anything I don't like, I'll shoot you. And don't think I won't, because if you escape, Crystal will kill me slowly. Okay?'

Adam nodded, and Salty pressed the gun into his belly. 'I hear it takes a long time to die from stomach wounds,' he said.

With the cuffs off, Rose heard the stream of pee hitting the contents of the bucket. She was sure Adam would try to overpower Salty. That was what she'd do. The junkie weighed less than a child, and one good punch would lay him out. Adam was strong and fit. She held her breath, waiting for him to strike. Instead, when he was finished, Adam put his hands behind his back, for Salty to bind them.

Rose lowered her eyes when she heard the screech of the tape as Salty wound it round and round Adam's wrists. Their best chance of getting away had just been surrendered.

Jay hurtled back to Wakefield in stony silence, the needle on the speedometer not dipping under a hundred. 'If he's laid one finger on our Crystal, I'm going to cut off his ears and make his girlfriend eat them,' he said.

'He won't have done anything to her,' Liberty replied, but

she wasn't convinced and didn't sound it. Vine had already fire-bombed Crystal's car. There was nothing that made Liberty believe he didn't want her sister dead. Maybe that had been his plan all along. To take out Liberty's sibling, the pregnant one, to show Liberty that there was nothing and no one she could protect from him.

She pressed the base of her palm against her forehead and tried to think. Suddenly, her head felt leaden, her breath painful in her chest.

'Try her again,' Jay barked.

Liberty called Crystal's number again. It went to voicemail.

Jay punched his side window. 'Shit. Shit. Try Mel again.'

Another call that wasn't picked up.

Jay pulled on the handbrake outside the Black Cherry and they ran. Liberty had to drag her body as if pushing through treacle and her chest rattled.

As soon as they were inside the club, Liberty knew something was wrong. The velvet entrance drape lay on the floor and the stage was empty. The girls were huddled around the bar, some of them crying, broken glasses at their feet. The dancer with the Cleopatra wig stood motionless, hands at her throat, eyes bulging.

The sound that came from Jay's mouth was like that of an animal at a slaughterhouse and he fell to his knees as he reached the bar. Liberty gasped, and had to lean against it.

It was Mel. On the floor, next to the open dishwasher, a small round wound in her forehead. Her eyes open yet blank, her mouth slack.

For a moment, Liberty could hear nothing but the sound of her own breathing. The faces around her contorted as they screamed and shouted. Jay's mouth opened and closed. But there was complete silence in Liberty's ears, except for the rise and fall of her own chest. She put a hand on Jay's shoulder, squeezed, then backed out of the Cherry. Only when she was at the door did the volume un-mute.

Two fire engines were outside the Cashino, half a dozen hoses trying to put out the inferno. A black pillar of smoke rose high into the air. The police had cordoned off the road and a group of onlookers pointed in horror at the blaze.

But Liberty didn't even stop, just made a U-turn, spinning the car with the heel of her hand on the steering wheel.

Chapter 18

29 November 1990

*Sinead tells me there's a party at her house tomorrow night. 'Not a party,'
she says. 'More of a gathering. But you should come.'*

*I say I'll try to make it, but I probably won't. Sinead's nice but there
doesn't seem much point in getting to know folk when we'll all be going our
separate ways in the summer.*

*At lunchtime, when everyone's gone off to the shop for a sandwich and
a crafty cig, I reread the letter I got from Connor this morning. He must
have written it as soon as he went back inside for it to come this quickly.
It's just a page filled on both sides with the same three words – I love you,
I love you, I love you . . .*

*I keep starting a reply, then screwing it up. Because I want to say the
same thing back, but I can't. It's not that I don't love him – I do – it's just
that I find it hard to believe we're going to be together again. And if I say
those words, me and Connor will be together until we die. That's how it
works. And if we don't, I'll disintegrate into a million pieces.*

*Anyway, I'm putting off a reply until tomorrow because I'm going to see
our Jay after school. I'm going to take him to McDonald's and he can have
whatever he likes. Three Big Macs if he's hungry enough.*

*I jump off the bus at the stop near the Turk's Head because I just want
to ditch my bag before I go over to Orchard Grove, but when I arrive, I
see police cars outside. I'm wondering what's gone off, maybe a fight or*

245

something, when I see Ian being led away in handcuffs, a copper pressing down on the back of his head as they push him into the squad car.

There's a second when the car pulls away and me and Ian look into each other's eyes. He says something to me but I can't make it out, and I realise my mouth's open.

Inside the bar, Janice is shaking her head, face white as a ghost's. A couple of regulars try to make her drink a brandy. A policewoman watches, scribbling notes in a little pad. When Janice notices me, she points and says, 'That's her, Ian's niece.'

The policewoman frowns at me. 'Can you show me your room, please?'

'What's going on?' I ask, as I lead the copper up the stairs.

'Room, please,' she says, not angry but not very nice either.

I open the door to the box room and show her in, wishing I'd made my bed before I left this morning.

'And is this your wardrobe?' she asks me.

'I suppose so,' I say. 'But I haven't put anything in it. I mean I will, but Janice needs to move all her stuff out first.' I try a smile, but she doesn't smile back. 'Can you tell me what's up?'

'A quantity of drugs and cash has been found in that wardrobe,' she says.

'What?'

'Is it correct that your boyfriend is currently in prison on drugs charges?' she asks.

I clam my mouth closed. I know there is nothing I can say that will help this situation. I might not be a solicitor yet, but I already understand that it's not my job to help the police fit me up.

'I think you'd better come down to the station,' she says.

As I walk through the bar towards the police car outside, Janice narrows her eyes at me.

Present Day

The garage door opened and Crystal sauntered in. 'Evening.' She pulled out her chewing gum into a long string, wound it around her finger and shoved it back in her mouth. 'Anything to report, Salty?'

'Only that I'll be clucking soon.'

Rose blinked at Crystal. Every muscle and bone in her body ached from the position she was in. The top of her arms felt like someone had filled them with gravel.

'We can sort that for you,' Crystal told Salty.

'Yeah, well, sooner rather than later would be good, or I'll start shitting myself.'

Crystal held a gun loosely in her right hand and delved into her back pocket with her left. She produced a baggie and waved it at Salty. 'Behold the magic cure.'

Salty shook his head and wiped a runny nose with his sleeve.

'Right,' said Crystal. 'Let's get this party started.'

She crouched in front of Adam and picked at the tape around his mouth. When her nail had lifted the end, she pulled. Bit by bit, the tape came away, taking half of Adam's face with it from the way he grunted. Finally, she pulled the cotton from his mouth and he sucked in a breath.

'Is that better?' Crystal asked.

'If you just tell us what you want—' Adam stopped in mid-sentence as Crystal pressed her gun up his nose.

'You need to stop talking,' she said. 'Okay?' Adam's head went back as Crystal pushed harder. 'Okay?' she repeated, and Adam nodded. 'I think we all prefer a pretty face when it's not yapping,' she said.

Rose prayed Adam would listen. His cheeky-chappie routine might work on all and sundry, but it wouldn't work on a Greenwood. She tried to catch his eye to warn him, but his head was too far back. How had she got him into this? A solid bloke, happy to go about his life, seeing his family, getting his tattoo sleeve filled in the highlight of his week. Now he was going to get shot. And for what? Rose's obsession with Joel? With Liberty? She desperately wanted to apologise.

Then, from nowhere, the razor blade appeared.

Adam whipped his hand from behind his back, and slashed the blade across Crystal's right hand. She gasped, eyes wide in surprise as blood spurted and the gun fell from her hand.

As if in slow motion, Crystal and Adam went for the weapon. Adam's hands were free where he must have sawn the tape with the blade, but his feet were still bound. Crystal was a ball of fury at being caught off guard, but she was heavily pregnant. Awkwardly, she reached out with her bloody hand, but Adam managed to kick the gun away with his feet. It skittered across the garage floor towards Salty. Adam lunged, but Crystal punched him back with her uninjured left fist. She probably weighed half what Adam did, but he still reeled backwards.

Then Salty picked up the gun.

Panting, Crystal held out her hand. Salty went to give her the gun, but a huge shudder went through his body and he let out a fart. The stench was horrific.

'I've got your gear, remember,' said Crystal, palm still out-stretched.

Adam straightened, nose burst, blood running into his mouth. 'Don't do it, mate.' Crystal laughed. 'I'm serious,' Adam told Salty. 'She's going to kill us and you're going to end up going down for murder. And why?' Adam nodded at Crystal. 'To protect her? Do you think she'll look after you when you're doing time for killing some coppers? Or do you think you'll get what's coming from the screws?'

Crystal laughed again and sucked the razor wound. 'Just give me the gun, Salty. No one need ever know you were here.'

'Bullshit,' Adam told Salty. 'Everyone knows this is where you stay. And our DNA is everywhere.' Adam flicked a fingerful of blood onto the floor. 'You think a Greenwood is going to take the rap?'

Salty groaned, put his hands over his ears. At last he got up and took two steps to Crystal. 'I hate you.'

Crystal smiled, her lips covered with blood. 'Thing is, Salty, I'm all you've got.'

He stood stock still, chest rising and falling in what? Panic? Anger? Fear? Salty was right: Rose had used him every bit as much as the Greenwoods had. She felt disgust at herself. Or was she just terrified?

Salty narrowed his eyes at Adam. 'When I was twelve I got taken into care and the policeman who dragged me away from my mum told me I was better off without her. About six months later I told him that the foster carer had been buggering me, and do you know what he said? He said, "Stuart, you've got a very active imagination." I tried to show him my bum-hole and all the blood and that, and he goes, "Stuart, stop making a mountain out of a molehill." So excuse me if I don't think you lot are the good guys.'

Crystal put her cut hand under her armpit and winced at the sting. 'I got taken into care at six.'

'I didn't know that,' said Salty.

'My dad chucked my mam off a balcony,' said Crystal. She said it with no self-pity and Salty nodded.

'The past isn't dead,' said Adam. 'It isn't even past.'

'Did you get that out of a cracker?' Crystal asked.

'A book at school, I think. Can't remember which one. Never did listen enough,' said Adam. 'It's true, though, don't you think?'

At that, Salty made his way to Adam and put the gun in his hand. Rose could hardly believe it.

'Don't come after me,' Salty said.

'Wouldn't dream of it,' said Adam.

'I fucking will,' said Crystal. 'Don't think I won't.'

Adam nodded at the door and Salty scarpered, leaving only a bad smell behind.

★★★

The car parked outside Crystal's flat contained the standard look-out, all thick neck and Puffa jacket, engaged in no looking out whatsoever. Liberty crept up to the driver's door in the darkness, yanked it open. Before the lookout even realised what was happening, she'd Tasered him in the neck. He slumped forward, fat face hitting the steering wheel.

The security gates to Crystal's flat were broken, swinging gently in the wind with a creak, and the lights in the entrance were out. Liberty assumed that Ricky Vine would have knocked out the cameras too. You could have a fortress, but if someone was determined to break in, they would.

She double-checked the silencer on both her guns and crept inside.

At the top of the internal stairs, another goon mooched about. Breaking all the lights had allowed Vine's crew to get in, but it also gave Liberty the element of surprise. If they were expecting anything, it was for the cavalry to arrive mob-handed, not a woman dressed all in black, able to slide like a sleek cat up the steps until she was almost upon the first man.

She raised her gun. One more step and she'd easily be able to take him. Crunch. The sound of a smashed bulb under her foot. Shit. The man turned to the noise, squinting in the darkness. Liberty knew he'd have a weapon in his hand so there would be no more than a second before he shot her. She leaped at him and fired. The gun made a small pop as the man crumpled with a thump onto the floor. Liberty dived back into the shadows and waited as the second man came to investigate.

'Masher?' The man found his colleague dead. 'Fuck.'

Liberty took the opportunity of his momentary surprise, dipped out of the gloom and shot. Pop. Another body on top of the last. Liberty stepped over the man-mound and into her sister's flat.

'Masher?' This time the voice was Vine's and it burned through Liberty. 'Masher?' She pressed herself against the wall, held her breath. 'Don't piss me about,' said Vine, as he stormed towards the door.

Liberty pushed her gun into the side of his head. 'Masher's dead.' She took Vine's gun from his hand. 'They both are. Maybe even the lookout in the car. I mean, I only Tasered him, but he didn't look like a man who took care of his heart.'

Vine's phone rang in his pocket. 'If I don't answer that, they'll know something's up and get round here,' he said, sounding faintly amused.

'We'd better get a shift on, then,' said Liberty.

She forced him through the flat into the kitchen, her eyes darting for any sign of Crystal. 'Where is she?'

'Not here.'

His phone rang again. She was going to need to do this efficiently, find out where he'd taken Crystal before his back-up arrived. Vine was watching her eyes, waiting for any indication of which way she might move. Poised to second-guess her and attack. She sniffed, smiled, and then, without moving her eyes a fraction from his, shot his foot. His face blazed and he collapsed against the floor-to-ceiling window, sliding down to the ground.

'Where is my sister?' Liberty asked.

He shook his head. Liberty shot his other foot. The white floor tiles were splattered with blood and bone.

'Knees next,' she said. 'Where is my sister?'

His phone rang again. Vine's men would be here any second. He knew that all he had to do was hold on until they came. He gritted his teeth and snarled at her.

She had seconds to find out where Crystal was and aimed at his knee. 'Last chance, Ricky.'

'For you maybe,' he said.

Another ring. Then Liberty realised it wasn't his phone but hers. Gun still trained on his knee, she checked it and saw an unknown number.

'What?' she barked into it.

'This is Sergeant Hooper at Crosshills station.'

Liberty tried to concentrate on the words. 'And?'

'And Crystal Greenwood would like to speak to you.'

The line went quiet, then, 'Lib?'

'Crystal?' Liberty almost screamed in relief. 'Are you okay?'

'No, I'm fucking not,' she said. 'They've only gone and nicked me. Can you get me a brief? And not that bloody Raj.'

'Raj is brilliant,' said Liberty.

'Fine,' Crystal huffed. 'But tell him to look sharp.'

Crystal hung up and Liberty laughed. 'You don't have her, Ricky.'

'I've torched your arcade and your house,' he shouted, choking on a laugh.

Liberty frowned at him. He didn't get it, did he? Her sister was safe and so was her brother. The rest was small change. She lifted the gun one last time and shot him in the head.

As Liberty walked from Crystal's flat, her phone rang again.

'Miss Greenwood?'

'Don't you dare start an interview until the lawyer arrives,' Liberty said.

'I'm sorry, I think maybe—'

'Who the hell is this?' Liberty snapped.

'It's the BMW dealership. I know it's late, but we just wanted to follow up our email letting you know that your car has arrived and we'd love to take you through all the specifications if you could come in tomorrow. Our records show that the vehicle is a gift for your sister. Perhaps you'd like to bring her too.'

Liberty rubbed her temple. 'I'm not sure that's going to be possible.'

★★★

Rose's hands shook as Adam handed her a cup of vending-machine coffee. His lip was still bleeding where Crystal had battered him with her gun. It looked like he'd need a stitch.

'Are your teeth still in one piece?' she asked him.

He ran his tongue along them. 'Seem to be.'

He'd been amazing back in the garage, disarming Crystal and convincing Salty to leave. Rose hadn't seen that coming.

Then, with the three of them just staring at one another, as Adam sliced the tape on his legs with the blade he'd nicked from Salty's pocket as he had a slash, Crystal had just laughed. 'So what are you going to do now?' she said. 'I know you haven't got the balls to shoot me.' She chewed her gum happily. 'And guess what? I found the phone in your place, so now you can't blackmail me with that either.'

She'd hauled herself up to her feet with a groan. 'So now I think I'll get off.'

When she was almost at the garage door, Adam moved towards her, gun pointed. For a terrible second, Rose thought he might actually shoot her, but what happened next took Rose and Crystal by surprise.

'Crystal Greenwood, I'm arresting you for the kidnap of Rose Angel. You do not have to say anything but anything you do say may be given in evidence.'

Rose tried a bit of tea but yelped as it touched her lips, now missing the top layer of skin that had peeled off with the tape.

'You got them, Rose,' Adam said.

She set the cup down. 'Who?'

'The Greenwoods.' Adam cheerfully slurped his tea, injured mouth or not. 'Maybe not in the way you thought you would, but Crystal's going down for this.'

Rose rubbed her wrists and wondered if she still cared.

Chapter 19

Me and Tiny sit in a café. I've got Grace on my lap as Tiny smokes fag after fag. At last Connor arrives, bag in hand. He's got two days out for Christmas and has come straight here to meet us.

He kisses my cheek and runs a hand through Grace's tufts of hair.

'So, what did they say?' he asks me.

I've been to the station again this morning. 'They're going to make a decision about whether to charge me by the new year.'

Tiny flicks her ash. 'They won't.'

'What does your solicitor say?' Connor asks.

'That it was my room, so I'm going to struggle to convince anyone I didn't know about the stuff in there.'

'So why haven't they charged you already?' Tiny asks.

'They want you to do a deal,' says Connor.

I nod. The police keep telling me that they know I'm not a drug dealer and if I'll just tell them where the gear came from they'll let me off. But how can I when I don't even know?

'Then do a deal, for God's sake,' says Tiny.

'And have Ian Lynch and his missus on her back?' says Connor. 'They're not nice people, Tiny. Not people you want to cross.'

Tiny shakes her head as if she's really angry.

'I've been thinking,' says Connor.

'Careful,' I say, but he doesn't laugh.

'If I tell the police it was my stuff, they'll let you off.' He can't be serious? He's not even finished his last sentence – God knows when he'd get out if he got another stretch. 'This could ruin your life, Lib. I can't let that happen.'

'No.' We both look at Tiny, whose voice is sharp. 'I'm not having that, Connor.'

'She's right,' I say. 'You can't do that, Connor.'

Connor reaches into Tiny's packet of fags on the table, takes the last one and lights it. 'This is up to me.'

'It's not just about you, though, is it?' she says, and I see now that she's crying.

'Tiny.' Connor pats her hand. 'You'll be fine. And so will she.'

My eyes dart between them. Tiny letting tears spill down her face as she looks at baby Grace, squirming in my arms. Then it dawns on me who her dad is and my mouth falls open.

'You're meant to be my friend,' I say to Tiny.

She wipes her bloodshot eyes with a serviette. 'It wasn't a big thing. Just a few times when we were out of it.'

'Does Rob know?' I ask.

Tiny shrugs. 'I never told him but he might have guessed.'

'The point is, Lib.' Connor puts his arm round my shoulders, 'I love you. And I'll do whatever it takes to make sure you're all right.'

I stand and hand the baby, Connor's baby, back to Tiny. The baby he made when he said he was madly in love with me. The baby he doesn't seem to care about. Then I walk out of the café without another word.

Present Day

The prison visits room was as hot and noisy as ever when Crystal wobbled in, uniform stretched across her belly. She raised an eyebrow at Liberty as she lowered herself into the seat opposite.

'How are you feeling?' Liberty asked.

'Like I've swallowed a bus.'

'Are they checking your blood pressure?' Liberty asked. 'I've heard it can shoot up near the end.'

'If anything will make it soar, it'll be the lasses on the wing singing "Mamma Mia" every time I walk past.' Crystal shook her head in disgust. 'But, listen, I need you to do something for me, Lib.'

'Name it.'

'I need you to take this baby.' Liberty had no answer to that. 'When it's born, I need you to go to court and take it in officially,' said Crystal. 'They'll never let our Jay, and I can't let it go into care.'

'I'm top of the list, then?'

Crystal stared hard at her sister. 'I don't have a list. I've thought about this, and it's the only way.'

'I don't know what to do with a kid,' said Liberty.

'And you think I do?'

A fight broke out close by, a table went crashing and the alarm sounded. Guards poured into the room, clearing all the inmates away. The visit was over.

Crystal shouted at Liberty over her shoulder: 'And you know what to call it.'

Yusef's cellmate Kyle had the TV blaring. Some game show or other. He tried to answer the questions but Yusef had never heard him get one right. Ever.

The game-show host gave a toothy smile. 'There are two official languages of Somalia, Somali and what else?'

'French,' Kyle shouted.

'It's Arabic,' Yusef muttered.

The game-show host revealed the answer. 'The second language of Somalia after Somali is . . . Arabic.'

'How d'you know that?' Kyle asked Yusef. 'You from there or something?'

'No,' said Yusef. 'I'm from Eritrea.'

But Kyle wasn't listening, already trying to answer the next question.

Sol had been to the barber's especially for today's appointment. And bought a new pair of jeans. He handed over the paperwork Natasha had given to him about adoption and the solicitor read it carefully.

She had blonde hair that seemed to catch the sun that poured through the window, and when she smiled, her teeth were beautifully white. He'd be willing to bet she didn't drink coffee or smoke.

'Have you ever met the child in question?' she asked.

Sol shook his head. 'I didn't know about her until my ex-wife gave me that piece of paper.'

'And what is it you want to do, Mr Connolly?' the solicitor asked.

And that was the question, wasn't it? The one keeping him up at night. Well, there was also the question of whether Yusef would go down for murder. Sol had given a statement explaining exactly what he and Hutch had done to Yusef. It would finish Hutch's career, but that was how it had to be. Hopefully, the jury would accept the kid's plea of self-defence. And then there was the question of whether he'd ever see Liberty again. She'd made it plain that this thing between them could never work, but the thought that this was the end made his stomach churn. But mostly what prevented sleep was the question of whether he wanted to be a father.

'I don't want my daughter to think I didn't give a shit,' he said. 'Sorry, pardon my French. I'm really stressed about all this.'

The solicitor laughed, opened her drawer and pulled out a packet of Marlboro. 'Shall we have a sneaky fag and then draft a statement for the court?'

Chapter 20

2 January 1991

There's still bits of tinsel strung across the custody area, but it's sagging and looking a bit sad as the copper leads me to the interview room. I've come without my solicitor this time, and when he goes to turn on the tape, I say, 'Can we have a talk without that on?'

'Course.'

'You said before that if I told you about Ian, you'd let me go,' I say. 'But what about Janice? She'll hound me into the ground.'

'She's hardly Al Capone,' he says.

I cross my arms. We both know that I'm just a kid and she can have me battered until I daren't appear in court.

'We can send you away for a bit,' he says. 'Until the trial.'

'Where?'

'There's a few places down south where we put witnesses usually,' he says. 'Nothing fancy, but provided you keep your head down, no one will find you.'

I tell him I'll need to have a think, and head over to the park. There's two old women with their grandkids on the bench. They're nattering away while the kids go up and down the slide. When one shoots off the end and bangs his head, he runs back to his nan, crying. She gives him a kiss and a packet of crisps and he's right as rain.

I sit on a swing and push myself off with my feet. I'm pretty sure I can tell the police whatever they want to hear about Ian. They'll probably write a statement for me if I ask. I wasn't expecting the offer to move away, if I'm honest. And how do I feel about that? Obviously I'll miss the kids, but our Jay's moving in with the Petersons next week, so I'd be all on my own anyway.

The main thing I'm worried about is college. It'll mean another move and then I'm bound not to get the grades I need for Oxford. Maybe I need to compromise and give up on Oxford. I mean, I don't even know if I passed the entrance exam, do I?

Present Day

Bunny looked chic in a cream linen dress and tortoiseshell sunglasses, the sole of a wedge sandal on top of the spade. 'It's with great pleasure I'm making the start of the foundations of our beautiful hotel complex here in Mallorca.' She pushed the metal edge into the soil and the small crowd clapped.

Liberty leaned into Jay and smiled. He smelt of sun screen and some new aftershave he'd bought on the plane over. The baby started to cry in his arms.

'Give her here,' said Liberty.

Jay passed her over, checking the front of his shirt for any signs of dribble, eyeing a pretty waitress with a tray of champagne. 'Want one?' he asked, already on his way.

'Go on, then,' Liberty said. 'And see if they've got some orange juice for Frankie.'

Hearing her name, Frankie stopped crying and gave a wet smile, showing her new tooth. Liberty kissed her and said, 'Well, now, that's like the sun coming out.'

Epilogue

I like London. You can lose yourself here, be whoever you like. Everybody's too busy creating their own story to worry about mine.

I'm staying in what Paddy the liaison officer calls a B-and-B. Bed in a room all of my own. Breakfast of individual boxes of cereal in the kitchen. I like the Frosties best.

I signed up for college under a new name. There was a bit of paperwork that Paddy helped me with, but not as much as you'd think. So now I'm Liberty Chapman. A few years ago I had a lovely solicitor called Miss Chapman and she was the one who first got me thinking about doing it for a job, so I took her last name. Maybe one day I'll tell her. But not until the trial's over and done with.

When I arrive at my new college in Peckham, Paddy's waiting outside. 'You've had a letter from Oxford University.' She hands over the envelope. 'You kept that one quiet. Didn't even know you'd applied.'

'No point telling you,' I say. 'I'll not get the grades.'

She puts her head to one side as I read it carefully. 'What does it say?'

'It says they're making me an unconditional offer,' I reply.

'Well, then,' Paddy says. 'Doesn't matter about your grades, does it?' She smiles at me. 'Congratulations, Lib. You're going to Oxford.'

Acknowledgements

So here's the fourth instalment of this series, written mostly during the trials and tribulations of lockdown during the 2020 pandemic.

To Krystyna and the team at Constable, many thanks for your support. And, as ever, the Buckman gang.

I'd also like to give a shout out to Jenny and Ruth at Snowed In productions for believing that the Greenwoods would make great TV.

Finally, a huge dollop of gratitude and love to my family for helping me do such a daft job.